MINE
forever

A Survivor Psychological Thriller

All the best

[signature]

Christmas 2022

Mine Forever
Helga Zeiner

Published by POWWOW Books Canada
Cover & interior design by Vanessa Ooms
Copyright 2019©Helga Zeiner
All rights reserved
ISBN: 978-1-948543-96-5

HELGA ZEINER

A Survivor Psychological Thriller

Copyright©Helga Zeiner
All rights reserved
ISBN: 978-1-948543-96-5
Published by POWWOW Books Canada

PROLOGUE

Living alone in the Australian bush forced me to develop a kind of level-headed gutsiness. Operating an opal mine all by yourself does that to you. I had to stay focused, determined, stubborn even, to survive in a male-dominated, tough environment, but I didn't mind, well, not until the new owner of the local pub arrived.

In past years, I'd dropped by the pub every Wednesday evening on my way home from the mine to get my people fix—meet old friends, chat with newcomers, keep up with local gossip, and have a few cold beers. It was a ritual I thought would stick until they closed the coffin on me, but soon after I met the new owner, I began considering spending my Wednesdays at home with only my two dogs for company.

That is, because since this hunky, blue-eyed guy took over the pub, inexplicable yearnings filled me with emotions reminiscent of my youth when I was crazy in love, blind, and stupid.

Dreams of John as my loving husband, a home permeated with the smell of freshly baked cake and decorated with flowers, Sunday visits to friends, days filled with laughter, and nights with him next to me, naked and moaning with pleasure...

Damn it! This has to stop. I can't afford such suburbia crap. How can I climb into the mine's dangerous belly every morning to pick and shovel its muddy walls in hopes of extracting enough opal to make a decent living if I start questioning the lonely grind of my existence with such frivolous delusions?

John. A single glance at this attractive man had me hooked. I'd walked into the pub sweaty, covered with reddish dust, and beat from yet another unsuccessful day below. A cold beer, a chat, a shower and a bed was all I wanted. Nobody in Lightning Ridge gives a damn how you look or smell, but the moment John's deep blue eyes focused on my face, I brushed the clay-coloured dust from my cheeks.

"Don't," he said. "It gives you a healthier complexion."

I felt pasty, ugly, and dirty.

"Although I'd like to see more of the lovely features you're hiding underneath your beauty mask."

A smooth talker.

"No, seriously," he said, leaning over the counter so other customers couldn't hear, "you are by far the best looking woman in here."

"I'm the only woman."

He looked around. "The best looking in town, then. And may I say, you beat every guy, too, and that's something, considering the charm and beauty prevalent in the amazingly sophisticated population of Lightning Ridge."

We shared a laugh, and I didn't feel quite as awkward anymore, but I made a point the following Wednesday to shower first.

When he saw me next, his eyes seemed to light up with admiration. I didn't care if it was genuine or great acting. He made me feel desirable, and for those brief moments, I remembered how it felt not to be pushed away and exploited.

He was pleased to be in my company and pleaded with me to come more often, and though I was tempted, I never had until that plain, boring, useless Monday.

The rain hammered on the tin roof of my little house on the outskirts of Lightning Ridge. I could forget working the mine. I'd drown like a rat. A few rainy days wouldn't have been so bad, but it had been pouring relentlessly, day and night, for nearly four weeks, forcing me and every other miner in town to sit idly. Another endless, wasted day. I settled on my beat-up sofa, looked at the heavy clouds outside, and seriously considered making an exception to my Wednesday ritual.

I closed my eyes. Don't think about John. Don't. Think of all the things that need doing once the rain stops. My mind drifted off.

A noise at the door startled me. Must be the wind rattling the metal frame, I thought. Or is someone trying to get in? I did lock the door, didn't I? I concentrated on the sound of the wind foraging through the trees in front of my house.

No other sound. Nobody there.

I leaned back again, tried to relax, and drifted into a semi-conscious state, envisioning making the fabled million-dollar find. One gentle tap of my hammer would break open what had been formed thousands of years ago—an iridescent opal street in the rock wall. Then, in the pub, I'd celebrate with all the miners, and with John…oh, John.

A hand fell on my mouth, stifling my involuntary moan and pressing me deeper into the pillow with brutal force. I opened my eyes, shocked to recognize the bulky man on my chest. My husband Kurt had disappeared from my life thirty years ago. He should be dead. He nearly destroyed my life. He was the one responsible for me hiding in a lonely miner's town in the bush.

He looked and smelled the same. I'd recognize the sour odor of his sweat anywhere. I choked under his hand and tried to free my mouth to get air, but his grip was vicelike, his fingers clawing into my flesh. His face, distorted from his hatred and the effort to hurt me, was so close I felt his hot breath burning my skin. Spittle dripped from his mouth into my eyes.

I pleaded with him. "Please don't kill me. I don't want to die, not like this."

But the muffled sounds escaping my throat only demonstrated my vulnerability. He controlled me as totally as he always had. He'd come back to execute his rights over me again—after all this time and after all the pain and suffering I had accepted as the price for his disappearance.

Where has he been, and why has he come back now?

I knew the answer. He had never let go. He had always been there, knowing every step I took. He'd always sensed my innermost feelings and used them to his advantage. He knew I'd been thinking of another man, and he was going to punish me for it. He'd kill me. And John.

I tried to banish John's name from my thoughts. Kurt may not have caught his name in his frenzy.

John. John. John.

I tried harder, but John's name echoed in my thoughts, louder and louder.

John. John. John.

Hohoho.

Kurt's laughter stretched John's name into a sequence of malicious sneers.

"John. Hohoho. John. John. John. Hohoho. Johohohn."

Kurt's face contorted and became a grimace with a gaping hole, rasping the guttural "Hohoho" like a hellhound into my ears until it swallowed the *JohnJohnJohn* of my thoughts.

Dead quiet in my brain. Death would follow.

I resigned myself to his brutal grip. He had finally won.

PART ONE
Bremen, 1978

1

JOHANNA

I'd never seen such a gigantic ship. *Queen Frederica* towered above the crowd at the pier, her white metal walls several stories high with bull's-eye windows blocking the view of the gray ocean behind her.

I'd been scared of the journey. I didn't trust the water and couldn't fathom how a heavy mass like a ship could float. Looking at this monster of a ship should have multiplied my fears, but instead, I was suddenly convinced this amazing construction could withstand the onslaught of an angry sea and navigate us safely. I would feel as secure in its belly as I used to feel in my tiny apartment in Heidelberg.

An employee of the Chandris Line appeared on the gangway. "Tickets, everybody! Get your tickets ready."

The crowd pushed forward as if there weren't reserved places. The ship wasn't scheduled to depart until eleven that evening and it wasn't even lunchtime yet, but the anticipation of the journey created an instant atmosphere of frenzy. An elbow pressed into my back, and I quickly grabbed hold of Kurt's arm.

"Here we go," I said, my voice coarse.

Kurt stayed calm and grinned.

"Do you have the tickets?" I asked him for the umpteenth time.

"Jesus, Johanna. Stop worrying." Kurt tapped his breast. "Tickets. Money. Luggage. Your parents are back home in their boring little village where they belong, and your wedding ring is on your finger where it belongs."

I understood the hint. How many times have I touched the narrow silver band to make sure it hasn't slipped off in the week since our wedding? Will I ever get used to wearing a ring—something nurses always avoid?

I placed my hand over the ring. Kurt noticed and shook his head. He mocked me when I behaved so silly, but at least I didn't cry because my parents weren't there to bid us farewell. I'd spoken to them early that morning and told them Kurt and I had married. Dad had let out a long breath and mumbled something like, "Good luck with that one." Mom had been more direct with her, "God help you, child."

It would have been nice if my parents and Kurt could have gotten along but they had disliked him from the moment they met, and I knew they wouldn't change their opinions of him. He is my husband, and it serves them right to be shut out of the glorious future I'll have with him.

My husband. A wave of happiness swept over me. I pressed myself closer to him and held onto his strong, muscular arm. If I could have, I would have crawled right into him. I could feel the heat of his body through our clothes and it made my skin tingle.

When I had seen him the first time, in the hospital's parking area where I worked, I'd felt that heat before he'd even looked at me. I was a virgin then, barely eighteen, and had never seen a man like him.

He was big, sweaty, and dirty. He worked for the maintenance company that serviced the hospital's heating system and had just finished a long shift crawling through ducts on a hot summer day. His naked torso, stuck in wide overalls, was covered with grime, and his hard muscles glistened in the bright sun. I couldn't stop staring. When I finally raised my eyes, I met his gaze.

Love at first sight.

This momentous revelation made me shiver with excitement. I quickly lowered my eyes to hide the sensual longing his body had evoked, painfully aware of my flushed face, and tried to get into my car, but his van was parked so close I couldn't open the door.

A grin broke his blunt expression. He leaned against the van door and crossed his arms, his eyes travelling to the opening of my nurse's uniform and the outline of my embarrassingly large breasts.

I couldn't breathe as he undressed me with his eyes. One of his eyebrows moved up approvingly, and his mouth twitched before his tongue appeared to wet his lips. His eyes lingered on my bosom. My mind groped for something intelligent to say to force his attention elsewhere but I couldn't think of anything, so I simply stood there, waiting for him to finish loading the van.

So, this is the one.

He finally broke his lecherous scrutiny of my body and loaded his metal toolbox in the van, got in the driver's seat, and drove off. He hadn't asked for my name or phone number or even said goodbye.

I couldn't move. My breasts ached against the tight nurse's

uniform, and my face glowed. I unbuttoned my blouse down to my bra and used one hand to fan a cooling breeze into the opening while my other dabbed the sweat pearls under my stiff collar.

When I finished my shift the next day, he was leaning against the wall at the entrance door, dressed in jeans and a short-sleeved shirt. His hair was crew cut, he had a high forehead, and his skin was the same reddish-brown colour as his hair. His eyes were alert and his facial features assertive. Look at me, his expression said, I know what I want and how to get it. I immediately felt the tightness of my uniform again.

"Hello." He walked toward my car and opened the passenger door. "I don't own a car," he said. "Came by bus."

I had to clear my throat before I could reply. "How did you know when my shift ends?"

"I've been standing here for the past three hours. Figured you'd come out eventually."

His single-minded determination to see me again impressed me so much that I surrendered my virginity to him the same evening, without shame or regret.

I made the mistake of introducing him to my parents soon after, thinking they would admire and love him as much as I did. Kurt was strong, decisive, confident, and manly. Very manly. He was a real man, not one of those curly-haired, hippy types some of the other nurses favoured.

He was the most exciting, most beautiful person I'd experienced in my life, and in those early, frenzied days, I was proud of his unbridled passion. I couldn't understand the intensity of my desire to belong to him, much less explain it to my parents.

Kurt loved my voluptuous curves. His firm hands grabbed and kneaded my breasts until my skin burned. Sometimes I cried out in pain and pleasure when he entered me His greed was nearly unbearable, that's how much he loved me.

When the longing for him became too strong, I locked myself in the hospital's washroom and used my hands to achieve the release I so desperately sought. He surely wanted to but couldn't give me that. My fault.

Every time he entered me, my moist desire turned into dread. He was huge and his forceful thrusts scared and hurt me. Entirely my fault. I concentrated too much on the pain, and urged him on with fake moans while suppressing cries so he would finish faster.

Afterwards, I curled up next to him, hoping he would gently massage the still pulsating region between my legs, but I couldn't ask him. A few times, I took his hand and guided it there, but he usually just gave me a pat and a tickle. Once, he said, "You got some greedy pussy," and laughed. When I explained it was difficult for me to get there due to his size, he shook his head and said, "Can't help it if I'm built that way. You're damn lucky I don't rip you to pieces. Not every guy is considerate like me. Most don't care once they get going. That's how we are. Women are different. They don't need it that often, but if they don't let the guy at it when he needs it, that kills a relationship faster than a fart blows out a candle, believe you me."

Of course I believed him. I had no prior experience, unlike him. I was glad he explained how wrong it was for women to demand things. To do so would only throw a bad light on me, and he'd stop loving me. Best to use my own hands and imagination and let him have it whenever he wanted. It didn't diminish my desire for him.

Hard as my parents tried, their belittling and bickering didn't affect my feelings for him either. Kurt reacted to their disapproval like a rat following the stink of a garbage dump. He bore right into it.

He went to Sunday afternoon coffee with dirty fingernails and when my mother politely asked him to wash his hands, he wiped them on the starched napkins. "Dirty from honest work," he said. When Dad discussed politics, Kurt labeled Dad's favorite party as a bunch of pussies and morons. Fairly soon, Mom stopped inviting him.

"What do you see in him?" she once asked me when we were alone. "All the expensive education we paid for and you choose a proletarian? Don't you see he's got no manners?"

Kurt is right to hold a mirror to their faces. It was their fault for making it so obvious what they thought of him. They were as superficial and boring as he said. To hell with them trying to ruin my bliss. I was over-the-moon happy in those months, aside from the rift with my parents and my inability to achieve orgasm by penetration.

Then, Kurt started talking about how much he wanted to go to Australia—with me. He'd already been to the Australian Consulate and checked the requirements.

"They welcome young, white workers with open arms and even offer some free passage just to help populate the continent," Kurt said. "I'd have no problem being accepted. I'm an experienced tradesman young enough to give the country many years of honest work. I just need a wife by my side."

"A wife?" I asked, my heart doing a drumroll.

"At your age, you'll need permission from your parents,"—he paused and grinned at me—"unless I marry you."

Then, he told me he'd already handed in his application with me listed as his wife and that they had stamped it. All I had to do was present our marriage certificate when boarding, and I'd be accepted, too. He neglected to mention, though, that he'd committed us to spend a minimum of two years in the country or we would have to reimburse the Australian government our fare.

2

Everything we had owned had been sold, except for some clothes and memorabilia. I had cleared my savings account and handed the money over to Kurt. He'd taken the meager amount with a frown and added it to the folder containing our marriage certificate, passports, and passage documents. After a whirlwind of activities to get our departure organized, we were finally boarding the *Queen Frederica*.

We were pushed along in the steady stream of boarding passengers, inadvertently kicking their neighbours but not giving an inch, like they needed to fight for their hard-earned right to start their new lives.

I couldn't hold on to Kurt while we maneuvered down four flights of stairs, each of us carrying two suitcases, and when I was pushed aside by the big guy behind me, I panicked. Dear Lord, let us get to our cabin quickly. I hate this. I just want to close the door and shut out those people for the whole journey. For our honeymoon.

How clever of Kurt to get the government to pay for our honeymoon—a six-week trip on an ocean liner, all expenses paid. None of my former colleagues could match that. They were all pretty jealous when I'd told them. I smiled. A luxury honeymoon with a strong man by my side. Beat that.

The sailor waiting at the bottom of the fourth set of stairs yelled up to us.

"All the women right, men left." His arms signalled the directions.

"What's he saying?" Kurt asked in German.

"I don't know," I replied, although I had understood the sailor's English clearly. The crowd stopped and got quiet.

"Alle Frauen rechts," the sailor said with a heavy accent, pointing to the right again. "Warum? Warum?" cried one of the passengers, pleading to know why.

"It's the rule," the sailor stared back at us. Most averted their eyes, embarrassed they didn't understand. A passenger asked in English what it meant, and after the sailor explained, he translated for us.

"He says we must be separated by gender or we forfeit our rite of passage. It's the rule. There have been too many problems with mixed cabins in the past."

"But we just got married," Kurt yelled, along with a few others voicing their objections.

The man spoke to the sailor again and said, "He says there can be no exceptions, but we can meet on the upper decks in the dining rooms. There are a few rooms allocated for social gatherings, and he says couples can meet there, occasionally, if you know what I mean. It has to be organized beforehand, but the crew will look the other way if we give them a heads up."

A hush fell over the crowd.

"We'll manage," the man said. "It's only a few weeks."

"Can't look a gift horse in the mouth," another man said, and some heads nodded in agreement.

"Fuck them," Kurt said under his breath, furious. "Six whole weeks."

"I'm sure they have a good enough reason," I said, trying to calm him down.

Before he could reply, the passengers moved again and within seconds, I was surrounded by women, all proceeding down the right-hand gangway. I noticed considerably fewer women than men in the crowd. Although I was sorry to be separated from Kurt, I understood the need for the gender split.

We moved forward until another sailor told our group to stop. He picked me and the five women next to me and allocated a cabin with three bunk beds to us. I quickly threw my handbag on one of the upper beds, as did two other women. The remaining three settled on the lower bunks. At least I would be able to stare at the ceiling when I thought of my love, but unfortunately, the upper bunks were only two feet apart. The women who'd grabbed those would be able to watch every move I'd make.

I stowed my luggage in the wardrobe the six of us had to share, climbed up on my bunk, and stretched out. Now what? Eventually, we would be asked to go upstairs again to get instructions on where to wash, eat, and meet our men.

Our men. Kurt. I let out a long breath. *My God! Kurt in such a small cabin. He'll go crazy.* Suddenly, my heart was heavy with dread. I didn't want him angry and upset. If only I could see him and figure out a way to calm him down.

The woman at my left stirred and made a funny noise, like a little animal in distress. I looked at her and saw tears running down her plump cheeks behind her oversized glasses. *Oh please, not that, too.*

"What?" The woman looked back at me, sniffled, and

wiped her cheeks and nose with the back of her hand.

I had been thinking aloud. "I mean," I said quickly, "all this is just too much to bear."

The woman's head bobbed up and down while she extended her hand. "I'm Eva."

I took her hand although it was glistening with moisture. I didn't want to offend her any further.

"It's tough on anybody," Eva said, "but I just got married."

"You, too?"

"Uwe wanted us to leave right after the reception. I told him to wait a few days but he said we shouldn't waste any time on useless festivities. He's not one to celebrate. I only agreed because it sounded so grand to have a honeymoon on a ship."

I swallowed hard.

"Uwe is not a romantic like me. My mom said I couldn't have done any better. One needs a man to take care of things, not one who likes to drink and dance all night, right?"

Eva didn't seem to expect an answer as she rambled on about how her new husband wasn't the prince charming she'd dreamt of but that he was husband material. He was the quiet type, which was nice, because he let her make the decisions—well, all except the one about the timing of their move to a new country. On this point, he'd been adamant, and she'd let him have his way because her mother thought it best and because she could barely wait to see all the exciting places the ship would stop. Las Palmas, Cape Town, Perth, Melbourne. Imagine, all that for the government handling fee of only two hundred German marks. Her mother had said Uwe couldn't have arranged it better, although it broke her heart to let her daughter go, of course.

I nodded when I felt Eva expected a reaction but didn't really register what she said. I'd never been one for chitchat. My eyes wandered to the upper bunk behind Eva and settled on a petite, foreign-looking, striking woman. She had features to die for: high cheekbones, large, dark eyes, and long, black hair pulled back into a ponytail, exposing a high forehead. Only beautiful women could get away with such a hairstyle.

The woman must have felt my scrutiny. She stirred and looked at me, then threw a side glance at Eva and rolled her eyes toward me. "Madonna mia! A whole life's trivia in the first ten minutes," she said. "We've got six weeks—God, have mercy on me—six long weeks to bore each other to death."

Eva clamped her mouth with a tiny whimper. I immediately felt sorry for her, but I also admired the direct approach the other woman had taken. "I'm Johanna," I said to smooth over any growing tension.

"Don't I know it already, thanks to that one." She nodded at Eva. "And you are Eva."

"How do you—" Eva stopped herself in time.

The woman broke into a laugh. "Get used to it. Every word we say in this goddamn cabin belongs to all of us." She looked around. "At least to the three of us. We've got ourselves a cozy little space up here."

She was right. We were out of earshot unless we raised our voices, but between the three of us, there would be no privacy.

"I'm sorry I disturbed you," Eva said.

"Oh please, don't start apologizing," the woman said. "Don't mind me. I don't mean half of what I'm saying. I've got a big mouth."

"Your German is good," I said.

"Why shouldn't it be?"

"Well, there are so many different nationalities on board—Italian, Greek, French. I thought you must be from the south. I mean, you look—"

"Italian. Correct. But I grew up in Germany, so my Italian is piss-poor."

Eva giggled. "You really do have a mouth on you. My mom would have stuffed a bar of soap into mine for such talk."

The woman laughed, too.

"So you are German?" I asked.

"No. Yes. Well, I was born in Italy but lived in Munich all my life. I only became a German citizen when I married Dieter. I'm still getting used to it."

I sat upright, tensed. "When did you get married?"

"Two weeks ago." The woman stretched her hand into the air. "I'm Isabella, by the way. Isabella Kraus. I know that sounds stupid. But what can I do? My husband is Bavarian, from Starnberg."

"Nice to meet you." Eva leaned sideways and took her hand. "Eva Seybold. My husband is from Hamburg. I'm still getting used to my new name, too, and I'm also from Munich."

Isabella shook her hand and looked at me. "And you?"

"Heidelberg. Johanna Strobel. And I got married just a few days ago."

"Sweet Jesus." Isabella's eyes grew even larger. "Three brand new brides in one cabin. What kind of weird coincidence is that? Shit. What are we doing on this ship from hell, newly married but separated from our lesser halves? Goddamn it. How dare they do this to us—legally married women? Those Australian blockheads treat us like nuns, locking us away from our husbands they assume to be sex perverts. What kind of prudish country have we chosen as our new home? A male-dominated, ex-convict colony. That's what it is. How on earth could Dieter do this to me?"

Eva's face contorted. She would cry again any second, so I quickly said, "Once we've arrived, it'll be different. It's only six weeks. We'll have to make the best of it."

"Only six weeks?" Isabella said. "Honeymooning with two women. Who would have thought? My goddamn luck."

Eva sniffled. "But what can we do?" She took out a handkerchief and blew her nose.

"I don't think it's the Australians who made that idiotic rule," Isabella said. "I bet it's that greedy captain who's enforcing it. I bet he has a few cabins reserved for couples like us, but he sells those on the side and charges the Australian government the full amount for us. No country would treat their newcomers like this. Shit. I'm gonna check into this, and when I find out I'm right, I'll make sure they fire him." Her face brightened at the thought. "I'll hang him from the galley like the old pirates did. On high sea, we can take over the command. He's cheating us out of our six weeks of bliss, the rotten little bastard."

It was getting dark when the captain announced for all

passengers to report to the main deck where dinner would be served.

Isabella, Eva, and I made our way up the flight of stairs, sticking together. Very soon, we would leave the harbour, and with it the lives we had known. It mattered little that we were so different. We shared the same dream of settling into a new life in a new place with a new husband.

When we arrived at the dining hall, we located our husbands and steered them to the same table.

Kurt seemed to have calmed down. He was friendly enough and smiled and shook hands. I had to check myself so my relief wouldn't be obvious. Kurt sat next to Eva's husband, Uwe, and started a conversation with him right away. I could see he liked him, maybe because he was as tall as him, though not as bulky. Kurt ignored Dieter, but that didn't surprise me. He was much shorter, like a dwarf next to Uwe and Kurt—thin and very mediocre. I had pictured a handsome man, one that could keep up with Isabella's exotic beauty. Poor Isabella. What does she see in him? I placed one hand on Kurt's arm. He didn't brush it off and probably didn't even notice, as he was engrossed in conversation with Uwe.

Dinner was a simple affair—only tea and sandwiches—but nobody ate much. When the ship's engines started to warm up, we could feel the floor beneath our feet vibrate, instantly energizing everyone. Many immediately rushed outside to secure a front row position at the open deck railings to watch the departure.

After an hour of waiting, huddled together in the cold breeze, the ship shuddered into motion without a noticeable difference in the engines' low hum. While tug boats pulled it out of the harbour, some passengers waved a final farewell to relatives or friends. Others, like us newly married couples, watched as the distance between the quay wall and the ship grew and the people on the land became indistinguishable dots. A hush fell over the crowd as the many lights of the city of Bremen merged into one. Only after this dim source of light vanished into the distance did we retreat to our cabins, silent and solemn, where each of us had to find our own way of coping with the finality of our decision.

3

The six of us spent nearly all our time together. We ate at the same table, got to know each other over long conversations, played board games, and sat on the upper deck and looked at the open sea. The weather became milder and sunnier the farther south we travelled.

Once we had passed the Canary Islands, we travelled down the African coast close enough to occasionally spot it on the horizon. To be able to spend most days on deck was a blessing that made the nights in the stuffy, narrow cabins more bearable. When the guys weren't playing cards, they were searching for suitable locations and dreaming up opportunities where they could take us wives for a good screw, as Kurt called it.

That wasn't as easy as the sailor had indicated at our departure. All social rooms were forever occupied by families with children. Kurt argued with a number of fathers, but none were willing to disperse the children's playgroups for the sake of his urgent needs. Other areas, like the washrooms or the storage areas, were hardly ever empty long enough. There were too many people on board.

The continence forced upon us increased the men's frustration level considerably. We women seemed to accept it much easier. We sat together for hours on end, chatting and laughing, even at night on our cots.

Deep down, I had to admit that I enjoyed Eva and Isabella's

company a lot more than I'd expected when I'd first met them. Eva was entertaining, in a scatterbrainy way, and somehow she knew details about all the other passengers we came in contact with. Isabella talked a lot less but when she did, her comments were sharp and interesting. In comparison, I was plain and boring—not as smart as Isabella and certainly not as amusing as Eva.

I felt a little guilty about enjoying my nights without Kurt so much. I was an only child, not accustomed to the comfort and warmth female company could provide, but he would be annoyed if he knew I preferred to be with my new friends. He was always so demanding.

All could have been well if only Kurt had been more patient. When others were out of earshot, he complained bitterly about the lack of sex. Trying to calm him down made him even more aggressive. He accused me of being a cold-hearted, frigid bitch, as if it were my fault we had to sleep in separate cabins. To hear him talk like that was painful, but it was only said in frustration, so I forgave him.

Whenever we walked past an alcove where curls of thick rope and buckets of sand were stored, he pushed me into its corner. He kissed me hard while his hands groped underneath my sweater and kneaded my breasts with feverish urgency, although we were easily visible to passersby. My objections only made him angrier, to the point that he scared me, but I still refused him. I didn't want it, not where we could be detected any minute. I wriggled myself free before he could get to his business.

Once, after I managed to get away from another of his persistent advances, he was so full of rage, he caught me at the railing and pressed me into the ropes. I felt his erect penis rubbing against my behind, pushing and shoving with increasing speed, like an animal.

When he pulled down my panties, I tried to escape but Kurt held his position with widespread arms and legs, pinning me against the tightly pulled ropes. I looked straight ahead. The horizon moved up and down with the movement of the ship. I couldn't fix my eyes on a non-moving spot and felt nauseated. I looked down and could see only the racing water below, white spray on wild waves. The ropes cut into me under the pressure of his weight, but clinging to them with all the strength I had left was my only hope of staying aboard.

Panicking, I bent my upper body back until I felt his head on my neck. He bit me brutally, then moved his mouth to my ear. "Stop fighting it, bitch, or I'll kick you overboard," he said.

I went limp and turned my head sideways to escape his teeth. A family stood close by. Blood shot into my head. I watched, ashamed, as the horrified father dragged his family away from the scene.

Kurt saw this, too, and let out a victorious roar. There was no stopping him, then. I concentrated on holding on to the upper rope, but with every thrust, I felt I'd lose my position and go overboard.

Finally, he groaned and took a step back, picked up my slip, and pulled it back into place. Then, he gave me a slap on my buttocks like I was a cow.

I wanted to move away from the danger, but my hands had cramped over the rope and refused to let go. I sank down, still holding on. The contents of my stomach heaved up and splashed all over my knees and thighs.

"Yikes," Kurt said and walked away from me.

My body was shaking so violently I didn't dare move. I didn't want to face anybody. Whoever had been watching would get tired of waiting for me to get up. I stayed at the place of my humiliation until it was dark enough to fade into the shadows of the ship's metal walls.

That night, I told myself, Kurt wasn't himself as long as we're on this ship. He'll be all right once we get off. I just have to avoid being alone with him. I might have succeeded if it hadn't been for Isabella.

She was forever complaining to anybody who would listen about gender separation, cramped quarters, and newlyweds needing privacy. And she was on a mission when she bumped into ship employees. Stewards, cooks, deckhands—nobody was safe from her bickering and nagging.

Somehow, word of this crazy woman unsettling others reached the captain. While we finished breakfast, the captain sent for her and Dieter. He offered them a two bed cabin on an upper deck that would become available when we reached Cape Town later that day. A paying couple had gotten into an argument and was flying home.

Dieter seemed subdued when he and Isabella returned. "Listen, guys," he said to Kurt and Uwe, "I don't mind you using our cabin during the day. We could all use some quality time, if you know what I mean."

They were pleased and excited with a grain of grateful jealousy. Even Eva let out a little shriek and gave Dieter an awkward hug before she took me into a warm embrace. "You understand what this means?"

I pushed her off.

Later, lying next to Eva and staring at the ceiling, I felt confused.

"Isabella must be so happy," Eva mumbled into the dark.

I pictured Isabella and Dieter in their new cabin on a soft double bed. Will he be gentle and loving? Will their night be filled with hushed declarations of love and excited moans?

"She got what she wanted," I said.

"She always does."

Isabella and Dieter faded from my mind, replaced with a vision I desperately tried to ignore. Same cabin. Same bed. A husband so full of anger I didn't recognize him—a stranger with a key in one hand and a rope in the other.

"It's nice of Dieter and Isabella to share their cabin with us, don't you think?"

Go away, picture. Go away.

"Go to sleep," I said, forcing the rising panic out of my voice. "I'm tired."

I woke, surprised I had slept at all. The memory of what Kurt had done to me and the anticipation of what he might do to me in Dieter and Isabella's cabin crept into my blood like molten lead. I felt heavy, unable to move.

"Hey, sleepyhead," Eva said. "Time for breakfast."

The thought of runny eggs and greasy bacon on a heap of baked beans made my stomach heave again. "I don't feel so good," I said.

"Suit yourself." Eva slid off her bunk to go to the women's communal bathroom. "Hope you feel better soon. Remember, Kurt reserved the two hours right after breakfast. He will be so upset if you miss it."

The inevitable would only get worse if I prolonged it. Kurt in a good mood or Kurt in a filthy mood? My choice.

I dragged myself to the dining room, picked at my meal, and waited for the guys' references to this morning's activities. No lewd remarks, no childish or vulgar quibble, not even a hint of what was planned. Maybe something happened that made it impossible for us to use the upper cabin.

When we all finished, Kurt turned to me and said, "Shall we go?" He pulled the chair for me, and I was surprised I didn't start shaking. The sooner he starts, the sooner it will be over.

Once inside the cabin, Kurt locked the door behind us, leaned against it, let out a long breath, and extended his arms toward me. His voice was gentle.

"Please, come to me."

I wanted to scream and yell at him. *You bastard! You disgusting piece of shit! I hate you! You hurt me! You degraded me! I hate you! I hate you!* But nothing came out. I stood in the middle of the room like a defiant child, trembling.

He came toward me and folded me into his embrace, carefully and tenderly, and stroked my back until I stopped shaking, and then he kissed me. His lips searched mine for the tiniest reaction, and when he felt me melting, he increased the pressure, still careful and tender, but with a passion I had never felt before. I forgot everything before that moment.

This was how I wanted him—caring and affectionate.

He slowly unfastened the buttons of my blouse—too slow for me, so I helped him. When he lowered my slip, he knelt in front of me.

"Please forgive me," he said, so low I could barely understand him. "I don't know what devil rode me, but I love you so much and I've missed you so much. You are mine forever, and I can't imagine a life without you."

He kept whispering but I wasn't listening any longer. He loves me. He needs me. That's all I needed to know. Of course I would forgive him.

That evening, the guys played cards, and we women met in our cabin. Isabella brought a bottle of schnapps she had bought from a sailor for four German marks. My parents had never allowed me to taste alcohol and none was allowed in the nurses' station, so I was one of those rare eighteen-year-olds who'd never had a single drop of alcohol, much less been drunk.

The schnapps burned my mouth. I wanted to spit it out but I held my breath and swallowed so as not to insult Isabella. It went down the wrong way and made me cough. Isabella laughed and Eva patted my back as the fire in my throat died down and a pleasant warmth spread from my stomach up to my face, making me giggle.

Isabella handed me the bottle again. "This time, only take a small sip."

The warmth spread throughout my whole body until I felt totally relaxed. What an amazing feeling. What an amazing day. Kurt's love felt even better now. I was so grateful to him. So very, very grateful.

My heart was so full of love and warmth, I wanted to tell my friends all about it, but it didn't seem to be the right moment. Eva was saying something silly we couldn't understand, and she got lost in a ridiculous explanation. Isabella's bottle made our little round again and again. We were laughing at everything and nothing, revelling in being so incredibly funny. Eva slapped her thighs when she thought something particularly hilarious, and Isabella roared and snorted like a walrus until the women below us complained. She handed them the bottle, and pretty soon, the mood in the cabin was a celebration of sorts. We didn't know what we celebrated, but hey, it didn't matter. We were happy. I was happy.

And then I noticed the white dots on Eva's pink dress. They were moving. Then, they got larger and smaller. I concentrated on the dots until I was dizzy. I looked away, but it only got worse. I looked back. Some of the dots blew up to the size of a fish, a poisonous one with spikes. I couldn't remember its name. I only remembered that people died when they ate a tiny gland inside the fish. I felt sick to my stomach.

"Jesus, don't throw up in here," Isabella said.

Eva helped me slide down from my bunk. I grabbed the bunk post to steady myself, but the cabin still danced around me. Behind the cabin was all-consuming blackness, a black hole.

I needed to get out before it swallowed me up.

"I need air."

I heard the other women laugh and some yelled advice. "Turn left. Take the lift. Hurry. Find a bucket. Don't lean on the rails. Don't fall overboard."

Please. Quick. Out of here.

I moved fast, feeling my stomach in my throat. When I reached the lift, I pressed the button, and by some miracle the doors opened instantly. I got in, pressed another button, leaned with my forehead on the cool metal, and listened to the motor's hum as I went up. I smelled diesel and oil and placed my hands tightly over my mouth.

Finally there, the doors opened and I staggered out onto the dimly lit, deserted deck. Far away, I thought I saw Kurt. *He's come to help me. My savior, my knight.* I wobbled forward, stumbled over a curled rope, and lost my footing. The images in view began to dance in and out of focus as I turned and fell into Kurt's arms. No, slipping through, no, no. There was no Kurt. Eyes closed, the dance didn't stop. I retched and knelt on the floor with my head down. When I lifted my head, I hit something hard.

Pain. Pain. Pain. Then, nothing.

When Isabella and Eva found me, dawn had already broken, but I could see the faint light only with my left eye. My right one was swollen shut.

"Oh my God!" I heard Eva say. "She's bleeding."

Isabella said, "Stay with her. I'll get help."

I could feel Eva wiping vomit and snot from my mouth and nose before I fainted again. I woke in the ship's hospital room, my right arm in a cast and bandages on my head, resting on clean sheets.

The doc stood next to my bed, looking at me with a mixture of curiosity and disgust. "You'll need to stay under observation until you're sober again."

He asked me how the injury happened, so I told him I tripped over a rope. He frowned.

"I've stitched up the laceration above your eye. You were lucky. No serious injuries…this time."

The nausea came back. "Please, believe me. I don't normally drink anything. This was the first time. I wasn't used to it. That's why," I pleaded.

His frown deepened. "If you say so."

Two days later, he let me go back to the cabin. Eva and Isabella picked me up. After two more days, I was strong enough to spend some time on deck.

"Kurt is pretty pissed," Isabella said.

I froze.

"Don't," Eva said quickly. "It's just because he is so worried about you."

"Bullshit. It's because that idiot doctor told him you were drunk, but I told Kurt you hardly touched it, that you'd just been a little tipsy. You have no practice—that's the problem. He understood that."

The three men were waiting for us on deck. With Eva and Isabella by my side, I wasn't quite so scared, but the shame was unbearable. Kurt will truly hate me now.

His expression changed from worry to compassion when he saw me. "My poor little darling." He didn't dare embrace me but took my hand to his lips and kissed it.

Uwe patted his shoulder, a big grin on his face. "Mark my words, she won't drink so soon again."

Dieter said, "It'll heal in no time."

"Main thing is nothing serious happened," Kurt said. He bent down to kiss my cheek.

I tried to smile at him but must have made a funny face because it hurt, and everybody laughed.

"Promise you won't wander around on deck alone at night again," Kurt said.

"I promise." What luck that he wasn't there with me stumbling around like a drunk and falling into my own vomit. He wouldn't love me anymore if he had seen me like that.

4

ISABELLA

By the time we reached Perth, the ship's fresh water tanks were nearly empty. The captain decided to shorten our stay in the harbour since bad weather had cost us a few days already and he wanted to reach Sydney on schedule.

Until Perth, the mood on the ship had been fairly peaceful. Sydney had seemed so far away that we weren't thinking about the future, but since we had touched the shoreline of Australia, our imminent arrival at our final destination created a lot of excitement. Suddenly, our involuntary inactivity became harder to bear, and having our water rationed because the crew had forgotten to fill the tanks in Perth further increased the nervous energy on board.

"I need to get off this damn ship" was a mantra I heard everywhere. I said it myself every hour of the day, mumbling it mostly, because I could sense the tension in the collective apprehension of what awaited us, aided by the stench of inadequate hygiene. God, how we all stank. To hell with the generous arrangement Dieter had made with our friends. I would have stayed in our cabin all day long if they would have let Dieter bring me something to eat and drink. The stewards were as cranky as the rest of us, and we were all at each other's throats.

When we finally reached Melbourne, the general mood

was happy again. Anticipation, expectation, hope and faith pushed aside the whiffs of foul breath, the reek of pungent armpits and the stench of unwashed diapers.

We were taken off board and squeezed onto a train taking us to a camp for new immigrants in Bonegilla.

"I'd like to know if they are going to put us in separate rooms again," I complained as soon as we settled on the train. Nobody said anything but I could see the worry in the faces of those around us.

"Be quiet," Dieter said, and for once I had to agree with him. Everybody knew we'd enjoyed preferential treatment until now.

Bonegilla was on the border between Victoria and New South Wales. Outside of town, deep in a forest of skinny gum trees, a cluster of various sized corrugated tin huts had been erected on an opening next to a picturesque lake. I saw campfire pits and a dock on the shoreline. The camp could have been a youth holiday camp somewhere in Europe if it weren't for those odd trees with their spotty white trunks and faded green leaves.

Still, I felt a little lighter when the camp officer announced that each family would get their own hut. Even couples without children would get one of the smaller ones closer to the forest.

"It's a start," I said. Then, the bus with everybody's baggage arrived. I pushed and shoved my way through the crowd to find our belongings.

"For Christ's sake, Dieter," I yelled. He leaned on one of those weird-looking trees, arms crossed.

"What's the hurry?" he said.

I found our two suitcases, dragged them over to him and dropped them at his feet. "I want the last hut in the row." He picked them up with a scrunched face, and I walked ahead of him to the hut of my choice. I was in desperate need of a shower, unfortunately in a communal washroom again, before we would unpack and get settled for the few days we'd be here.

In the evening, our little group met by the lakeshore, away from the campfire pits where all the others had grouped.

We sat on the soft ground in a semi-circle, facing the water. I searched my friends' faces but couldn't make out their reactions to the dump we were in. Kurt held Johanna's limp hand loosely and Eva leaned on Uwe's shoulder, both of them looking exhausted.

"What do you think?" I finally asked.

The guys didn't reply.

"It's quite nice here," Eva said.

"Johanna?"

"Huh?" She lifted her face, surprised.

"What do you think?"

She quickly turned to Kurt, who pressed her hand. "Uh-huh, yes, it's nice."

"Are you all nuts?" I said. "This is a concentration camp. The huts are dilapidated. The roofs have holes the size of golf balls and look like they'll cave in on us in our sleep. My mattress is so worn it hangs down to the floor. I don't want to know how many creepy crawlies live in it. And the toilets? We have to squat on the floor. I refused to use one of those when I visited my relatives in Italy, and I'm certainly not going to start now."

"Take it easy," Dieter said. He turned away from me to address the others. "My dear wife is a little spoiled, being the only girl in a family with three sons. Princess only had to snap her fingers and daddy loved his only girl so much, he told her she'd never have to dirty her hands with work. A plain camp obviously isn't to her liking."

I got up and stared at the lake. "You are wrong," I said, loud enough for the group to understand me. "And you know you are wrong. I'm not spoiled. I'm only honest. This is a cheap dump, worse than the ship, and I bet the food is just as bad."

"The food was great," Kurt said.

I could feel his eyes on my back. *Feast them on my tight arse, you creep.* Dieter had asked me a number of times to get rid of those jeans. He thought they made me a target for sex-starved, hot-blooded males.

"You'd eat anything." Swirling around to him, I caught a glimmer of greed in his expression and was taken aback. He made no effort to hide his craving for…for what? For me, his friend's wife? His eyes lingered on my breasts, and his lower lip quivered. I saw his tongue come out, a fleshy, wet bulge moving over his lower lip, leaving it glistening with saliva.

I did a half turn again, embarrassed, as if I were at fault. None of the others noticed as they stared at the sand in front of them.

"I liked the food on the ship, too," Johanna said, eyes still on the ground. Then, she looked up at me. "Most of the time, anyway. The camp is all right. At least the ground doesn't move."

I remembered how ill Johanna had felt after her accident.

She was on pain medication for a while, and she'd developed seasickness and would puke if she didn't take those pills regularly. Poor thing. Today must be her first day not feeling queasy from the pills.

"I'm going for a swim," I said.

"Great idea," Eva said, getting up.

I was halfway to our hut when I turned back and snapped my fingers at Dieter, signalling him to come along. "Help me unpack." He wasn't out of the woods for his idiotic comments. *Me, a princess?* I vowed to sit on our filthy mattress and watch him unpack those damn suitcases all by himself.

Dieter walked past me like a puppy dog. I let him go ahead.

He was already out of earshot when I heard Kurt say, "Dieter doesn't know what he's got himself into with that one. She needs a strong hand, a real guy who knows how to handle her, not a wimp like him."

He knew I could hear him, and so did the others. Uwe laughed. Eva and Johanna didn't, but they didn't contradict him either.

I followed Dieter into the hut.

We stayed three weeks in Bonegilla. We had no responsibilities and next to nothing to do. Three meals were served daily in the community hut, and our basic laundry could be done in the lake. The huts had dirt floors, so we didn't bother sweeping them, and there were no toilets to clean. Everything was taken care of by a bunch of disinterested government employees in charge of the camp, knowing and abusing their power to their own advantage. I was sure a lot of money allocated to our well-being was syphoned off, but what could we do? Most of us didn't understand a word of what they said, their accents being so thick our basic school English seemed like a different language.

We hung around the fire pits, the guys played cards all day, and the women gossiped. I couldn't be bothered listening to the young mothers complaining about their children or the childless ones complaining about their husbands, so I stuck to Johanna and Eva. I could tell them to zip it when I wasn't in the mood.

"I wish they'd give us knitting needles and wool," Eva said once.

"No fucking way," I said. I was so bored, in all honesty, I would have started knitting, but they didn't give us any, so why admit it?

"Uwe really likes Kurt," Eva said to Johanna.

"They are both craftsmen," Johanna said.

And that wasn't the only thing they had in common. I didn't say it, but looking at those two tall men with their broad shoulders and confident swagger when they strolled around the camp, I could understand why they became the go-to guys and why Dieter ranked lower on the masculinity scale guys establish for themselves. Dieter didn't notice, though, because they let him run with the pack, and he basked in their popularity.

"Photography is kind of a craft," I said.

"Oh no," Eva said. "That's different. Dieter is an artist. You should be so proud of him."

"His English is not bad," Johanna said.

I was floored when it registered that even Eva, who spoke the best English of the six of us—better by far than Dieter's embarrassing fumbling for words—was far from being fluent. Eva shrugged when I pointed this out to her. "They promised we can all take a course when we get settled in Sydney."

"If we ever…" I said.

"Did I tell you about our plans once we're there?" Eva asked. I'd heard it before, but hell, anything to kill time.

Kurt was yelling something in our direction and Johanna jumped up as if a spider had crawled up her legs. Eva got up, too.

"You don't have to go," I said to her.

"Maybe Uwe needs me."

"Sit."

She sat down again, but her story had dried up. After about a minute, Uwe called for her, and she looked at me.

"Go. For heaven's sake, go."

"I'll be back soon."

She returned after ten minutes, no explanation given. I didn't need one. Eva and Johanna had built-in spring coils that reacted to their masters' commands, I had once told them, making them jump through fiery hoops. The sad thing was they didn't even object to my mocking.

5

JOHANNA

Three months from our wedding day, I finally understood how wrong I'd been about Kurt. That morning, camp management informed us that we'd depart the following day. The bus would arrive at 7:00 a.m. to take us to our destinations. Most had picked Sydney, Melbourne, or Brisbane, but some of the more daring ones were headed into the country.

The three weeks in Bonegilla had given me enough country life experience to be thoroughly disgusted by it. I couldn't wait to get out of the dirt and depression, and neither could Eva and Isabella. Sydney was what we all needed.

Right after breakfast, Kurt got into gear. He was a natural leader, and even Uwe listened when he spoke. He took our group aside and explained how important it was to stick together.

"Let's go to my hut," he said. "We need to get organized."

Our hut was too small to accommodate six people but we had no choice, as it had been raining hard since dawn. Kurt pushed the double bed back to the wall, we women sat on the mattress, and the guys leaned against the opposite wall.

"We pack this afternoon, everything except one towel per couple. Take a shower in the evening and hang the towel to dry in the hut. With a bit of luck, the rain will stop overnight."

"What's your worry?" Uwe said.

"We need to be ready before the bus arrives. You know how excited everybody will be. They'll push and shove. Stick together at all costs. When they take us to Sydney, they'll drop us off at different camps, smaller ones than Bonegilla, spread all over town. We'll get split up if we let others get between us, and we can't afford to be separated."

He was so smart. Nobody asked how he knew those things.

"What shall we do if they insist on separating us?" Dieter said.

"They won't. That's why it's so important to be the first on the bus, together. That way, we'll be the last to leave. We'll be okay, just do as I say."

"After we pack and help clean up the campsite, we should meet again by the lake," Kurt said. He'd organize a six-pack of beer—again, nobody asked from where—to celebrate our departure.

Each couple went their own way. When Kurt disappeared to get the beer, I took the empty suitcase from the corner and placed it on the bed. I folded the few clothes we had worn in the last few weeks and put them inside. Kurt had stowed our other three suitcases under the bed. They were full of memorabilia from my past life, and we hadn't opened them since we left Germany. Kurt said all those trinkets were pretty useless in our current situation.

I closed the packed suitcase, pulled one of the other three out, placed it on the bed, and felt an instant lump in my throat. My stomach contracted so badly I doubled over, pressing both hands on my abdomen. The suitcase brought back painful memories. My old home. Neat. Tidy. Glorious autumn days. My parents being bossy and pushy, making me learn a decent profession. The nurses' home. Strict, but friendly. A home with brick walls under white stucco, green wood shutters, and a well-kept park surrounding it.

Hot tears shot into my eyes. The longing for what I had left became overpowering. I would never be able to go back—at least not for the two years Kurt had committed us. We couldn't afford to pay the fare back to the Australian government. I sank to my knees. Two years. I can't survive two years. That's a lifetime away.

"What's the matter with you?" Kurt said. He stood in the doorway, the six-pack dangling from his hand.

I didn't want to show him my swollen, wet face. I'd never considered myself attractive, but crying made me outright ugly. "I don't know." I covered my face with my hands, mumbling through my fingers. "I was thinking of Heidelberg…of home."

"Are you nuts?" His voice blew over me like an arctic storm. "Who cares about the old home? We are in Australia now. That's our home. Got it?"

The tears didn't stop. The shivering didn't stop. The pain in my stomach spread to my heart, so heavy I gasped for air.

"Stop crying over nothing."

The pain was all-consuming. I didn't register his command and stayed on my knees, not realizing I knelt in front of him like a sinner. "But I don't feel at home here. It's so ugly, so disgusting, so dirty. So…so…different from home. There are crawling insects everywhere. And it smells. Everything smells…moldy, rotten…I don't know…"

He should have taken me in his arms and comforted me, explained it would be better in Sydney and that it was normal to miss home initially—that this was only a transition, and once we got settled and started a life together, he'd make sure I wouldn't miss anything.

Instead, he grabbed my arms and pulled me up with such force my hands were jerked from my tear-streaked face. He stared at me, pulled me closer, and squeezed my upper arms together until I cried out.

"Look at me," he commanded.

His face was contorted.

"I'll say it only once. I have no use for a stupid, whining woman. What don't you like? The insects? That's your problem? A few cockroaches? Are you kidding me?"

His sudden burst of anger took me by surprise. I didn't know what to say or how to react. I was caught in his strong arms. The truth hit me with terrible clarity. I wasn't suddenly scared of him, I'd been scared of him for some time already—maybe ever since I'd met him. His dominance was so intense I had succumbed to it from the beginning. I feared him, and had called it love. He scared me, but I was in awe of his power and his ability to protect me. In bed, when his strong body was on top of me, forcing me into his rhythm of lust—wasn't that love?

"I'm sorry." I couldn't think of anything else to say. He raised his hand. I expected him to hit me, but he didn't. He'd never do that. He let me go and pushed me back on the mattress.

"Sit. Don't move. I'll be back soon."

I stayed in position, my brain devoid of any thought. I

was numb. He'd been like a different person. That contorted face wasn't the Kurt I loved.

This was all wrong—this country, this hut, this bed. *What am I doing here? Stop it. Stop this, now. Don't put up with it. Leave. Go back home and work hard. You can pay back your share. You have a profession to fall back on. Your parents will help you. You can do it. Get up and tell him it was a mistake—the wedding, the journey, everything. Leave Australia. Tell him.*

The door opened again and the angry giant filled the doorway. I'd never stand my ground when he was in this mood. I made myself smaller.

"Get up. I want to show you something."

I did. My brain was empty again.

He stood very close, leaned down to me and held up his closed fist. "Do you know what I got in here?"

I shook my head.

"A tiny brown animal only a few centimeters long with skinny legs and long tentacles—a cockroach. A simple insect, one of billions in this world."

I'd chased away enough of those since we'd arrived in this country. They were revolting and fearless, some as large as a mouse. Many held their ground until they felt the bristles of my broom, putting their antennas up and staring at me as if ready to attack.

I took a step back. "I don't want to see."

He closed up on me again, leaving no room between us. "You don't have to. As soon as I open my hand, it'll escape. Open your mouth."

No. He wouldn't do that.

"Open it. Cockroaches are a delicacy in many countries. They taste good, they say. In any case, they are nutritious and this country's got plenty of them. If you want to live here, you better accept that they do too."

His free hand grabbed both my wrists. "Open your mouth."

I wanted to protest and tell him I couldn't live here—that it had been his idea entirely and that Australians don't eat cockroaches. Maybe the aborigines in the bush did but not the city people or immigrants. I opened my mouth, just a tiny bit, enough to plead with him. He placed his closed fist over my lips, flattened it, and forced my mouth open…and then I could feel it. I couldn't scream. Terror spread from my lips to my mind and made me clamp my teeth together. I heard a sharp crunch and felt the shell crush. I opened my mouth again to stop the horror, but the cockroach still wriggled against the tip of my tongue.

I fell back on the mattress, and Kurt fell with me, never letting go and never lifting his hand from my mouth.

"Eat it," he said, breathless. "Chew it, swallow it. Whatever. Get it down somehow. I won't let you go until you do."

I couldn't breathe. I sucked for air and sucked the roach in, choked, swallowed, and choked again, but it wouldn't go down. I was suffocating. Not much longer and I'd die.

The mass of squashed cockroach eventually slid down my throat and Kurt let go of my mouth. I frantically drew in air and desperately tried to squirm out from underneath him. He finally let me move sideways and I puked the disgusting mush up next to the mattress and heaved until only bile came up. Then, I sank back, exhausted.

Kurt got on top of me again, his hand fumbling for the button on his jeans as he breathed hard and fast.

Although I had air in my lungs again, my body didn't react. Motionless and breathing shallowly, I was just a heap of flesh and bones, unable to think or feel anything. Kurt grinded away, shoving and pushing and groaning with savage pleasure while avoiding the sour smell coming from my mouth by covering my face with the bedsheet.

When he finished, he zipped his jeans, picked up the beer cans, and went outside.

He came back much later, when darkness had fallen. I still hadn't moved.

"Get up and join us. Wash your face and fix your hair. You look like shit and the others are wondering about you."

I did as I was told.

Everybody sat around the campfire, but nobody asked where I'd been or why I didn't join the conversation. I rarely ever did, anyway. I wished I could have a sip of beer to get rid of the foul taste in my mouth, but nobody offered me any, and I wouldn't have taken it. Kurt wouldn't have liked it.

6

EVA

An old beat-up bus took us to our destination. As we approached Sydney, I searched the landscape for a change of scenery but the bush on both sides of the road was low and dry. It was barren land with no sign of civilization. There wasn't a single village for hundreds of kilometers.

At four in the afternoon, we arrived at our new camp on the outskirts of the big city I longed to see. Low houses lined the wide, paved streets, I noticed with a secret sigh of relief. I'd had enough of dusty dirt roads.

"Villawood." Isabella read the sign painted on the top beam of the gate we passed. "How appropriate." The camp consisted of hundreds of roughly erected small, wooden huts. "Looks like we get a villa each," she smirked.

Kurt got busy right away, instructing Uwe and Dieter to look after our luggage while he secured three huts next to each other.

One other couple was as fast as him and took the third hut in the row he had picked. Kurt walked over to them, exchanged a few words, and they left with hanging heads.

A little later, the camp manager showed up. Kurt didn't understand a word he said. I stood next to them and could have translated the basic meaning, but the idea of telling Kurt that the manager wanted him to give the hut back to the couple was too intimidating. I moved away from the confrontation, trying to ignore the choice insults Kurt hurled at him. Soon after the manager left with a resigned look on his face, Kurt clapped his hands together and told Johanna to go inside and unpack.

It didn't take long for us to get settled. Uwe and I strolled through the camp to the manager's building, a wooden hut similar to ours but larger, and looked at the blackboard. Uwe asked me to translate what was written on it. We'd get three meals a day as well as all the necessities—bedsheets, towels, soap, and shampoo. We had to keep ourselves and our surroundings clean at all times or we would lose privileges, though it didn't specify what privileges. Maybe they meant the right to join the language course starting the next morning, although the invitation to join sounded more like an order.

When Uwe told everybody about the instructions on the blackboard, Kurt told him to enroll the six of us in the course immediately. Finally, this was a real step toward taking charge of our lives again.

We were in the classroom from eight in the morning until early afternoon. The course's intensity left us all visibly drained, but we still got assignments to complete for the following day. We'd forfeit our right to the free course and would have to pay to master the language if we didn't do them. They told us we were free to leave the camp anytime and that job openings were posted on the board, but nobody would hire us if we couldn't communicate.

Kurt said we should meet every evening in one of our huts to do our homework together. We agreed not to speak in our native tongue anymore, like the course teacher had recommended, but Kurt was the first to break our pact.

"Fuck this," he said. "I don't need to write an essay to repair a heating element."

Dieter laughed. "Did it ever occur to you that we are in a country without central heating? Or any other kind of heating? They don't need to heat their houses here. You'll have to learn a new trade." He laughed even harder, and Kurt boxed him in his rib cage.

"Asshole. As if I hadn't thought of that. Heating and cooling units work similar. All the offices have air-conditioning here, you smartass. I'll get a job in no time with my qualifications."

Four weeks later, we all received our language course completion certificates and were let loose in the job market. I had top marks, but the others put their documents away without dwelling on them, so I assumed their results weren't so good. I didn't press them to save them any embarrassment.

Uncertain what to do next, I suggested we go to town together a few times to check out where we wanted to live and work and practice our language skills in everyday situations.

"What a waste of time and money that would be," Kurt said. "Our first priority is to get jobs. Then we can go exploring and blow our hard-earned money to our heart's content."

He sounded insecure about navigating the town by himself. It must have been tough for such a patronizing character to feel so helpless.

We studied the job offers first thing every morning. Uwe bought the daily paper, *The Sydney Morning Herald*, and I translated all offers posted there. We discussed and argued over every single possibility. Nothing seemed suitable for any of us, so we settled into a routine of hopes and dreams, waiting for the right opportunity to come along.

Six weeks later, Kurt surprised us. "We gotta get out of here," he said. The longer we stay, the less likely we are to get decent jobs. Employers will look at our arrival date and wonder how come we haven't got jobs yet. Villawood is dragging us down. The camp brands us as useless immigrants. We have to show initiative."

"Shouldn't we get jobs first?" I asked.

"Tell your wife to shut up," Kurt said to Uwe.

Uwe scratched his head. "It's quite comfortable here and it costs nothing."

Kurt ignored him and addressed me. "Don't be so dense, Eva," he said. "I didn't say we should move out without having jobs, but we have to stop being so picky. We need to accept what's offered, get a flat, and then start to better ourselves."

I nearly said, "Oh, now I understand. You are worried you'll only get a menial job and need to justify selling yourself below value." Maybe the others thought the same thing but, of course, none of us said anything of the kind. We all nodded and went back to the blackboard with renewed eagerness.

We had vowed to stick together. Moving out was only possible if all of us earned money.

Two days later, I bumped into Johanna at the camp gate when she returned from an interview.

"I got a job," she said, smiling.

I congratulated her with a tiny stitch of jealousy inside me. My day hadn't been successful.

She must have read it in my expression. "It's cleaning at a seniors' home."

My face went all soft. "Oh dear, that's terrible."

"It's okay. The manager asked me why I don't want to work as a nurse when he saw my resume. I said that I do but that my English isn't good enough yet."

"It isn't too bad."

"That's what he said, too. Giving injections and bandaging wounds doesn't take much language skills. He said the old people will be grateful if somebody has medical experience, and he offered me a nurse's position."

"But didn't you say you got hired as a cleaner?"

"To officially work as a nurse, I need to do a special exam, and for that, I need to study and save. So on paper, I'll be employed as a cleaner, but that's okay. I start tomorrow."

That evening, we met in our hut. Uwe congratulated Johanna. "Well done, girl."

Kurt made a face. "She'll have to wipe arses and change diapers for forty lousy bucks a week. Big achievement for a former nurse."

"But still. She's the only one of us who'll make money tomorrow.

Two days later, Kurt had a job on a construction site. They took one look at his massive shoulders and offered to pay him eighty dollars a week.

I was pleased for Johanna. Kurt was so competitive it wouldn't be easy to come home from work and have to deal with his dissatisfaction. She'd have enough to handle with the old folks.

After that day, I didn't see much of her anymore. She usually came back late, but several times when we did meet, I noticed bruises on her arms or neck, and once even a shiner on her left eye.

"Those old folks can be pretty strong," she said. "I have to be careful. But they don't mean it."

7

JOHANNA

A week later, we all had work except Isabella. Eva had found a cleaning job and Uwe was sorting spare parts in a factory, but Dieter had won the lottery. He'd been hired in his field at the Sydney television station, Channel Ten.

"Only to look after the props needed for their regular programming," he said. "Way below my qualifications, and way below the money I'm used to making."

"But you got your foot in the door," Kurt said. "Smart guy."

Dieter grew a few inches.

Uwe gave Dieter's shoulder a slap. "Well done. You'll move up soon. We all will."

"We will need to," Kurt said. "We're all working below our capabilities."

Eva and I felt sorry for Isabella. We tried to console her every chance we got, but she seemed to care little about her misfortune. Dieter had work, so some money was coming in, and she was busy looking for a place for all of us to live. It wasn't an easy task to find three small flats close to each other, much less in the same complex. Most days she took the bus all over town, coming back looking like she'd been enjoying herself.

Kurt must have noticed. "This has to stop," he said. "We'll

still be here at Christmas if we insist on staying together. We won't be able to better ourselves as long as the camp address is on our application forms, and I don't plan to stay in this job forever. We have to get on with our lives. From now on, it's each couple for themselves."

Again, it was me who first found an apartment. An adorable old lady in my seniors' home who liked to dress up like a countess asked me one afternoon while I was doing her hair why I always looked so sad.

I hadn't noticed it showed. "It's nothing. I just wish my husband and I could find a place to live."

"Camp life must be hard." The countess smiled at me. "I own a place on the north shore. The tenants moved out last week. I'd be happy to rent it to you, dear. It's nothing fancy. Two rooms only. But decent enough for a start."

Kurt and I moved in the following weekend. On Friday evening, our friends came to help us get settled. Together, we picked up a few pieces of furniture from the second-hand shop I had discovered around the corner and carried them to the top floor of our three-story block. The apartment was bright and airy. If I stood on tippy-toes at the bathroom window, I could see a glimpse of the harbour bridge in the distance.

"The rent is twenty-five dollars a week," Kurt said. He glanced at Isabella. "Very doable with two incomes." He enjoyed showing off our new home. "All houses here have built-in kitchens." He opened the oven door. "See. Would cost us a bundle if we'd had to get our own." Everybody followed him into the bedroom. "Curtains, carpet, everything included. All we had to get was that sofa, the table and chairs, and a bed."

"Heavy enough to schlepp up all those stairs," Isabella said, earning a frown from Dieter.

Kurt grinned back at her. "You may have to do it again soon. I talked to the neighbour, and he said the apartment next to ours will be available soon."

After everybody had left, Kurt went to get a cold six-pack. I put five cans in the fridge and took one to him. He was slumped on the sofa—legs wide, arms folded, with a pleased expression on his face. I sat down next to him.

"It feels good to finally have a place where I can cook for us," I said. Since our marriage, I hadn't made a single meal.

"You bet." He emptied the can with one long gulp. "Get me another, will you?"

He seemed in a mellow mood. I brought one back and dared to ask, "Are the neighbours really moving out?"

He burped. "I'm not giving it to Dieter. Isabella is a bitch and she treats Dieter like dirt."

"Can you decide who gets it?"

"I prefer Uwe. He's reliable, and I can count on him to pay the rent. Otherwise, it might fall back on me to cover for him if he's late, with me recommending him and all."

"I don't think that would happen," I said. "Eva and Uwe both have jobs. They won't be late. And even if they were, why should we have to pay for them?"

"God, you're dumb." He got up to get another beer. "Anything can happen in this country. They are so backwards. No social security. If you lose your job, you're on your own. Not like in Germany. You can starve to death here, and they don't give a shit."

He walked to the window and stared out. I didn't see his expression and had just about forgotten how quickly his mood could change. The past weeks had been so good. With me coming home from work so late and him leaving so early, we had hardly seen each other.

"I don't agree," I said. "The Australian government has been generous. All the weeks in camp we got fed and housed without having to pay a cent. I'm sure they have unemployment benefits. You just don't know about it."

He drank his beer and squashed the empty can. "I see. Madam there knows everything better than I do? You haven't got a fucking clue. I'm telling you. There's no office to go to, no help, no fucking nothing. Now that they got you into their country, they'll let you perish if you don't perform. You got a job. They take your tax money. And what do you get for it? Fuck all. They don't give a shit what happens to you, but they won't let you go home, either, unless you pay them. It's a scam, a fucking scam."

"We'll always make enough so we won't starve."

He turned around, his face twisted. "You don't know what you're saying. You've never starved a day in your life. You don't know what it feels like when your stomach is growling and all you can think about is food."

He didn't even have to raise his arm to make me cower. The tone in his voice alone brought the fear back—the fear I had felt when he forced me to swallow that cockroach. I had pushed that incident far from my mind, even excusing Kurt for his temporary insanity, but now the fear was back with a vengeance. It gripped me as strong as ever before, knowing what he was capable of. My insides froze, and my mind stopped. I should have run, but I could only hang my head in a gesture of total obedience.

"Go to the bedroom and lie down," he ordered. Dusk hadn't settled yet, but I didn't object. It would only aggravate him further.

He took one of my scarves from the open suitcase on the floor, tied my ankles together, and wrapped it around the right end bedpost. Then, he left and returned with a long rope. He told me to put my arms up and he tied them together to the left top post, though not very tight. I was lying stretched across the bed with enough room for movement. I wondered what his plan was and why he was considerate enough not to hurt me.

He stood at the end of the bed and inspected his work, then bent down to tighten the scarf. I moaned, and he immediately loosened the knot again—a warning that he could always make me suffer.

I understood.

He nodded and left the room. I waited all night, terrified of what he would do to me when he came back. But nothing happened. Saturday morning at 7:00 a.m., I heard the entrance door open, then the bedroom door. He walked up to me, his eyes distant and cold.

"Do you need to pee?"

I whispered a yes.

He untied me and let me go to the bathroom. Then, he tied me up again, brought me a glass of water, and made me drink it. He left again and didn't come back until Sunday morning.

I'd been lying there for twenty-four hours. His eyes were cloudy when he returned. He'd been drinking, so I didn't dare move.

"Are you hungry?"

What do you want me to say? "Yes."

"Good. You can make us breakfast."

He untied me, rubbed my ankles and wrists, and steadied me when I stood. "You understand why I had to do this?" he asked. "You know so little and you trust the wrong people. I'm your husband, and I'm responsible for you, especially in this dog-eat-dog country. I need to make you understand what life is all about, even if it hurts you. We need to be prepared. You understand that, don't you?"

I nodded several times. I did understand. He worried about me and wanted to protect me. He couldn't show his love for me any other way because he had never known another way. I figured the indifference of his alcoholic parents while growing up was interrupted only by brutal beatings. He couldn't help it. He meant well.

"Scrambled eggs and bacon," he said.

I fried enough bacon and eggs for two, set the table, and served us. I sat down opposite him. He reached over, pulled the plate away from me, and loaded my serving onto his plate. "Not today," he said. "I know you're hungry, but it's better that way. You'll learn faster what's important in life."

I tried to look hungry so he wouldn't catch on that I'd been worried how I would keep the food down.

He smiled, and so did I. The danger had passed.

8

EVA

Uwe and I moved into the apartment next to Kurt's about three weeks later. Uwe had to leave at 5:30 a.m. to get to the factory and didn't come home until 8:00 p.m., but he never complained about the long hours.

"It's only until I find the right thing," he said. "Maybe I'll get something closer, like you did."

I had applied at the dry cleaning shop on our street when we moved in and got the job the moment the German owner heard where I was from. Being able to learn everything I needed to know about my new job in German was an incredible blessing, and, as an added bonus, when the owner came back to close the shop, I could chat with her about our old home.

The dry cleaner was only a ten-minute walk from our apartment so I did the grocery shopping on the way home, prepared a meal to warm up for Uwe, packed his sandwiches for the next day, and cleaned our little place. I was usually done by six.

Johanna was always on the early shift and didn't have any more household chores than me, so with Kurt working long hours, too, I thought it only natural for us to spend some time together before our men got home. I knocked on her door the day after I had started work, coffee mug in hand, but she didn't let me in.

"It's a mess," she said. "Let's go to your place."

The second day, she said she'd run out of coffee. On the third, she simply stepped out and closed the door behind her as soon as I knocked.

"Kurt doesn't want me to come over?" I asked her one evening but got no answer.

"How is work?" she asked instead.

"Like being back home," I said. "Of course, I wouldn't be caught dead working in a dry cleaning shop there but Mrs. Bauer is nice, and Uwe said that if I'm smart about it, she might let me run it one day."

Some evenings Johanna didn't answer my knock, and some evenings I was too proud to go. I stood instead at the bathroom window, counting the white clouds drifting over the Sydney Harbour Bridge, wishing it was the Marienkirche. The bridge's steel construction was as perfectly shaped as the two onion towers of the church in Munich—both so pleasing to look at—yet I couldn't appreciate what I saw, for my heart yearned for the one I couldn't see.

Somebody once told me there is a difference between being alone and being lonely. I stood there wondering what that meant.

"I think Kurt doesn't want her to spend time with me," I said to Uwe one Sunday when we went for our afternoon walk along the ocean at Cremorne Point.

"Nonsense," Uwe said. "You're making a fuss over nothing. Why should Kurt care?"

"She always comes over to our place like she isn't allowed to have guests at theirs."

"We've been over there."

No point in spelling out my suspicion when Uwe was in denial. He would only take Kurt's side.

"Stop wasting your time with idle gossip," he said.

He'd become such a bore since we'd arrived in Australia. Or had he always been so uptight and such a stickler for proper behaviour, and I hadn't noticed? "We are foreigners here, we have to adapt to their way of life," he preached. "They do things differently." As if I didn't know.

I couldn't talk to Uwe about the emptiness I felt inside—the disconnect from the country I was supposed to call home—or about my deep-rooted fears that I would wither away and die of homesickness. He would have rejected those feelings as futile emotions.

Johanna didn't talk much but she was a good listener. When I felt especially troubled, I opened my heart to her and complained bitterly about the country we had to live in. She never contradicted me, and even if she didn't share my misery, the burden was lightened by talking about it. Only once did her indifference annoy me enough to ask her outright if she really liked living here.

"Nothing bothers me," she said.

"That's not what I asked," I said. "Don't you miss anything about your previous life?"

She suddenly looked very sad. "Our lives have changed so much."

"What's that supposed to mean?"

"Everything in my life is so different now, I wouldn't know where to start with what I find missing."

I could understand that. "Start with the bread. Don't you

miss our bread?"

Johanna's eyes glazed over. She didn't want to understand me. I was tempted to grab her shoulders and shake some sense into her. Damn it, girl! Don't you care about the daily deprivations the Australian way of life throws at us?

"We are immigrants, but the Australians don't want us here. I haven't felt welcome a single day since our arrival. Even working at the dry cleaners, the customers reject me. They aren't rude, insulting, or even uncivil, but they ignore me the moment I open my mouth and they hear my accent."

Of course, my litany of wrongs didn't shake Johanna out of her unexplainable stupor. Nothing affected her like it did me.

I carried on with my monologue regardless because voicing my frustrations was better than burying them inside. After she left, I took out a slice of bread, bunched it into a ball and threw it against the wall.

It made a gentle thump when it fell on the floor—so unspectacular it made me cry.

9

ISABELLA

Almost everybody had left Villawood. Some days it felt like I was the only one still there. By now, every aspect of camp life annoyed me. I could hardly swallow the disgusting mush they served us in the cafeteria, and I got hives after every shower. We had to get a place of our own before I went crazy, but with only one income and no savings, we couldn't afford it.

In Munich, my parents had taken care of everything, but we had no support system in Australia. Landlords required two months' rent as a security deposit, and it would take us a year to put that much aside from Dieter's salary. Hell, we couldn't even prove we could afford to pay the rent without starving.

Every Saturday, we went to Cremorne to visit our friends. It was the highlight of Dieter's week, but I hated those visits. Kurt was so full of shit about the money he made and how much he could save. I usually tried to ignore his bragging but the way he stared at me, I knew he was trying to impress me more than the others. With Johanna right there, that was outright embarrassing. She must have noticed, but she never scolded him and actually became more and more monosyllabic. Eva, on the other hand, talked incessantly, while Uwe was a jerk who corrected her on just about anything.

Camp was the only thing I hated more than spending time with this irritating bunch, but I think Dieter enjoyed it so much because it gave him an audience for his constant complaining about his employers at the TV station—how they didn't recognize his talent, cramped his style, and underutilized him.

Once, sitting on the bus, when his whining started before we'd even arrived in Cremorne, I lost my patience and yelled at him. "What the hell do you expect? You are employed to dust off props for the next shoot. You're not there as a top-notch photographer."

Dieter pointed to a large billboard featuring one of the ad agencies along Pacific Highway. "That's where I should be, Isabella," he said. "North Sydney is the mecca of advertising. I've got to get in there. My talent is wasted with those idiots at the TV station."

"Then go apply for freelance work. Maybe they're looking for a photographer."

It sounded like a good idea so I kept nagging him, but for weeks I heard nothing but excuses. He couldn't reach anybody on the phone. Nobody called him back. One had to have connections to get a foot in the door. First, I was supportive and understanding, but when that didn't work, I pressured him with demands and accusations. Didn't work, either. Nothing worked. The truth was he didn't have it in him to sell himself, and eventually, he turned the tables on me. I was the lazy one, sitting around camp when I could go to the agencies on his behalf. Other wives took their artist husbands' portfolios around until they found a suitable opening. If I was so desperate for my own place, I better get my game on.

I visited the first agency the next morning. And then another, and another, morning after morning. I talked Dieter up to anybody willing to listen and quickly learned the difference between art director, creative director and managing director. My language skills also improved dramatically. By evening, I was jittery from all the office coffee and compliments I'd received, but the vague promises of keeping Dieter in mind slowly dampened my initial enthusiasm.

By the time I met Hal Singelton, my confidence was pretty low. He was the boss of a North Sydney, medium-sized specialty agency with a terrific reputation of being artsy and daring.

He turned from the reception desk when I walked in, still bearing a victorious grin from flirting with the girl behind the counter, but from her quick change of expression once she was out of his field of vision, I figured he'd only imagined he had scored. When he noticed me, he straightened, pulled his stomach in, and looked me over. I suddenly became aware of the flimsy material my summer dress was made of and that my nipples had reacted to the cold blast coming from the air-conditioning unit above the counter.

He looked at the large portfolio I was carrying, nodded at me, and waved me closer. "Are you here for a job?"

His stare had an unnerving quality. I felt like a piece of furniture being considered for the comfort and pleasure it may give, but simultaneously, I wanted to pass his examination and be worth something.

"Yes, uh, no...not for me."

"Come on in," he said, opening his office door.

He didn't even have the courtesy to look at the whole

portfolio. He merely glanced at the first page and closed it again, putting his hand on it as a final gesture of rejection and then offered me a job. "I need a personal assistant," he said, "and you display the qualities I'm looking for."

I understood what he meant.

"It won't pay much until you pass probation."

"I'll think about it."

"Don't think too long," he said with all the arrogance his superior position allowed him. "Show up Monday morning or the job goes to somebody else."

Saturday evening, we gathered at Uwe's place for a casual dinner. Dieter told them about the job offer and everybody agreed instantly what a lucky girl I was.

"The salary isn't grand," Dieter said, "but it's in the right business, and eventually, it'll give me the opening I need."

"Wait a minute," I said. "I haven't accepted the offer."

"Are you nuts?" Kurt said. "You've got to support your husband."

"Why?" I asked. As usual, Kurt rubbed me the wrong way.

"Don't be so goddamned ignorant. Dieter just told you. You'll meet the right people and make the contacts he needs to get back into his profession."

Uwe agreed with him. "And two salaries are better than one, aren't they?"

"You can finally move into your own place," Eva said. "If you save your salary for a few weeks, you'll have the deposit together."

"Or don't you want to work?" Kurt asked.

How could I tell him that the job had nothing to do with

work if I'd interpreted Hal's signals correctly? But what if I hadn't? What if he is the flirty type but knows the boundaries? Can I afford to reject this chance? Do I want to stay in this rotten camp forever? If push comes to shove, I can always resign.

About an hour after I started work, Hal had his secretary brief me on my duties. She told me when and how he wanted his coffee and where to book his extensive luncheons, take his suits for dry cleaning, shop for client gifts, and so on. By the end of the week, she felt I was competent enough and withdrew into her previous duties.

As soon as Hal and I were alone, he touched me every chance he got, more intimately every time. Soon, he put his hands on my breasts or my bottom and let them linger there. I tried to avoid his advances but he playfully pointed out that it was part of my job to make him feel good.

I couldn't tell anybody in the agency, or anybody in our small circle of friends. If I resigned now, they'd think I was lazy. I briefly considered telling Dieter, but he would accuse me of provoking Hal's behaviour because he hated the way I dressed and made myself up—too colourful, too sexy, and too extravagant for his taste.

We had looked at a perfect place in Mosman, close to the agency and to our friends' places in Cremorne—two bedrooms, fully and rather elegantly furnished, with a balcony and a view of the adjacent green space. We would be able to invite not only our four friends but also Dieter's acquaintances from the TV and advertising world, who could further his career—none of whom he'd spoken more than two consecutive sentences to—to our housewarming party.

He'd be mad as hell if I quit this job now.

We signed the lease. That night, before Dieter drifted off to sleep, he turned to me and said, "Do you know how proud I am of you?"

So, I'll make you proud, and Hal feel good.

About a week after we moved into our wonderful new place, Hal moved in for the kill. "Let's go for lunch at the Rosehip Hotel," he said one morning, his hand resting on my back. "And book us a room there for after lunch."

After that day, my life settled into a routine, as did the friendship our little German group practiced.

Living so close to each other, we met even more often. With all of us working, we could afford to go to a pub or have barbeques in the park or on the beach, drink beer and cheap red wine, and eat homemade sausage rolls.

After a few drinks, we'd tell each other how lucky we were to have made it in this fantastic city. Compared to good old Germany, we'd hit the jackpot. Who there could spend their February weekends on the beach without a sweater? On those leisurely days, we talked about all sorts of things but never about our jobs. To them, I was just a boring secretary who passed probation and made decent money. Hal and I travelled a lot, sometimes overnight, to different Australian cities for conferences, but always only during the week. His wife wouldn't like him being gone on weekends. Dieter asked me not to mention those trips to the others. He worried our friends might be jealous.

I wondered if he was jealous.

10

JOHANNA

Kurt liked to go to the pub in Spofforth Center on Friday evenings to catch up on what every member of our little German circle had been up to all week. I'd felt a cold coming all week so I asked if I could stay home, but Kurt didn't want me to make a fuss over it.

"Pull yourself together," he said when he saw me wiping my dripping nose on the short walk to the pub. "You're disgusting."

He seemed in a rush and looked disappointed when he spotted only Uwe and Dieter at our usual corner table.

"Isabella will be a bit late," Dieter announced, adding a proud, "busy with work, you know."

Uwe said Eva had a headache and preferred to stay home.

What I would give to have that choice. As the only woman present this evening, I just sat in the corner, made myself small and pretended to show interest in their conversation.

Uwe ordered the first round of English ale, brought it back to our table and put it in front of the guys. I got a soda that would last me all evening.

Uwe raised his glass, inspected the small measure—a constant bone of contention for all three of them—let out a deep sigh, and said, "How I miss a true Bavarian beer stone."

"Served with a fresh pretzel," Dieter said.

Kurt fell into the usual litany. "And a warm meatloaf with sweet mustard."

"Cheers to that."

They emptied their glasses with one long gulp.

Kurt got the next round. And, as always, he had a quick one in between before he came back with three glasses. The second round lasted longer.

Dieter lit his cigarette, then bent forward and lit Kurt's.

"How's the new job going?" Kurt asked Uwe.

Uwe had finally found a job in a carpentry shop in Dee Why, only a half hour bus ride from our home. He told us his boss already understood the extent of his knowledge and gradually gave him more complicated jobs to do. "The place is run well," Uwe said, "but I can see room for improvement and will discuss that with my boss when the time is right."

"Then you should get more money," Kurt said.

"That would be great, but that's not my priority. I'd like to see the shop working more efficiently, like the company I worked for back home. Changing some of the equipment and the flow of tasks would increase profitability without increasing labour costs. Once I can prove my worth, the money will come all by itself."

Kurt laughed. "You're such an asshole."

"No, he is right," Dieter said. "I did a great job with the first freelance order I got, and I did it for a pittance. Then I got three more, charging a slightly higher fee for each of them, and now I have several requests for quotes on my table. I'm building my reputation so I can adjust my fees to reflect my worth."

"Was a good plan to send Isabella to that ad agency," Kurt

said. "She got you those connections, right?"

Dieter coughed into his hand.

Kurt laughed. "Don't be like that. It's what a wife is for. Took her long enough to get her act together. Where is she, anyway?"

"Told you. She's got to work late." Dieter got up. "Time for the next round."

The evening dragged on and I stopped listening altogether. Whenever I could, I was practicing to slip into a calming state of mindlessness—something I had nearly perfected by now.

The next day, we went on a picnic at the park in Cremorne Point, right next to the ferry pier. I had marinated pork chops, Eva had made two large salads, and Isabella was in charge of dessert.

Uwe knocked on our door when it was time to go.

"Johanna, get the beer from the fridge," Kurt yelled back at me. He had chilled four six-packs—two were Dieter's contribution so he didn't have to bring his share on the long bus ride. I loaded the beer into my bag, and with the meat container, it became quite heavy. Kurt carried the grill and didn't offer to take any of my load. Uwe carried his two six packs and the salads and Eva walked empty-handed downstairs with us to meet Dieter and Isabella.

"You never showed up last night," Kurt said to Isabella. "Where've you been?"

She ignored his question, looked at me, frowned, looked back at Kurt. "Don't you want to take Johanna's bag?"

"It's not heavy." Kurt smiled at me and placed his arm on

my shoulder. More weight to carry. "Right, Johanna."

"It's not," I said. "Really."

Kurt let go of me, and we started walking. The bag kept slipping off my shoulder, and I fell behind the others so they wouldn't notice my puffing and my flushed face. I could have handled it easily if not for this stupid cold.

I could still feel my ear throbbing where Kurt had twisted it and dragged me out of bed and into the bathroom by it when I'd asked if I could stay home to get healthy for Monday. "Not a fucking chance," he'd said. "We are celebrating our one-year-arrival anniversary today. You can't chicken out on such a day just because you've got a dripping nose. We arrived together, we do everything together." I'd suppressed a cry but couldn't stop a moan. "God, you're such a wimp." He'd laughed. "That didn't really hurt."

As we sat on a blanket on the cool ground, watching the boats sail into the sunset, the pain in my ear subsided but my throat got much worse, my bones ached, and I could barely swallow. On the walk home, I began to sweat. My skin was burning, yet I was shivering when we finally got into bed. That didn't deter Kurt from taking what was his.

Afterwards, he rolled onto his back, crossed his arms behind his head, and talked in a subdued voice, as he often did when he had too much to drink. Those monologues weren't meant for me. He was telling himself stories, not caring if I listened or not.

"Was on the road with Jack yesterday afternoon getting shingles for the job. Bummer when we noticed we didn't have enough. Drove down Pacific Highway to the supply store. On the way back, Jack stopped in Chatswood to get a pack of smokes. Guess he had a quick one in the pub while I waited in the truck, but what do I care? It was nearly five o'clock and we were done for the day once we unloaded the shingles. Otherwise, Jack wouldn't dare. Way too dangerous. I'm his boss. He knew I wouldn't allow that. I never drink on the building site. Got to be an example to the boys. So, anyway, there I'm sitting, watching the traffic go by, and what do I see? A couple comes out of the hotel opposite our parked truck—the hotel with the pub downstairs, the Rose something or other. I squinted because I thought I knew the woman. But I told myself, No way, that can't be her. Then, they started kissing, and the woman turned her head when they finished. She looked in my direction, but I was quick enough to cover my face and saw her eyes move past me, not recognizing me. But I sure recognized her. That's Isabella, goddamn it, I thought. What the fuck is Dieter's wife doing here kissing a stranger on the mouth? She's cheating on her husband, that's what she's doing. Boy, oh boy, I nearly couldn't keep my mouth shut at the barbie tonight. It took some doing not to embarrass Dieter in front of everybody. She sure had it coming, but I couldn't do that to him. I'll bide my time until the right moment comes. Then, I'll stick it to her, and I don't mean just with words. If she screws around, I sure as hell should get a piece of the action, too. Gotta think of the right time, the right way to go about it…"

His last words had been so mumbled I wasn't really sure if I'd heard him right. He started to snore, gently at first until his sleep got deeper.

My own sleep came slowly and turned into a feverish nightmare, plagued by images of things Kurt would do to

Isabella if he got hold of her. By morning, I was a sweat-drenched mess, not knowing if I had only dreamt Kurt's monologue. I didn't say anything to him or to Dieter, and especially not to Isabella.

11

ISABELLA

Hal and I got into the rhythm like a couple. In the weeks when we didn't take a short trip, we went to the Rosehip Hotel at least once a week and spent about two hours in the afternoon having sex. Hal found it unwaveringly exciting and it was not unpleasant for me. He showered me with compliments, and, as the months went by, with privileges at the agency. Ironically, what was meant to make me feel less dirty had quite the opposite effect.

Contrary to my expectations, Hal turned out to be nice and considerate, most of the time, just like Dieter. At times I felt could manipulate them both, but I was kidding myself. When it came to their God-given masculine superiority, I had to back down and ultimately, they manipulated me.

Dieter had worn me down, demanding that I introduce him into the advertising crowd, and I resented him for pushing me into this job. My affair with Hal was entirely his fault, but it was my guilty conscience that made me continue to praise my talented photographer husband to all my contacts. And that made me resent Dieter even more.

Hal was oblivious of my inner turmoil, and sometimes I thought he'd fallen in love with me. I became the highest paid personal assistant in all of Sydney. He gave into my whims and smiled at my moods, but I had to be available to him whenever he wanted. Never once did he ask if it suited me or if my marriage would be in trouble because of his schedule. And, although his demands weren't perverted, he insisted I do a few things I wasn't keen on, like oral sex.

I never told Dieter about my ridiculously high salary. I opened a secret bank account and took the price tags off the expensive clothes, shoes and handbags I bought. And I still accompanied him to the boring parties with our German friends, ate cheap sausages with potato salad and drank dreadful red wine out of two-gallon bottles.

To pacify Dieter, I began inviting my colleagues to our home more often. It was tough getting their acceptance, but I wasn't one to give up easily. Eventually, we had a nice group of casual friends who came quite regularly, giving us a great excuse not to go to Cremorne every weekend.

But Dieter insisted we spend Easter with our German friends to uphold certain traditions. Silly beyond belief. When did I last search for painted Easter eggs or bake an Easter *fladen*? But I gave in to have peace and agreed to meet a week before Easter to plan our activities together.

It wasn't as bad as I'd expected. After the initial boring start, Kurt surprised us with a question out of the blue.

"You guys want to go to Lightning Ridge?"

"Where is that?" Eva asked.

Kurt leaned back, arms resting on his protruding gut, and waited until we all gave him our undivided attention. "It's a small opal mining town in the bush, north of here, close to the Queensland border."

I couldn't imagine where this was going. "And what exactly are we supposed to do there? Spend Easter in the bush, searching for egg-shaped opals?"

He ignored me and spoke to Uwe and Dieter. "I read in the papers that they found a huge black opal there recently. You wouldn't believe how valuable those are. They've never been found anywhere else in the whole world." His face was flushed with excitement. We all stared at him, all except Johanna, who never really showed any emotion. "That's the place where, ages ago, silicon dioxide mixed with water and trickled through the rock formations underground. When the water evaporated, the silica deposits turned into precious stones of varying density. That's why opals come in so many different colours. Black opals are the most precious because they are semitransparent and reflect brilliant colours like bundled bursts of sunlight."

"That's interesting," Uwe said lamely. He probably wondered, as I did, if Kurt had memorized what he had read in the newspaper. He wasn't usually so eloquent and was obviously out to impress us. But why?

"Yes, *terribly* interesting." I rolled my eyes but nobody took me up on my sarcasm.

Uwe asked if Kurt thought we could find opals if we went there.

He nodded. "A hobby miner staked a claim for some weekend digging only a year ago. He was there on his annual leave to dig for a few days and found this giant black opal very close to the surface. No hassle at all to get it out. Apparently the opal is so large, it's worth millions. The guy never has to work again, and it's not the first find of that magnitude in Lightning Ridge. It happens all the time there."

Dieter was skeptical. "How did the guy know what to do?

Doesn't one have to have mining experience?"

"Not from what it says here." Kurt pulled a carefully folded newspaper page out of his back pocket and opened it. Immediately, Uwe bent over it. "But I got myself a few good books on the subject, too, in case you're interested."

"Do you think there are any claims left in that area?" Uwe asked.

"Have you lost your mind?" I asked. "Eva, say something. They want to spend Easter in a mining town."

Eva didn't say anything but threw a warning glance at Uwe.

"The early bird catches the biggest worm," Kurt said, taking out a map, "or however the saying goes. I figured after this newspaper article appeared, there would be a run on getting claims staked, so I called the claims department right away. Cost me only fifty bucks for a whole year. Here, look at the map. That's where my claim is." He looked around. "So, who's in?"

I didn't have to think about it. "Dieter, if you want to go, you are very welcome to it, but you'll have to go without me. I've got better things to do." Dieter avoided Kurt's eyes when he said he just remembered a party planned for Easter Saturday that was too important for his career to miss.

Eva surprised me. She simply said, "Uwe and I are not going either." I could see Uwe was not happy but he didn't object, at least not in front of us.

Come Good Friday, Johanna and Kurt left for Lightning Ridge. Eva told me she'd tried to talk some sense into Johanna but couldn't get through to her. "I reminded her how disgusting, primitive, and filthy living in the camp had been. It would be just like that in an opal mining town. And I told her I didn't fall for those get rich quick schemes, but Johanna said Kurt wanted to go and that was it, so I gave up."

"One day, she'll kiss his feet," I said. "I'm glad you stood your ground."

Eva sighed. "I had to promise Uwe that we'll go up with them next time."

I didn't tell Eva I had to pay my price, too. My fool of a husband had invited Hal and his wife to the party he had organized for tomorrow in a haste so his buddy Kurt wouldn't catch him in a lie and, I guess, because he felt it was about time for him to finally meet my boss.

12

The party would be a disaster. I could feel it in my bones. I'd been apprehensive all afternoon, wondering if Hal would show up. He hadn't been in the office the past two days, and for obvious reasons I couldn't call him at home. I asked Dieter how many guests were expected. "About twenty," he said with a weird grin on his face.

I checked the flower arrangements, the catered trays with appetizers, the rows of polished glasses and the stacks of folded napkins—all perfect. The apartment looked great— right out of a real estate brochure for yuppie couples. Dieter was on the balcony, firing up the grill, so I went into the bedroom to get dressed. I had bought a new dress, a slim-cut, crisp white linen number from France with a daringly low neckline.

Dieter appeared in the doorframe, a full beer glass in his hand—his third in the past hour. "Be careful or your tits will fall out," he said.

"Do you always have to be so vulgar?" I hated when he was like that. I hated him. "And since when are you interested in my breasts? Excuse me, I mean my tits. Your crude vocabulary proves how little you value my body, and your comment implies you think you have a right of possession. Well, I have news for you. You waived that right months ago."

My face flushed in anger. How dare he. He hadn't touched

my bosom, or any other part of me, since I started working at Hal's agency. He liked to be the benefactor, but ultimately, his ego couldn't handle my success. I was so mad I wanted to throw some more choice insults at him, but he fled the room.

I turned sideways in front of the mirror. Not bad, but not daring enough. I got a pair of half-moon foam push-ups from the drawer and slipped them underneath my breasts, checked the mirror again, and admired my new silhouette. Now we're talking, Dieter. My breasts were popping out of the dress like overripe peaches, my nipples barely concealed. Carefully, I slipped the spaghetti straps of my dress from my shoulders. The dress was holding. I got a pair of scissors and cut them off. I took a deep breath. My nipples showed ever so slightly, dark and dangerous on my olive skin.

I better not lean forward too far. But what if I did? How would Dieter react? Would he come to my rescue with a towel or a napkin or his bare hands? I had to laugh. That's one way to get your husband to touch you. I paused and then came a revelation. *I don't want his touch anymore.*

The doorbell rang. I sailed out, my back straight and a wide smile on my face, past Dieter, who gasped but got himself quickly under control again. "Doesn't my wife look spectacular?" he said to the first arrivals, placing an arm around my waist.

I shrugged him off. "Nice of you to notice."

After greeting the two couples who'd been at the door and offering them a drink, I went back into the kitchen. Dieter followed me, his smile frozen. "Do me a favour. Try and hide your inner slut," he hissed into my ear and disappeared again.

I got a bottle of Chablis from the fridge and poured myself a large glass. It looked cold and delicious. Staring at it, I heard the doorbell again, and then I heard a voice I knew only too well. I gulped the glass of wine down. He'd come. Not with his wife, I hoped. The timid little thing was a homebody—one of those nonexistent women who didn't want to shine at her successful husband's side. Hal had mentioned her only a few times but that had been the general gist.

I found my smile again, brighter than ever, and walked out into the living room, right into them being steered toward the kitchen. "Look who's here. Your boss and his wife," Dieter said.

The woman by Hal's side was indeed tiny, fragile and delicate, but adorable, like a late Audrey Hepburn. She had a strand of pearls around her neck—no, three stands—and small sparkling diamonds in her ears.

I couldn't stop staring at her. This wasn't how I had pictured Hal's wife. True, she was older than him, and a lot older than I was, but her obvious self-confidence and elegance made her age irrelevant. She was beautiful. Looking at her jewelry, I instantly became aware that Hal had never given me any, and suddenly chocolate bars and silk scarves didn't matter anymore.

Jealousy is a mean emotion. The bitter taste in my mouth needed to be quenched. I mumbled something about getting fresh ice and turned away from them. Dieter ushered them into the living room. Thankfully, he didn't follow me into the kitchen. I probably would have thrown the half-full ice bucket at him. While I refilled the ice trays, I had a quick glass of Chablis and then, for good measure, another before I dared join the fast-growing crowd of guests. I put on a smile, busied myself rearranging the appetizers, and watched Hal and his wife out of the corner of my eye. The bastard was chatting with the small group surrounding him, laughing at somebody's joke, and ignoring me totally.

Dieter ignored me, too. His smug expression made it clear he knew perfectly well how uncomfortable it was for me to have my boss present at the party. How dare he put me in this position? I had to function as a hostess with both of them there—the man I slept with to satisfy the man I was married to.

Damn both of them.

After the fourth glass, I lost my inhibitions sufficiently to walk over to Hal and slide my arm into his in a gesture that signalled intimacy. I felt him straighten but he didn't look at me and kept talking to the others. His wife, however, watched me with a slight frown. I let go of Hal, walked away, and joined another group. As soon as I felt she was losing interest in me, I sneaked up to Hal again, wrapped my arms around his waist from behind, got on tip-toes, and kissed him on his earlobe. His wife's eyebrows shot up. The poor darling had no idea. I grinned at her.

"Hey babe," I whispered into Hal's ear, making sure my voice was loud enough for his wife could hear. "I like it when you get me going with your tongue, but you were a bit rushed last time. I prefer you take your time when you go down on me." I let my tongue wet my lips while giving my best erotic sigh, not losing sight of my rival. She was mortified.

I felt like a race car driver crossing the finish line ahead of the pack—alive, empowered. I went back to the kitchen, shaking with excitement, to savour my victory. When I returned, Hal and his wife had left. One of my colleagues walked up to me and raised her glass. "Congratulations," she said. "Ten points for courage and honesty, zero for your future in advertising." People around us laughed.

Dieter came in from the balcony with a full tray of grilled steaks. "What's funny?" he asked.

"Your wife upset her boss a little, that's all. I hope you bought the weekend papers. If I were her, I'd start looking for a new job," my colleague said.

Everybody laughed again, and I laughed with them, loud and hard. Dieter was oblivious to what had just happened, and my friends from the agency didn't snitch, but it wouldn't have bothered me if they told or even if he had stood right next to me.

The party fell flat after that. People kept whispering, and one couple after another came to Dieter with an excuse to leave. Before midnight, Dieter and I were alone and he urged me to tell him what I had done. I shrugged it off as too much to drink. "A stupid comment, that was all."

Dieter begged me to apologize to Hal first thing Monday morning.

Although the guests leaving so suddenly had the effect of a cold shower on me, I was holding enough alcohol to be careless and very angry. "How dare you. You have no idea what I said to him, but you want me to apologize? You are so worried about losing your pitiful little photo shoot orders that you expect your wife to fall on her knees and kiss his arse. Why don't you do that? Crawl to him and lick his balls! He might like that! You think you can snap your fingers and I jump and do as you order? It's all about you. Your career. Your shit. And Hal thinks he's the greatest gift to advertising and I'm supposed to be at his beck and call. No more, I'm telling you, no more. Not you. Not Hal. I've had it with both of you. I'm not your slave."

After my outburst, I expected that the truth finally had dawned on him and that he would pressure me for more details, accuse me of cheating, and yell and scream at me so I could admit my guilt and explain my behaviour—that I had done it for him and that I could now close that wretched chapter in my life and make a new start, with him, if he wanted—but he turned away from me and left the apartment, not returning until the next morning.

We hardly spoke for the next four weeks. I spent a few days after my termination visiting agencies, like I did a year ago for Dieter, but I gave up quickly when I discovered I had become an untouchable. After about a month, I found a job at an import/export company, dealing with several European countries. The pay didn't reflect my fluency in three languages, but beggars can't be choosers.

When I told Dieter about the new position, he mellowed enough to ask me if I'd be home that night. Uwe and Eva were coming over. I didn't exactly have a swinging social life anymore, so I nodded. I hadn't seen them in a few weeks and worried what they might have heard, but when I told them about my job change, they were only mildly interested and seemed unaware of the reason. Trusting that they were too far removed from the sick world of advertising, I explained that I simply needed a new challenge.

Eva congratulated me in her usual soft manner. "How nice. You'll get the chance to speak a lot of German again."

"Did you hear what Kurt and Johanna are up to?" Uwe asked.

I was glad he changed the subject. "What?"

"They left for Lightning Ridge again last weekend—this time, for good. Johanna wanted to hand in her two months' notice at the old folks home but Kurt was so eager to get up north to his claim, he told her not to bother. He bought an old truck, packed up their belongings, and off they went."

"Do they have any savings?" Dieter asked.

"Couldn't be much," Uwe said. "Kurt is sure he'll find enough in his mine, and I bet he will. He's such a tough guy. I admire him."

Eva bit her lip. "I worry about Johanna. She liked her job and had no problem settling in Sydney, and now she'll have to get used to a totally different environment—not one I'd like to live in."

"She'll be fine," Uwe said. "Kurt will take care of everything."

That annoyed me beyond reason. "Oh really? Like he did here in Sydney? He worked her to the bone, if you ask me. Haven't you noticed how haggard she's become? Something is wrong with her. I bet she's sick and he doesn't care enough to take her to a doctor. I wonder if they have any doctors up there in the bush."

"The fresh air will do her good," Dieter said.

Uwe nodded. "I'm sure she's looking forward to the

change. And we'll find out soon enough how she is coping. I promised Kurt we'd visit soon. We should plan a trip up there as soon as we can all get some time off."

13

JOHANNA

We arrived in Lightning Ridge a month after Easter, at the tail end of summer. Our first winter passed quickly, with us setting up in the old, dilapidated shack Kurt bought on our first day. I had no time to make the place somehow homey because he was so eager to work in his mine.

He made me work with him underground all day at a frenzied pace. We were both so exhausted by the time we got home, he fell asleep on the hard mattress on the floor without bothering me further, and I was grateful for that. At least I got a few hours of sleep.

Some nights I laid awake listening to his snoring, thinking I couldn't take it anymore. Brief moments of despair came and numbness filled me when I realized I couldn't remember what my life had been like before Kurt. He was my beginning and my end.

In early September, Kurt and I came home one evening and found our four Sydney friends in front of our shack. Uwe explained that they had asked in town where we lived and had been waiting for us for over an hour.

"What a surprise," Kurt said with a flat voice.

"You've got no phone," Dieter said. "We thought we'd check to see if you're still alive." His laughter sounded forced.

Kurt opened the door. "Come on in and sit down. I'll get you a beer while I change. We've come straight from the mine."

Uwe did a quick assessment of our shabby dwelling—a couch and two chairs, rescued from the dump, and a plastic table with a crack running through it. "We don't want to inconvenience you. We're staying at the motel next to the pub. How about we meet you there for a cold beer after you've freshened up?"

"Go ahead," Kurt said, a touch more accommodating. "I'll be there in a sec."

Isabella looked at Kurt before she cocked her head in my direction. "Only you? Aren't you coming, Johanna?"

I opened my mouth to say I didn't need to come along but Kurt was quicker. "She's busy."

"You must be mad if you think we drove a thousand kilometers so see only you. Johanna comes, or we women stay behind with her," Isabella said.

"We can help her finish her chores faster," Eva said.

I didn't dare look at Kurt. He'd be livid inside. I detected an angry undertone that made me shiver when I heard him say, "All right, then. Come on, Johanna. Get a move on. We don't want to keep our friends waiting." Hopefully the others didn't catch it.

Kurt was like a different person when we arrived at the pub. He walked up to Uwe and Dieter at the bar, slapped them on their shoulders, and asked them what they wanted to drink.

I looked around for Eva and Isabella.

"The girls are still next door, taking forever to get ready,"

Uwe said, noticing my bewilderment. "Why don't you go get them, Johanna?" He handed me a key. "Room twelve. I bet they're in the bathroom and won't hear you knock."

Kurt gave his permission with a quick nod, and I took the key from Uwe and walked out. When I got to the motel, I opened the room door after a quick knock, and stepped inside. The bathroom door was slightly ajar. I heard Isabella talking and stopped in my tracks.

"I told Dieter a gazillion times this surprise visit was an idiotic idea. Did you see the state their place is in? Johanna must be mad to stick it out here. And did you hear Kurt answering for her? He's the same shithead he's always been. If I were her, I'd get out of there in a flash."

"But you are not her," Eva said. "She doesn't have your strength. She won't talk back like you do to Dieter."

Isabella giggled. "I told him I'd come only if he goes with me to our next company party. Import/export bores him, and my new company is super conservative. The evening will be hell for him."

"Don't you miss your old job?"

Isabella drew in a breath. "No."

"Honestly?"

"Even if I did, there is no way back. The whole advertising profession is incestuous." She sounded unusually cheerful, adding, "Whoever leaves, for whatever reason, never gets back in."

I quietly opened the room door again and then slammed it shut behind me, calling their names to announce my arrival.

Isabella came out of the bathroom first, startled to see me but not suspecting I might have listened to their trashing of my wretched existence.

I forced a smile. "I've been sent to get you."

Isabella called into the bathroom, "Hurry up, Eva. Our darling hubbies are missing us."

Eva appeared a few seconds later, and we walked over to the pub.

The large jug of beer on our table was nearly empty and the men were so deep in an animated conversation we might as well have sat at another table. As always, I tried to listen to Kurt because he didn't like it when I didn't pay attention to him. He spoke so enthusiastically about opal mining that I began to wonder if he really believed his exaggerations.

"Sounds like great fun," Uwe said. "When can we see the mine? I'd love to do a bit of digging."

"How long are you staying?" Kurt bit his lip, thinking.

Dieter smirked. "Depends. How much have you found?"

"Quite a bit," Kurt said. I quickly lowered my eyes to hide the truth. The opal yield from the broken rocks and dirt we had brought up so far hadn't covered our living expenses. We wouldn't be able to hold out much longer. I sent a silent prayer of gratitude for every day he discovered nothing in his self-built agitator, although it put him in a filthy mood.

Kurt gave the men a wide smile. "I've been lucky with this mine. Just yesterday I took this month's nobbies to the local cutter. Otherwise, I could show you some. If you want, you can work with me, starting where I've discovered the latest opal deposit of significance, a small, glittering line that promises to be the beginning of a so-called street, a line that goes deep into the rock."

Dieter had the same eager look on his face as Uwe. "We

can stay about three days."

"Settled," Kurt said. "Normally, Johanna and I start at five in the morning but I will be kind to you city slickers. We'll pick you up at six thirty."

"Nice," Eva said. "We women can sleep in and have a late breakfast."

"And we have the car all day," Isabella said. "What time shall we get you, Johanna?"

I didn't look at Kurt but I could feel his eyes bore into me, willing me to decline.

Isabella must have felt it, too. "Don't even think about needing her at the mine," she said to Kurt. She laughed and patted Dieter's shoulder. "Not when you have those two strapping guys as helpers."

"What if we find something?" Dieter said. "How does that work?"

"Miner's law says the mine owner gets sixty percent and the rest is shared between the other miners."

"Done." The guys sealed their deal with a handshake.

14

EVA

The next day, I didn't hear Uwe get up. Isabella and I slept in, and after breakfast at the local pub, we went to pick Johanna up for a long walk in the bush. She declined, saying she had things to do. We said we'd come back later in the afternoon and she said, "Sure. Come back around five."

"Sounds like she doesn't want to spend time with us," I said to Isabella after we'd left Johanna's place.

"Or she isn't allowed to," Isabella said.

I shrugged it off. Whatever made her act so strange wasn't our concern. Johanna had always been distant and private, and she wouldn't want us prying into her affairs. We walked until it was time for lunch at the local pub, then we returned to our motel rooms. Luckily, I'd brought a good book with me. Isabella said she'd catch up on some sleep.

We arrived at Johanna's just after five and chatted until the guys came home around seven. Then, we all went back to the pub for dinner.

After their first day of hard labour, as Dieter called it, they were a bit disappointed they hadn't found anything.

"You should see the manhole," Uwe said to us women. "So tiny."

"Admit it," Kurt said. "You were shitting yourself."

"I only tested the stability of the ladder." Uwe looked at me. "It goes down so deep, you can't even see the ground."

"I didn't have to test it," Dieter said. "Good enough for me if it holds Kurt's weight."

They bantered a while longer, but somehow, the conversation wouldn't flow. The evening ended early, and we went back to our motel rooms.

Uwe took a long shower and stretched out on our bed. While I folded his clothes, he recounted the day's experience, still bugged by Kurt's ribbing.

"It's easy for Dieter to talk. He is so much smaller than me, and Kurt is used to climbing down there. Lucky he went in first so I could see how he does it. He had to roll his shoulders forward to squeeze in because the damn thing's only a meter wide. The ladder won't support two guys, not even if the second one was a lightweight like Dieter, so Kurt told us to wait until he'd pull the string next to the ladder to indicate he'd arrived at the bottom. I insisted Dieter go next. I've never seen him so pale, but he couldn't refuse, not after making fun of me. Then I went. Once down there, the main cave was so large I could stand upright in it. Kurt and Johanna must have worked their guts out, digging that underground area in just a few months with only a pick, shovels, and buckets. I'm surprised they've had time to dig for opals. As we went deeper into the mine, along the main tunnel Kurt calls the drive, the ceiling became lower. And by the time we reached the side tunnel where Kurt wanted us to work, we were crawling on our hands and knees. For the rest of the day, we carefully dug along a gray seam with a glassy consistency. According to Kurt, this seam shows promise to turn into a ribbon of sparkling rock. "An opal street," he called it. "Hit one of those streets, and we'll all be rich." When we heard that, Dieter and I had to hold back not to hammer away too fast, but after a while, we had to slow down—our wrists and knees hurt that bad—and we fell into a more natural, much more careful rhythm. I guess that's what we'll do all day tomorrow, too—slave away in the dark." He took a deep breath. "Until we find something."

The next day was indeed a carbon copy of the first, except that Isabella got bitchy. She was bored, and she blamed Dieter for being stuck there, Johanna for not entertaining us, and me for everything else—the lousy food I chose in the pub and the dump of a motel I had picked. Pointing out that this was the only motel and the pub was the only eatery there didn't matter.

That evening was the low point of our trip. Uwe and Dieter were so exhausted they hardly spoke at dinner, and Kurt and Johanna hadn't even joined us.

"Last day, tomorrow," Dieter said. "If we don't find anything, we call it quits at lunchtime."

Isabella smirked. "Dreamer. We might as well leave now."

The next day, Isabella and I sat in front of our motel room on a small bench, idling away the few hours until lunchtime when we could hopefully leave Lightning Ridge. The guys had taken our car to the mine this morning so Kurt wouldn't have to bring them back in case their adventure came to a premature end. Which we both were secretly praying for.

By ten o'clock, Isabella was so stressed out she was convinced they wouldn't come back all day. But then they drove into the motel parking area at high speed, slammed on the brakes and jumped out of the car, looking jubilant.

"We hit pay dirt," Dieter said.

"We had barely begun digging when I suddenly saw a reflection in the level I was working on," Uwe explained. "I called Dieter, and he saw it, too. We didn't dare hammer around the small, glittering area for fear of breaking a larger opal deposit hidden in the rock. Kurt came running when we called, and when he saw what we saw, he went all quiet, reverent-like. He moved us aside, and we watched him break a few rocks loose. Three buckets full. He worked until the reflective rock turned into dirt again. Kurt thinks he got everything of value out of this deposit. It's not huge, but it's something. He's gone to the cutter to have the opal freed."

"Do you trust him?" Isabella said.

Dieter told her he'd asked how much it could be worth, and Kurt had said whatever it was, he would share it as agreed. "He is a man of his word," Dieter said.

The next few hours, we waited for Kurt at the motel, our bags already packed. We planned to return to Sydney as soon as Kurt was back with news about the rocks. The tension was unbearable, more so for Uwe and Dieter than for Isabella and me, but their excitement was catching. When Kurt finally arrived early afternoon, we saw him grinning from ear to ear.

"You made a hundred bucks each," he said. "Not bad for a few hours of digging."

Uwe and Dieter congratulated each other.

"You can take the money once it's paid out in a few weeks, or I can give you the value in opals now if you like. I have a few stones your wives might like." He opened a small satchel filled with already cut, tiny black opals.

Uwe and Dieter accepted Kurt's choice without questioning it. Two opals for each of them, similar in size and value. Kurt stressed that they made a good deal because those little beauties were worth a bit more than what he owed them. The guys were beaming, and I have to admit that I was quite pleased myself with such pretty stones. When Isabella pointed out that the clock was ticking, we said our farewells and left. Uwe promised Kurt to return soon.

Our drive back home was much more relaxed than our journey to Lightning Ridge had been.

Isabella and I sat on the back seat and chatted, mainly about the stones and what we would do with them. Earrings? A necklace?

"Did you notice that Johanna doesn't wear any opal jewelry?" Isabella asked me. "She said Kurt sells everything he finds. All those rocks, and he hasn't put a single one aside for her—for Christmas, her birthday, or their anniversary. What a tightwad."

I knew better than Isabella because I had asked Johanna myself. "She told me, it's because she doesn't like opals."

"Show me the opals again," Isabella said to Dieter and stuck her hand between the front seats.

"Oh, stop it," Dieter said.

Isabella turned back to me, silently mouthing, "Idiot," and said aloud, "Just wait until he's made them into some kind of jewelry. Then he won't be allowed to touch them anymore. Right, Eva? Once they sparkle on our skin, they're ours to wear and keep."

I remembered my last birthday. Uwe hadn't even bought me flowers. Would he really let me have his precious opals?

15

ISABELLA

More than half a year had passed since I'd been forced to leave Hal's agency, and much had changed since then—or had I changed so much that my new life didn't seem so badly out of balance anymore?

I had little contact with Eva but when we did phone each other, I noticed her tone was different. She no longer whined about all the things she missed—the German gossip magazines, the strong filtered coffee, the creamy dark chocolate, the speciality shops for haberdashery—things I had also secretly craved. Had we both finally stopped missing those things or had we simply discovered enough suitable substitutes?

My new boss had emigrated from Holland over twenty years ago and told me it takes two years to get settled in a new country and three if the country has opposite seasons and a different language. He still compared the two continents often, favouring Australia over Europe, pointing out the freedom of the informal lifestyle and the outgoing, friendly personalities of most Australians. After all the bickering in our German group, I found his attitude refreshing. He was patient, sensitive, and, above all, happily married and faithful—so different from Hal.

All would've been well if my work in his import/export company wouldn't be so boring and if my office had a window. From nine to five, I worked in an artificial environment, forcing me to spent my lunch hour walking the main drags of downtown—Pitt Street and George Street, down to the park by the Opera House—just to get a bit of fresh air and sunlight. After work, I walked the same path to reach Cremorne Ferry to head home. With the same routine every day, I'd become dulled to the unique charm this harbour city has to offer.

At home, my life was even more mundane. Dieter had decided to play the artist card, I guess to prove he was the only one with talent in our household, and since I didn't work in the advertising field any longer, I was nothing in his eyes. He'd become the sensitive artist who constantly needed pampering, expecting me to cater to him while handling all the tedious chores of daily life. To make sure I understood my lowly position, he stuck notes on the kitchen cabinet and bathroom mirror, telling me what to do. When I objected, he'd say things like, "If I have to get the dry cleaning myself, I'll miss the photo shoot and lose a thousand bucks. I'm sure you can afford to pay next month's rent."

I usually smiled at his sarcastic remarks and did what he asked because he did make good money. Unfortunately, he watched our expenses like a hawk, so I could rarely syphon even small amounts to put in my secret stash. Thanks a bloody lot, Hal. I wished I hadn't squandered a small fortune on stuff I didn't need when the money was coming in so generously. I couldn't even afford decent clothes anymore.

How would I ever change my life dressed like a plain office mouse?

One evening in November, Eva called. "Let's meet at six o'clock in the Crow's Nest pub at the end of Spofforth Street. The fish and chips there are really good," Eva had said. I agreed right away, feeling disgusted with myself. Meeting Eva as the highlight of my week, really?

She probably was out of a job again and needed a shoulder to cry on.

She confirmed my casually worded assumption as soon as we had placed our order. "And I'd been so happy to get that job," she said. "I only started there when we got back from Lightning Ridge two months ago and I've lost it already."

I tried to cheer her up. "Only two months? Guess you broke your own record, then." I saw her eyes well up. "Oh, come on. I was joking. You'll find another one. You always do."

"Not this time."

"Plenty of businesses need secretaries."

"This is different from all the other times."

I wasn't overly interested, my wine glass was nearly empty, and the food hadn't arrived yet so I lit a cigarette. Christmas was in just six weeks, and with it, the beginning of the long stretch of summer holidays when the Australian business world went into beach mode. Eva wouldn't get a new job until the middle of January. That wasn't my problem, and I certainly didn't want to make it mine, but she looked so desperate, I felt sorry for her.

"Why? What's the reason this time?"

"I'm pregnant."

Without thinking, I hugged her. "You two must be thrilled."

"Uwe doesn't know yet."

"Then you better tell him."

Eva's shoulders slumped and her previous expression darkened even more.

"He won't be pleased. Uwe always said we must wait until we can afford a child."

The waiter arrived with our food. The barramundi was hidden inside a greasy batter and the fries were soggy. Disgusting food and depressing conversation—just what I needed to lift my spirits. Suddenly, my empty apartment with Dieter's silly notes posted everywhere had a strong pull.

I checked my watch. "Shouldn't you go home and tell him?"

"He's working late, like every night." Eva forked a piece of fish and shoved it into her mouth.

"You have to tell him eventually."

"I know." She picked a fry, held it in midair, and wrinkled her nose. "When the time is right." She put the fry back on her plate. "I need to get used to the thought that everything will change. Don't get me wrong, I'm looking forward to the baby and I'm sure Uwe will, too, but the timing isn't good."

"It never is."

She pushed her plate aside. "This is especially bad. Uwe is determined to move to Lightning Ridge."

"You can't be serious."

"He believes he can strike it rich there, like Kurt and Johanna. He told me he's planning to resign at the carpentry shop by the end of summer. We will buy a camper, move up there, and live in it until his claim makes money. Uwe even said I should work in the mine with him."

I leaned into Eva. "Then he's just as mad as Kurt. Those two up north didn't strike it rich. If they did, why would they live in such a shack? And Johanna is working so hard, she's aged ten years since they moved there. Do you want to look like her?"

"Of course not. And now, with the child coming, I don't know what to do."

"You have to be adamant. Don't let yourself be pushed around like Johanna. If I were you—"

Eva put her hand on my arm and squeezed. "You have to help me. You have to talk Dieter out of it."

"You mean Uwe."

"No. Dieter. They talk often and he's encouraging Uwe. They're convinced they can make it big there. Dieter even said he'll come up and help Uwe as often as he can."

"Whatever kind of virus they caught in that stinking hole, I sure hope it's not contagious."

"Uwe told me he and Dieter are planning to go back to Lightning Ridge this coming Christmas to get the ball rolling. They want to pick a claim together and be partners, even if Dieter won't live there full-time. They've got it all sorted out."

I let out a strained breath. "Idiots, both of them." I waved at the waiter and asked Eva, "Are you not going to finish your food?"

She looked miserable. "I'm not hungry."

"And you're not drinking?"

She looked even more miserable, the poor girl.

I asked the waiter to clear the table and bring me another wine and a water for Eva. We sat in silence, and when the drinks arrived, I took a mouthful of my dry cabernet sauvignon and felt better immediately. "Just as well this foolishness took care of itself. Praise to your tummy."

Eva stared at the tabletop and said nothing.

"What's wrong? You're not seriously considering this? If you go, you're on your own. I won't accompany Dieter, not in a million years."

"But—" Eva hesitated.

"But what?"

"Now I'll have a baby, and he'll think I did it on purpose to stop him going."

"It's not you alone who made that baby."

"But it was my responsibility to remember to take the pill."

God Almighty. Eva was a walking disaster. How could she forget? And why was she always such a scatterbrain?

Her eyes explored me. "Can't you please, please come along? If the four of us go over Christmas, and the men dig in Kurt's mine for a while and don't find anything, surely they'll lose interest. When we visited Kurt and Johanna in September, Uwe was already at his breaking point on the second day. If they hadn't found those small rocks on the third day…"

Tears rolled down Eva's cheeks and she quickly got a tissue from her handbag.

"Listen," I said. "We both know opal mining is a waste of time, but you want us to spend the Christmas holidays in that godforsaken rat's ass of a place so the boys can discover for themselves that their brilliant idea isn't so brilliant? You and me—we'll be collateral damage."

"It'll be so much easier for him to accept the baby if he doesn't feel he has to give up his dream for it."

"Must be true love."

I don't know if Eva misunderstood me on purpose. She nodded, placed a hand on her tummy, and said, "I already love this baby."

With that, I decided to write Dieter a note, telling him I was spending Christmas in Lightning Ridge whether he liked it or not. Eva must have read my face. "Does that mean you're coming?"

"Only if I can be your baby's godmother."

She hugged me and said, "Please keep it a secret until after Christmas."

As if I would share such good news with my darling husband.

16

EVA

We planned to go to Lightning Ridge the day before Christmas and stay until New Year's Eve. A good week should be sufficient for Uwe to figure out for himself how ridiculous this adventure was. I was sure he'd be his responsible self again after a few days of backbreaking labour without results.

I woke up on the day of our departure with an overwhelming urge to vomit, like every other day that week. When I sat up, my stomach did a somersault and I raced to the bathroom. Usually, Uwe had left the house by then, but today, he caught on to the telltale noise.

"I know you don't want to go," he yelled through the bathroom door. "You don't have to make it that obvious."

"I'll be fine," I called back. "Must have eaten something that was off."

By the time I'd brushed my teeth and washed my face, he had forgotten about my indisposition. He was so excited about mining for opals, he had developed a one-track mind. While he packed, he chatted like a schoolboy.

"Will I need an extra pair of work boots? What should I do if Dieter and Isabella have too much luggage? I need room for my toolbox. Has Kurt called to confirm our motel booking? We got to make sure to take enough sandwiches for the long drive."

"Isabella wants to stop at one of the wineries in Hunter Valley for lunch," I said. She'd mentioned she also wanted to buy some wine there to take along.

Uwe didn't bother to reply.

An hour later, Isabella and Dieter picked us up. Of course, we drove right through the wine valley without exploring its lovely little villages. The guys were in such a hurry to reach our destination, Isabella's noisy objections fell on deaf ears. They told her we'd do some sightseeing on the way back home. She had been in a subdued mood from the start, but when lunchtime passed without stopping, she turned outright broody. She wrinkled her nose at the water bottle I handed to her when she'd mumbled something about being thirsty, and refused one of the sandwiches Dieter passed around. I didn't take one, either, fighting a mild case of car sickness.

Dieter and Uwe didn't notice, or care, about the developing tense silence in the back seat.

"Next stop is Gunnedah," Dieter announced. "We can look for a motel there."

"How far is it?" I asked.

"About fifty kilometers."

"And from there to Lightning Ridge?"

"Another three hundred or so."

I was glad when Dieter finally stopped the car. My knees locked when I got out and stretched, and my back was as stiff as an ironing board. The guys stretched, too, but Isabella stayed in the car and said through the open window, "I'm not staying in this dump."

"Suit yourself," Dieter said, grabbing their overnight bag and walking to reception. Uwe waved at me to follow him.

"Come on," I said to Isabella. "It's only one night."

She made a face and got out.

We checked in, walked to the diner next door, and ordered burgers and fries. I worried briefly if the meal would stay down but I was too hungry to pretend otherwise. It smelled good and tasted delicious. Isabella complained, of course, but she, too, ate until her plate was empty.

We went into our rooms immediately afterwards, tired from the long drive and satiated by the large portions the diner had served.

Uwe mumbled something coming out of the shower and I looked up from my book.

"I said I've never seen Isabella in such a filthy mood. I don't get it. Dieter said *she* suggested they make this trip—that he didn't have to persuade her. She's always been a fickle one, though. She probably doesn't even know half the time what's driving her. I just hope she doesn't ruin our trip by being such a drag."

I smiled to myself, and turned a page.

17

JOHANNA

Our friends are coming. A warm, desperate longing to see them spread through me, immediately dulled by dread. Our shack was still only barely furnished. All the money we had brought, and the little we'd made from the mine went into the mining operation. It would always be like this. I'll never again have a home with a roof that doesn't leak and with walls insulated against the cold winter storms. I'll never again enjoy the luxuries of a washing machine or a stove with more than one cook plate.

I heaved myself off the hard mattress we rolled out on the floor every night and put the kettle on while Kurt continued to snore. I rubbed my sore ankle with the healing cream I had made from local herbs and put my socks and boots on. I wouldn't take them off in front of our friends. Kurt had been in such a rush to get the mine tidy and secure before our friends arrived, he'd worked me harder than ever yesterday.

He had made me make countless trips carrying full buckets from a new side shaft to the manhole all day. I'd worked until I crawled on my knees from exhaustion, and the chain links around my ankle had rubbed my flesh with every step. I had to fill bucket after bucket so he could pull them up.

When I felt I couldn't go on much longer, I placed my empty bucket next to his toolbox before I collapsed. He finished hammering a plank across the new tunnel entrance's wooden frame before he turned and saw me lying there. His face darkened.

I turned my upper body and tried to crawl away, but my foot got tangled in the chain and then he was on top of me, his massive body squashing me into the moist dirt floor. He pressed my face into the mud. I couldn't see or breathe, but I could hear. His breath was hot and heavy as he hissed into my ear.

"Listen, bitch. You do your job, exactly as I told you to, or you stay down here all night. Got it?" He pulled my hair until my head came up. I gasped for air. He pulled harder, then pushed my head down again. "Understand what I'm saying?" Again and again he lifted my head and then lowered it into the dirt again until I thought my cervical vertebrae would snap. "Say yes. Our friends—those idiots who have no fucking business coming here, playing hotshot miners—come tomorrow. And whatever I say, you agree with me. You say yes. Got it? Yes. What do you say?" He yanked my head again, up and down. "Yes. Yes. Yes. That's what you say."

I moaned something like a yes.

He let go of me and went back to his work. I wiped the mud from my eyes and nose and untangled the chain to make my way back. I continued to crawl on my hands and knees until the job was done, his last warning ringing in my ears.

"If you don't, I'll make you disappear for good," he'd said. "Nobody will ever find you."

This morning, my neck was still stiff, but I could at

least move my head without restriction. I was in less pain than other times Kurt had been overcome by his explosive disposition.

But I wanted to forget all that. Daylight broke, and knowing I wouldn't have to go into the mine filled me with golden light. I would be up all day, seeing the sun and chatting with our friends. Kurt was allowing me to stay home for the entire week of their visit. All I had to do was clean the house and go shopping so we would have enough to entertain our friends. He wanted to show them how successful and generous he was. And I would say yes as he had ordered me to.

I briefly thought about using this opportunity—the first that had presented itself since we arrived just after Easter—to run away, but I suppressed that foolish notion very quickly. Kurt would look for me, and he would find me. He would not stop until he caught me, and then his fury would be unimaginable. I shivered and pulled a sweatshirt over my T-shirt. Mornings were still nippy around Christmas time in Lightning Ridge.

Kurt was not back from the mine yet when our friends arrived, looking exhausted, stressed, and confused.

We sat in front of the house on a bench, facing the sun. Eva gave me a pink, silky-soft scarf, which I quickly put aside, and Isabella gave me a bottle of whiskey. "For both of you," she said with a wink. "Merry Christmas."

I got up to make us some tea, taking the bottle inside with me. Isabella called after me that I better bring the whiskey back with the tea.

"Shouldn't we wait until Kurt is home?" Uwe asked.

Isabella laughed. "We'll leave some for him." Her mood improved as soon as I opened the bottle and poured some into her tea.

I made us sandwiches from the supplies I had bought earlier. We ate, drank, and chatted, but the atmosphere between us was strained until Kurt came back at dusk. Uwe and Dieter jumped up and greeted him like a long-lost friend. Isabella made one of her faces and stopped herself smirking when she realized I'd seen it.

Uwe poured hot tea into an enameled cup, added a generous serving of whiskey and sugar, stirred, and handed it to Kurt. He patted Uwe's shoulder and suggested we all go to the pub for a beer.

"A quick one," he said, "to celebrate the start of our mining adventure tomorrow."

"The sooner the better," Dieter said.

Each of the next three days, Kurt drove to pick up Uwe and Dieter before dawn, taking the large container of sandwiches and water bottles I had prepared the evening before with him. The three of them didn't return until after sunset.

Isabella and Eva showed up on the first morning after they'd had their breakfast. We spent the first day on a long walk in the bush and then hung out at our house. On day two, our bushwalking was cut short because Eva saw a snake. They arrived much later on the third day and we drove around for an hour without getting out of their car. I noticed Isabella on the back seat frequently taking swigs from a bottle. She must have brought another one because the whiskey bottle was still at our house. Her daytime drinking didn't stop her from asking for more back home.

I brought the already half-empty bottle out, and we moved our makeshift bench into the shade. The afternoon sun was merciless. I spent so much time underground, I wasn't used to the dry, dust-filled heat and could feel my lungs compressing and my heart struggling to keep a steady rhythm—a feeling not unlike when Kurt terrified me. I should enjoy the moment and savour the precious hours of serenity, but somehow, the future seemed bleaker in bright daylight than down in the mine.

Like every evening since their arrival, we went to the pub for dinner. Kurt was still full of fake enthusiasm, telling stories of amazing opal finds and riches to be discovered, while Uwe and Dieter were noticeably quiet. They slumped in their chairs as if they had no energy left.

Will there even be another day of grace for me?

Isabella was distant and restless, poking at her food and twisting her empty glass in her fingers until she got a refill. In between refills, she disappeared to the ladies room, taking her handbag with her. When she returned, her cheeks were flushed. And by the end of our meal, she was slurring her words.

"Shouldn't we go back to where we found something last time?" Dieter asked in one of Kurt's rare pauses.

He waved it off. "Checked it already."

"Nothing there?"

"Nope." Kurt got up and asked the guys up to the bar for a night cap.

"I think I'll call it quits," Uwe said. "It's been a long day."

"That's why you need another beer. Come on, I'll tell you

about the find Old Joe made last week."

Old Joe had closed his mine last week after thirty-five years of toiling—thirty-five years of crushed hopes until nothing was left but disappointment. Kurt would make it into a success story, though. It gave me a stitch of gratitude. I heard the guys laugh, and I knew I was safe for another day.

18

ISABELLA

I heard a knock on my motel room door. "Go away."

Eva opened the door and came in anyway. "Don't you want breakfast?"

The thought of food annoyed me. I wanted another drink, and I wanted her to go away. "I'm staying in bed until Saturday. If you would be kind enough to go to the liquor store and get me another bottle of vodka, I'd be much obliged."

Eva sat down on my bed and studied me with kind eyes. "Don't be ridiculous. You can't stay in bed."

"Give me one good reason."

"It's still four more days until we drive back to Sydney."

"Oh dear God." I pulled the covers over my head. "Please. Bring me alcohol. I can't handle this sober."

"You don't want me to go alone to Johanna, do you? What would she think?"

"Nothing. I guarantee you she'll think nothing whatsoever. She doesn't give a damn if we show up or not. She'll just sit there on her stupid bench and listen to us trying to keep a conversation going."

"But you're not contributing. I'm the only one who tries to be civil, and every time I say something, you cut me short with a snide remark. You're forever criticizing me and you're in a foul mood all the time. It wouldn't hurt you if you were a bit nicer."

"To whom?"

"To Johanna and me."

I stuck my head out from under the covers and blinked in the bright sunrays falling through the window. "All right. I'll try. But I'll only be nice to you two, not to the guys. They are shitheads, the lot of them."

"Come on. Uwe isn't so bad. You don't know him enough—"

I zipped my mouth with my fingers. "I shall not judge the father of your unborn child, and you are right, I hardly know him. But I know enough about Kurt to find him an obnoxious bastard, a detestable bigmouth, and a bully who gives me the creeps."

Sudden, pure hatred filled my mind. Where did that come from? I had to check myself. Kurt had never harmed me. Sure, he'd undressed me with his eyes every chance he got, the lecherous bastard, but he'd never tried to touch me. Why would his desiring me create such havoc inside me? Was it suppressed anger toward Dieter, who so loathed me? Or toward Hal, who had taken such pride in using me?

"What about your own husband?" Eva asked. "You think Dieter is such a superhero?"

"Don't worry. I'm not glorifying him. Dieter is a weakling. He hates conflict and always takes the easy way out. He's a wimp." My impulsive outburst cleared my head more than any contemplation could have. There it was—everything I had tried so hard to lose in a fog of drunkenness. "Dieter is an arrogant, mendacious asshole."

"Stop talking nonsense," Eva said. "Are you getting up

now or not?"

"I feel nauseated."

"So do I," Eva said. "I'm the one who is pregnant here. Please, get up—for me, for your godchild. We'll get through these last few days together."

I let out a long breath. "The heavens will shower me with gifts for my selfless sacrifice."

Eva went to the door, grinning. "I'll wait outside."

After a hot shower I felt human enough to tackle the day. I found Eva sitting on a bench in front of the motel door. "Let's buy the ingredients for a decent spaghetti sauce and cook it at Johanna's place." I was so tired of the basic pub food.

"Great idea," Eva said. "Uwe loves home cooking. He might realize what he's missing and cut the trip short."

Or we'll give him an excellent demonstration that home cooking can happen here in this shithole, too.

After the grocery store, we dropped by the liquor store where I got a two liter bottle of Chianti to take along, and another half bottle of vodka to slip into my handbag. Then, we drove over to Johanna's. As expected, she sat in front of her house.

"I'm so glad to see you," she said.

I dropped my shopping bag next to her. "Why's that?"

She shrugged, looking sadder than ever. "It's just…I was just thinking…for me, these are the best days ever."

"You're not serious?" Eva asked. "Don't you remember our time on the *Queen Frederica*? We had a lot of fun there, didn't we? And in Sydney. Those were good times, too."

Johanna stared at her. I could see pain and hopelessness in her eyes. "You meant since you've been here in Lightning

Ridge, didn't you?" I said.

I could see fear crossing her face, but I didn't want to dwell on her problems.

Suddenly, Johanna grabbed Eva's arm and clawed into it. "For old times' sake, you'll be staying all week, right?"

"Of course we will." Eva placed her hand over Johanna's.

"Promise?"

"Cross my heart and hope to die."

Johanna's shoulders slumped and her grip went soft, then she looked at me, and so did Eva, when she said, "A promise is a promise, right, Isabella?"

"Let's get started on this sauce," I said cheerfully, feeling like a traitor. "I even got oregano in this godforsaken country shop. Who would have thought?"

The herb made for a good sauce, but the dinner was far from what Eva had hoped for. The guys came home with sour faces and wolfed down the food without a single word.

"What's with you?" I asked, addressing all of them. "Did you guys have a fight?"

Kurt's head jerked up. "Don't be so bloody stupid."

I turned to Dieter. He bent lower over his plate and kept eating.

"We're fine," Uwe mumbled.

That did it. I filled my glass with Chianti again, thankful for my secret liquor stash. Wine wouldn't cut this shit, not by a mile. I'd get through this evening, but tomorrow, I'd refuse if Eva tried to schlepp me to this dump of a place again. Whatever her gentle soul was trying to achieve, she was on lost grounds with me. She may be thinking of her unborn child, but I'd tried enough, and I planned to stay blissfully intoxicated until we headed back to Sydney.

19

A shuffling noise in the room woke me. Dieter was getting dressed. I looked at the clock. Already eight. "What are you still doing here? Hasn't Kurt picked you up?" I asked, still half-asleep.

He buttoned his shirt and slipped into his sandals. "Meeting Uwe and Eva for breakfast at the pub." With that, he walked out. Something was wrong. Then, I saw his packed travelling bag next to the door, and although my head thumped a warning to take it slowly, that beautiful sight made me jump up and get ready like lightning. We were leaving. I threw my stuff in my bag, placed it next to Dieter's, and went to the pub.

"So, what's all this about?" I asked, smiling, when I joined them.

Eva stared into the distance and bit her lip. None of the guys answered, so I nudged her. "Say."

She looked at me and said in a whiny voice, "Uwe just told me they want to drive back to Sydney today, right after breakfast."

"Suits me fine," I said. "You must be glad to get out of here." But she didn't look it. Why the hell didn't she look elated? Wasn't the whole exercise to make Uwe come to his senses, which, I figured, had been achieved?

"I told Uwe we promised Johanna to stay all week." She stared at me. "He thinks we can't break a promise."

"Watch me," I said.

"Johanna needs us here."

"What for?"

"Uwe said Kurt told him she might be ill."

I turned to him. "Is that so? Good old Kurt is worried about his wife? He should take her to a doctor then."

Eva let out a long breath. "Apparently it's something women deal best with—something emotional. It's only three more days, and I don't mind staying behind if the guys want to head home."

I bet she didn't mind. She must be so relieved, she'd do anything to make Uwe happy. "When the guys are gone, we won't have a car. How are we supposed to get back?"

"We'll take the train."

"No, thank you," I said. "You can stay if you like."

"We owe it to her," Eva said.

"Eva's got a point." Dieter said. "You should stay with Johanna."

He couldn't be serious. I felt a rush of anger and put all the disdain I could muster into my reply. "You must be dumber than you look if you think I'm staying here."

Dieter and Uwe glanced at each other, but I couldn't grasp the meaning of their exchange. I didn't care. I got up, nearly knocking my coffee cup over, and said, "Meet you at the car."

Half an hour later, the guys showed up at the motel without Eva. I felt a twinge of regret for abandoning her but had no qualms about breaking a promise I hadn't made to Johanna. I had fulfilled my duty—to stay by Eva's side while

Uwe got his opal fever out of his system—and nothing in the world could stop me from getting into that car.

We had just left the town behind us when Dieter started his verbal attack on me. "That's so typical of your egotistical self, leaving Eva behind. You're a spoiled brat. You don't deserve friends. I'm ashamed for you." And on and on he went.

I sat in the passenger seat and searched the radio for a decent music station, without responding to him. It only surprised me that he let go like that in front of Uwe. My indifference must have annoyed him even more, because he slapped my hand from the radio like I was an obnoxious child. How dare he. On impulse, I hit him back, hard. In the face, with my fist. "You pig," I screeched. "How dare you!"

Dieter hit the brakes and let the car roll to the side of the road. He raised his hand to hit me back but reconsidered, reached across me, and opened the door.

"Out!"

I stiffened in my seat.

"Out with you. I refuse to take you back to Sydney." He pointed west. "Kurt's mine is over there. He can drive you back to Eva and Johanna. After that, I don't care. I don't have to tolerate this behaviour."

My pride kicked in. "I wouldn't ride another meter with you." I could see blood running from his nostril. "You started it."

I got out, thinking he'd drive a few meters and come to his senses, but then the car disappeared around a bend in the distance. My anger dissipated, making room for huge disappointment. I was stuck in Lightning Ridge for another three days. Damn Dieter. I wouldn't stand for it. I'll take the train tomorrow. Eva could join me or stay—her choice.

I walked in the general direction Dieter had pointed. The mine couldn't be far because I could see the tip of the derrick. The temperature was still pleasant, being so early in the morning.

Walking through the low bush, I shivered, annoyed that I got in the car without a sweater. All my clothes were in my bag, and the bag was on the way to Sydney. Even my handbag was still in the car. I'd have to borrow money for the train ticket from Eva. Maybe I can catch one later today.

Moisture collected in the thick, grassy vegetation dripped on my open sandals. Thorny bushes scratched my ankles. Thinking of snakes and scorpions and other ugly creepy crawlies, I shivered even more. Why did I pick such a thin dress this morning? Because Dieter's damn car doesn't have air-conditioning, the miserable bastard.

I walked in a straight line for over an hour but the derrick didn't seem to get any closer. With the bush around me getting thicker, I had to use more effort to part the shrubbery. The sun was up in full force, and I began to sweat, hoping the scratches on my skin wouldn't bleed and attract Australia's finest. The bush was home to every goddamn poisonous insect and wild animal on the planet. I walked faster, panting like a thirsty dog.

Christ, Dieter, I'll make you suffer for this.

When I finally reached the mine, my armpits were soaking wet, and my dress stuck to my back and around my waist. I was relieved when the flat dirt area around the derrick with the manhole in its center appeared in my view, but at the same time, I was mad as hell at Dieter, and Uwe, and all men in general, for making me stomp through the bush alone. Bastards.

"Kurt," I called out in all directions.

Having to rely on Kurt, of all men, caused toxic waste to bubble up inside me. *Why did I hit Dieter so hard? What is the matter with me? Where did this sudden rage, come from? I hate myself. I hate him. I hate everybody. That idiot down there, too.*

"Kurt, you rotten bastard, where are you?"

The mine was quiet. I walked over to the manhole, looked down, and listened.

"Kurt?"

I suddenly felt dizzy. Leaning forward, dehydrated, exhausted, and full of animosity, resentment and irritation, my head felt light and white stars appeared in my vision.

I grabbed hold of the ladder leading down the shaft. My head was spinning. The manhole lost its contours and the ladder floated in open space like a feather. I tried to keep my grip on the ladder but my hands slipped. I slipped and floated into the shaft. Hold onto the ladder. I wanted to cry out but my throat was parched. The shaft walls touched my body and an angel got hold of me—an ugly, black angel with gigantic wings and a grinning, pockmark face. He caught me, held me tight. I could feel his ugliness while his huge strong wings folded around me. Can't breathe. Can't move. No escape.

Disgusting black angel smell—devil smell. His sweat was mixing with my own, his mouth pressed onto mine, breathing his ugly soul into my mouth. The ugliness penetrated my whole being. I put all my strength into getting free of him. One arm, then both. I fought and fought but the ugliness engulfed me even tighter. Behind closed lids, I could see the angel-devil, and with every pore of my skin, I could feel his deadly hug.

Then, nothing.

20

JOHANNA

Kurt was in front of the house, working on his truck, when Eva arrived.

"Where're the others?" I heard him say when I came outside to greet her.

Eva cleared her throat, obviously uncomfortable. "They've had to go back to Sydney. Sorry, something important. I thought you knew."

Now Kurt cleared his throat.

"Just as well I have to fix the truck before I head to the mine," Kurt said. "Would have been a damn waste of my time to drive to the motel to pick them up."

Eva looked at me. "But I'll be staying a few more days, as promised, and will then take the train back."

My heart stopped for a second. I didn't dare say anything and waited for Kurt's reaction. He looked up sharply and mumbled something about not giving a damn.

After an awkward pause, Eva said she'd wander back to the motel to shower and change, and then come back.

Kurt waited until Eva was out of earshot. "Get rid of her," he said to me in a hoarse voice. "One more day, and she's on that train. Tomorrow, you're mine again, all day long."

Instant terror froze my insides. His hunger to torment me had been supressed for days already, it would need to be

141

fed an extra-large portion. My whole body was shaking long after he had left for the mine, and I had to breathe deeply and slowly to get enough oxygen into me. Part of me wanted to stay home with Eva, and part of me wanted to get it over with. Not knowing what to expect was harder than living through the actual torture. But how I could I send Eva away after she'd made this special effort to keep me company?

Eva returned around lunchtime. I was calmer by then, having decided that I would make good use of my last hours with her. I tried hard not to think about what I would have to endure later on, but every time Eva fell silent for a moment, my thoughts circled around flight and resistance. Should I have gone to Sydney with them? Uwe and Dieter would have told Kurt immediately. They wouldn't even have taken me to begin with. Get on a train with Eva tomorrow? Kurt would drag me back by my hair. The world isn't large enough to hide me.

Eva and I spent all afternoon sitting and drinking tea, talking about the good old times, which Eva now admitted hadn't been all that good. I felt she wanted me to open up to her, and I nearly did, but the thought of sharing the secret of my shameful existence made me so nervous and frustrated, I clammed up again.

At six o'clock, Eva suggested we go to the pub for dinner. Kurt wouldn't be back before eight, but I declined. We moved into the house and eventually, all conversation dried up. I hoped Eva would leave me alone and go back to her motel because it felt like we were sitting in a waiting room—quiet, depressing, and confusing.

Suddenly, a breeze rattled the mosquito screen on the

open door.

"What was that?" Eva asked.

We could hear a car approaching at rapid speed. It came to a halt in front of the house with screeching tires.

Alarmed by the noise and by intense foreboding, I raced to the door but before I could open it, Isabella stumbled into the house and sank into my arms. She looked ghastly. Her left eye was swollen shut and deep welts ran from her neck down across her naked breasts. The top of her dress was ripped apart and hung from her waist, and large red spots soaked her skirt. Isabella tried to cover them with her hands.

"Oh my God, Isabella!" Eva jumped up and helped me drag the semi-conscious Isabella into the room.

"Quick," I ordered, "get my blanket and pillow."

We placed her on the sofa, and I got a bowl of water and a clean towel.

"She needs a doctor," Eva said. "She's injured. I'll call for an ambulance. Where are the numbers?"

I shook my head and began to clean the wounds.

She understood. "Sorry, I forgot. I'll get a doctor. Where do I have to go?"

"No!" Isabella clawed at my arm, her breath laboured. "It's nothing. He didn't get me."

"You need a doctor," Eva repeated. "What happened, Isabella?"

"I got away." Isabella shuddered. "No doctor."

Eva sounded panicky. "Johanna, say something. She needs help. She's bleeding."

Isabella still hadn't loosened her grip on my arm, and she stared into my eyes.

"No," I said. "She doesn't want it."

Isabella's eyelids fluttered. She was losing it fast. "I'm thirsty," she whispered.

"Kurt did that." I carefully extracted my arm from her weakening grip and stood to get her some water.

"Kurt?" Eva looked stunned. "What are you talking about?" When I didn't answer, she asked again. "What did Kurt do? Damn it, talk to me"

I came back with the glass of water and propped Isabella up so she could drink. After a few greedy sips, she fell back on the pillow, pale as a ghost with streaks of her wet, dirty, black hair sticking to her head. Some of the water she hadn't been able to swallow in her haste ran out of the corners of her swollen, cracked mouth and her whole body shivered. "I had a fight with Dieter."

I put my ear closer to her mouth so I could understand her better. "He stopped the car on the highway…threw me out… walked to the mine…thought Kurt would…" Her voice faltered.

"Dieter said Kurt would bring you back?" I assisted.

By now, Isabella barely had the strength to hold her gaze with me. I could see all the pain in the world in those eyes. "It happened so fast…oh God, Johanna…I'm so sorry….I didn't want to…"

Finally, Eva understood, too. "That can't be true. Not Kurt."

And why not? How can you be so blind? So clueless? I wanted to yell at her, but nothing came over my lips. Every fiber of my being was stretched to the limit but at the same time, a calmness came over me, close to satisfaction—

confirmation of my suffering. *See what I had to endure?*

Isabella's eyelids moved, but I couldn't see any light in her eyes. "I ran…ran…the truck…he's after me. He's here. I took a hammer. I hit him. I hit…hard. Get off….please…" She suddenly sat up, eyes fully open, and stared at the door, a wild yet terrified expression on her face. "Please…please, don't let him in. He's coming. Don't let him in. Don't let him hurt me."

She fainted and fell back.

Eva started to cry. "Oh my God. Oh my God. What are we gonna do? She needs help. Look at her."

I remembered from my nursing days that Eva would go into hysterics if I didn't stop her panic, so I slapped her. "It looks worse than it is."

"Are you sure?"

"Of course I am." Eva looked confused but at least she'd stopped crying and could help me tend to Isabella's injuries. My first aid kit was as extensive as any miner's. Living in the bush had taught us all to be self-reliant. Isabella's wounds were mostly superficial, and when we had patched her up as best as we could, I pulled the blanket over her and told Eva to look after her.

"Where are you going?"

I went to fetch my nylon all-weather jacket and Kurt's rifle.

Eva gasped when I walked past her to leave the house.

"What are you doing?"

"I'm going to take care of Kurt."

21

EVA

Johanna returned after about an hour, stored the rifle, and said, "He's dead." Then, she went to the stove and busied herself making coffee. I, too terrified to even ask how Kurt had died, stayed in my chair next to where Isabella was sleeping.

Johanna came back with two steaming mugs and placed one in front of me. She sat down on the sofa next to Isabella's feet, blew at her drink, and stared at the floor while she told me in a subdued voice what she'd found.

"He was lying close to the manhole. I checked his pulse, but there was no life in him." Her expression was serene, close to a quiet inner joy only she could be familiar with, and her posture and gestures were soft and tranquil. This demonstration of peacefulness helped calm the panic I felt. I had never dealt with death before.

"I think we should bury him," she said after we finished our coffee.

"How did he die?"

"Does it matter?"

Of course not. It wasn't something I wanted to discuss. I didn't want to picture Isabella killing Kurt. I couldn't imagine how she had done it, or if she even knew.

Johanna must have read my mind. "Isabella thinks he's

still alive."

"Why do you say that?"

"She was terrified that he might be following her. She said she hit him pretty hard, but she wasn't aware that her blow could have been fatal. He probably bled to death after she left, like a pig." Johanna mused over her words, and a tiny smile formed on her lips.

"Oh God, no. She'll be so upset when she wakes."

Johanna's smile disappeared. "Don't you dare say anything to her. It's hard enough to cope with the emotional stress of being raped. She doesn't need to feel like a murderer on top of it. She doesn't deserve this and she doesn't know what she's done."

"But how can we keep it from her? The police—"

Johanna was quick to interrupt me. "No need for that either. Imagine the outcry this would create, the drama poor Isabella would have to go through. She'd never recover from that."

"We can't keep it a secret. Kurt's dead body at your mine—how do we explain that?"

"I told you. All we need to do is bury him. The bush is large and forgiving."

Johanna was right. If we wanted this to go away and help Isabella, we had to get rid of his body. What Kurt had done was inexcusable, and what Isabella had done was understandable, but people would still blame her. It surprised me how rationally I was considering to be an accomplice to manslaughter. We had to work fast.

"Who will look after Isabella while we do it?" I asked.

Johanna got up and checked Isabella's pulse. "She's

stable, but she needs fluids. Let's try and wake her. I'll dissolve a sleeping pill in her tea. That'll knock her out for a few hours."

We rubbed Isabella's face and arms with cold towels until she opened the eye that wasn't swollen shut. I could see terror on her face. She moaned, "Is he back?"

"No," Johanna said. "Kurt is dead."

Isabella lifted her head and blinked. "What happened?"

I could see Johanna searching for the right words. "It was an accident." She put the mug to Isabella's lips. "You need to drink."

Isabella drank long, slow sips, then her head fell back again, exhausted. "Good riddance. You better bury him. Nobody has to know what happened."

Ten minutes later, she was fast asleep again. Outside, dawn was breaking.

"Are you really sure he's dead?" I asked Johanna when we arrived at the mine. I refused to look at the massive body on the ground. Somehow, I expected Kurt to come back to life, jump up, grab me, and shake some sense into me. My God, what are we doing? I prayed to a higher power that he was truly dead. I dared to risk a cursory glance and shuddered when I saw this lump of flesh covered in dried blood, dirt and flies at Johanna's feet.

Johanna didn't answer me but stared at the body of what had been her husband. She bent over him and studied his face and body. Was she searching his face for signs of past passion? Was she thinking of the times when she had fallen in love with him and had made love to him? Did she feel sad seeing him in the dirt, knowing his eyes were empty and his extremities limp and cold?

She straightened again. "Of course he's dead."

"Are you sure he was already dead when you...I mean, definitely dead...when you—"

"Oh, don't be ridiculous. Of course he was dead when I found him. He's still lying in exactly the same position." She sounded impatient. "Come on now. We need to get rid of him and head back to Isabella."

"Wouldn't it be better to go to the police?"

"To tell them what? That Kurt had an accident? Does it look like he did? What conclusion will they draw if they come to my place to interview us and find Isabella in the condition she's in? Please, be sensible." Johanna's voice got more aggressive. "Come on. Help me get him into that damn wheelbarrow. He's as heavy as a porker."

I winced. Not in a hundred years did I want to hear her calling him names now that he was dead. And I didn't want to touch him. "I can't."

Johanna stood and placed her balled fists on her waist. She looked angry. "You refuse to help Isabella? You want her to go to jail for this...for this...piece of shit?" She spit on the earth, narrowly missing the body at her feet.

Kurt didn't look like the Kurt I knew any longer with the twisted expression of his death mask and weirdly placed limbs. I couldn't fathom how the living human I had known could have become so unrecognizable. Was that really him underneath all that blood? "How could she?" I let the sentence linger in the air between us.

Johanna picked it up without hesitation—without

emotion. "You heard what Isabella said. She hit him. Hard. Sheer luck that she got him with one blow, or she'd be the one we'd have to bury."

I winced again.

Johanna bent down, grabbed Kurt's arm, and started to pull him into the wheelbarrow. "Come on, now. You said you'd help me."

I did, but I had no idea how hard this would be. All I had thought about was how to protect Isabella. To get the wheelbarrow and shovels, quickly hide the evidence from prying eyes, and then… What was I thinking? Sure, I wanted to hide the truth from Isabella. She wouldn't be able to live with the guilt of having killed somebody. Therefore, I should be able to shoulder the much lesser crime of removing a dead body—the body of a rapist, Johanna's husband. That was another consideration that should help me get through this ordeal. Poor Johanna would have to deal with the shame of being the wife of a monster. She would be exposed to unfair scrutiny from people who didn't even know her. The gullible public would wonder why she hadn't known what a monster he was. They would imply she was stupid, or partly to blame, or even guilty. No, I couldn't expose both my friends to such treatment. Johanna was right when she said it was best for Isabella to forget it all.

I wondered if she or I would ever forget it.

Once we had managed to heave Kurt into the wheelbarrow, we rolled it along a path deep into the bush. Several times, one of his arms or legs fell over the edge and we had to stop and rearrange him to balance the weight. The path we followed was getting more and more overgrown, showing it hadn't been worked in a long time. Finally, we were in deserted bush, too dense to part with our heavy load without leaving visible signs.

"Enough. This will have to do." Johanna stopped at a small clearing, leaned over the wooden handles of the wheelbarrow to catch her breath, and wiped the sweat from her face. She looked spent.

I had no energy left, but we still had to bury Kurt. Johanna pulled the shovels and a pick out from underneath his body. We began to work the ground, dry and hard as it was. Johanna hacked away at the overgrown earth while I scraped the loosened lumps, rocks, and broken roots aside. I thought we'd never be able to dig a hole deep enough but we were lucky. After the first few inches, the earth turned crumbly. Johanna gave the ground a few hard hits with her pick, and suddenly, the surface broke, opening up a hollow space underneath.

"Wow," she said, looking into it. "A cavity. Looks like it'll do."

My back ached badly, sending urgent signals to my brain not to question her judgement. It didn't matter if this was the old den of a wild animal or an abandoned mine shaft as long as it allowed us to dump Kurt into it, cover him with earth, and let nature take care of the rest.

Johanna worked the hole with frenzied blows until she considered it wide enough. Then, we maneuvered the wheelbarrow next to it and tipped it over. He was halfway in the opening when his legs jammed. Johanna had to climb into the cavity and push and shove until his whole body fit.

She climbed out again, picked up a shovel and started to throw the earth we had loosened into the hole. I took the other shovel and we covered him as best as we could. When we had no earth left, the ground showed an indentation of only a few inches. We put our shovels down.

"Shouldn't we say a prayer?" I asked.

"If you want to."

It had been a while. I collected the words in my mind and began to say the Lord's Prayer. "Father in heaven…"

Johanna took a step forward and trampled over the burial site.

I felt a lump in my throat. "Johanna, I can't pray if you…"

"Then don't." She stomped her feet, rhythmically and indifferently. "The ground needs to be solid, or wild animals will dig him up. No need to pray for a damned soul anyway."

I mumbled the rest of the prayer, thinking she might be right.

On the way back to the mine, we made an effort to cover our tracks where they were too obvious, all the while realizing that it was impossible. We could only hope nobody would come along there until nature had sealed our path. In a few weeks, nothing would lead to Kurt's burial site, and on the slim chance a miner would cross there, it would be impossible to notice the small disturbance in the rough terrain surrounding it.

Just a few short weeks and this nightmare would be over for all of us, forever.

22

Life stood still for the next three days. Isabella was in a drug-induced haze and didn't seem to be in pain. She was never hungry or thirsty, didn't cry, complain or smile.

Johanna and I should have wondered if we had done the right thing, how this could have happened, and what we could have done to avoid it. We should have talked about it, but we never did.

Not until the evening of the third day, when I heard Johanna mutter, "What now?"

I understood. We needed to look ahead.

"I'm sure Uwe expects me home any day now," I said, glancing at the sleeping Isabella. "And I'm surprised Dieter hasn't called at the pub yet to find out where she is."

"I'm not," Johanna said. "They had a fight, remember? He's convinced she came back here and is staying with us."

"She can't go back with me, not in the condition she's in." I looked at her injuries. They were healing but not fast enough. She needed a few more days.

"I drive you to the post office later. There, you can call Uwe and tell him you are staying a bit longer because Kurt has disappeared. We'll drive to Dubbo first thing tomorrow and tell the police Kurt is missing. In about a week, Isabella will be fit enough, and I'll drive you two to the train station in Brisbane."

My mind was racing without getting anywhere. "Do I

have to go with you to Dubbo?"

"I need you to confirm my statement."

I paced, thinking. "What if the police come here to get Isabella's statement? If they'll see her in that condition."

Johanna walked to the window and stared outside. "Those windows need a good cleaning. Everything here does, but that'll have to wait." She looked around the room and sucked in a deep breath of the stale, sick-smelling air which lingered in the room. Chamomile tea, antiseptic tincture, body odours. She turned back to me. "The police won't come here."

"How can you be so sure?"

"They don't know Isabella is here. Think about it. Aside from Kurt and the two of us, nobody here knows she came back. And Kurt is dead. That leaves only you and me. If we stick to our story, the police will assume she's back in Sydney."

"But Uwe and Dieter know she isn't."

"So?"

"What if they are interviewed? Dieter will tell them he kicked her out of the car and so will Uwe."

Johanna came a step closer. Her face was all bunched up, and I could see real anger in her expression. "Don't be ridiculous." Even her voice sounded highly agitated. "Why would anybody interview them? The police don't know they've been here. You and Isabella came to visit me, nobody else. She's gone back home, you stayed. Stick to that, and confirm my missing person's report. We'll go to Dubbo and tell them I drove Kurt to his usual hunting spot three days ago and when I went back to pick him up yesterday, he hadn't come back. So, I went this morning again but there was still no Kurt. All you have to do is tell them you saw Kurt leaving with me. That's not so difficult, is it?"

"Oh dear. I just hope they don't start a big search party for him."

"Nobody cares if he returns or not. He isn't the first husband to go AWOL. The police will sympathize with me, the waiting wife, label him missing, and put the file aside. Stuff like that happens all the time." Johanna came back to the sofa and looked down at Isabella. "While we are in Dubbo, we need to get a change of clothes and some makeup for her. We can't send her back to Dieter a mess like that."

The policeman on duty at the station in Dubbo, Bill Wiseman, was young and still eager. Before he wrote down our statements, he asked several questions.

"Where did your husband usually go hunting?"

Johanna described a large area north of Lightning Ridge that must be half the size of Queensland. Bill jotted it down.

"How did he get there?"

Johanna explained where she dropped him off.

"How long did he plan to stay away?"

She dabbed her eyes and told Bill he was supposed to come back yesterday and that he'd never been late before.

Bill took out a tissue and handed it to her. Then, he asked me to describe the clothes he was wearing when I saw him last. That wasn't difficult with the image of his dead bulk in the wheelbarrow burned into my mind. I gasped before I told him, and he slid the tissue box over to me.

He finally wrote down our statements and finished the hour-long ordeal with a reassuring, "We'll call you if we have any news."

"I don't have a phone," Johanna said.

"How can we reach you then?"

He looked at her address, disturbed. An hour and a half drive away.

Johanna reacted quickly and gave him the number of the local pub. "Somebody there will forward your message to me."

"And we'd appreciate if you let us know if he shows up," he said.

When we left, he called after us. "It's still early days. I'm sure he'll show up."

"Told you so," Johanna said on the drive home. "Nothing will happen. They won't call me, I won't call them, and the file will be put aside and forgotten."

"Surely, you won't stay here in Lightning Ridge? What if they do call and can't reach you? Won't they become suspicious if you move away so soon after his disappearance?"

Johanna's face dropped. "I'll stay in Lightning Ridge and pretend to wait for my husband."

"But you can't live here on your own."

She smirked. "You think?"

"What will you do? I mean, how will you make a living? You can't work in the mine, and you won't find a job here."

Her smirk turned into a wide grin. "Maybe they'll open a hospital here."

"Be serious."

"I'll tell you what I'll do for starters. I'll get myself a phone. Kurt never let me have one. Then, you can call me anytime you're worried about me. Next, I'll clean up the place and take all the old junk Kurt forced me to live with to the dump. Then, I'll fix up this house. I know where Kurt has been hiding most of the money he made from the mine. It isn't much, but it's enough to survive a while and get the place livable. And when I've used it all up, I'll go back in the mine and work it myself. I know I can do it, especially on my own."

Bill left a message for Johanna at the pub, and she called him back the day before she drove us to the train station. He gently prepared her for the possibility that Kurt might have suffered a tragic accident. By now, Bill was convinced Kurt hadn't disappeared on purpose. Other miners in town had told him he wasn't the type to sneak away from his wife and his business. Johanna started to sniffle and told him she believed her husband would come back one day, and that she would wait for that day as long as it took.

23

Johanna had stopped sedating Isabella the day before our departure. When she woke up that morning, we thought she'd ask us what had happened and why she was injured, but she didn't. She simply got up, got dressed, and asked for a cup of coffee. When she didn't mention Kurt and wasn't curious about the time she had lost, I chose not to mention it either.

I said goodbye to Johanna at the railway station. She gave me a casual hug and waved to Isabella, looking rather relaxed and somewhat pleased, and off she went. She was already settling into her new life as a widow, or as a deserted wife.

We boarded the train and I sat opposite Isabella, who had taken a book from her bag and started reading. When the train shuddered into motion, I decided to make a careful approach to suss out her feelings. "This whole experience must have been dreadful."

She looked up, her eyes cold and empty. "I sure won't go back to that boring place." She lowered her eyes and continued reading.

"I mean...it's been quite horrible." I fumbled for words. Should I ask her point-blank if she remembers what Kurt had done to her and what she had done to him? Johanna had stressed again last night that Isabella was traumatized, that she believed Isabella didn't know what had happened, and that confrontation with the origin of the trauma could create severe mental stress for her. She might go into shock. I can't handle that, not on a train.

I stared at her. She has killed somebody. She is a murderer. Can I ever see her as a friend again?

She must have felt my intense gaze because she lifted her head, scowling at me. The coldness in her eyes broke for a second when she met my thoughts, reading me, absorbing my doubts, and accepting the rift that had opened between us—maybe even welcoming the distance it created.

I broke our eye contact and turned my head to the window.

The rest of the journey was spent in total silence.

Uwe picked us up from the railway station. Isabella wore large sunglasses to hide the discolouration around her eyes. The scabs had fallen off the scratches along her neck and arms, and she had covered what was still visible with the makeup and long-sleeved blouse we had bought for her in Dubbo. When she got dressed without commenting on her new blouse, which was clearly not her style and didn't fit her well, it became apparent to me that she still wasn't herself.

If Uwe noticed the changed mood between us, he didn't show it. He drove to Mosman and stopped at Isabella's home. She thanked him, waved to me, and walked away without asking us up for a drink.

Her strange behaviour must have rubbed off on Uwe. I waited for him to say something or ask about the extension of my trip, but he was silent until he parked the car at our house. I couldn't stand the tension any longer. "So, what do you say?"

"About what?"

"About Kurt's disappearance, of course."

He turned the motor off and kept looking through the windshield as if he still needed to concentrate on the traffic. I got the feeling he didn't want to look at me. "Terrible," he said. "Really terrible. Who would have thought? Only two weeks ago, we were all together having a good time."

I winced. "The police think he could have had a hunting accident, and I think he's dead." Could I trust Uwe with the truth?

He didn't react, so I made another move. "I don't think it would be all that terrible for Johanna if he—"

Uwe finally turned his face to me, flushed and angry. "What kind of bullshit is that?"

"Well, he's been gone over a week, and I think Johanna knows he's dead."

He totally ignored my rather direct statement. "How long will they look for him?"

"They haven't really looked for him at all. They never look for lost people. The terrain is too vast and inaccessible. They'll just wait until he shows up, and if he doesn't, well, then I don't know. I guess he will be declared dead, eventually." I stopped and waited, but Uwe was back to studying the windshield. "I guess if one wants to make somebody disappear, Lightning Ridge is a good place for it."

Finally, I had his full attention. He turned his upper body, poked my shoulder with his index finger, and snapped at me. "How dare you come to bullshit conclusions like this? You are too stupid to understand what you are saying. You're accusing somebody of murder, and I won't tolerate such mindless gossip. We could get into trouble with such ignorant talk. Think before you open your mouth. Making somebody disappear, really? How could you even think that?"

How could I? I hadn't accused anybody. I'd simply stated the truth.

"Because it's true," I barked. "Because he's dead. If you want to hear it or not, what I'm saying is true, and you can insult me all you like, I'm not—"

"Shut up!" He hit the steering wheel with his hand. "Shut the fuck up! I won't listen to another word. Kurt will be back soon."

Tears shot into my eyes. I wanted to tell him the truth, but he shut me out. He hadn't hugged me at the station or even said a single nice word to me since I'd arrived. He didn't want to hear anything and was only concerned about his reputation. But Kurt was dead. Isabella had killed him, I had helped dispose of his body, and I couldn't share the worst two weeks of my life with my own husband.

He opened the car door and got out. What was the matter with him? Is the thought of his friend being dead so upsetting, he refuses to even consider it?

Thinking back, he had always taken Kurt's side and practically worshipped him. They had spent hours talking right from the beginning. He had given Kurt a lot more attention than he had ever given me.

I stayed in the car. My tears flowed freely now. My husband, the father of my unborn child, rejected me for a guy he still saw as his future. Mining with Kurt was the dream he would have to bury, and I would have to bear the consequences. I suddenly knew I didn't want to share my future with Uwe. My baby deserved better than an unsupportive father.

I felt a kick against the wall of my gut. *Here I am.* And I smiled.

Uwe and I would separate. But I couldn't go back to Germany, to my family and all the I-told-you-so's. Not yet. My silly dream of emigrating halfway around the world, laid bare for all to snicker at. No, I couldn't handle that.

"You and me," I said to my stomach. "We need to stay here a few more years. Uwe has to support us financially. I can't be dependent on my family back home again, but when you are ready to go to school, we'll make our move. The education system is better in Germany. Everybody will understand that, and I can go back to work. So, do we have a deal?"

Another kick. "Good." Uwe and I were done, but I'd have my baby for company.

I waited until my tears dried up, then I went inside to not talk to this man who had become a stranger to me within a few short hours.

24

ISABELLA

I heard the music and laughter before I opened our apartment door. Dieter was on the sofa in front of the window, his guest opposite him, with his back to me.

"Hello, darling," Dieter said. "Back already? How was the journey?"

I walked past the two of them.

His laughter followed me. "Still pissed at me, are you?"

Obviously, he wanted to taunt me, to remind me of his insulting behaviour. I remembered very well how he had thrown me out of the car. Dieter was probably still proud. "See, that's how you treat an obnoxious wife," I imagined him saying. His guest was laughing, too. Had he made a joke at my expense?

I went into my bedroom, closed the door, threw myself on the bed, and kicked my shoes off. Dieter was unbearable, superficial, and stupid—an arrogant, conceited bullshit artist. I bet when he came back from Lightning Ridge, he'd told everybody he knew how he cut me down a notch, abandoning me in the bush. He'd likely exaggerated the story until I'd become the laughing stock of the Sydney advertising community.

Music wafted through the apartment's thin walls, tearing at my nerves. I was so tired. I wanted to sleep, but his angry reaction in the car haunted my mind. Did he tell his friends I hit him or did he leave that part out of his bragging? I bet he told them I had to walk for hours through deserted bush in the heat, all alone, to get to Kurt's mine. I bet he was proud of treating a woman this way. I was sick at the thought.

The damn music got louder and my body felt heavy like lead. I'd turn things around and tell everybody what really happened, that I was married to an inconsiderate pig. But who'd care? Everybody who knew Dieter was aware of that already. It was over.

I had found my way back and had survived this terrible ordeal. It was best to forget everything from the moment Dieter had kicked me out of the car. I was too tired to deal with it, anyway.

I need to find the energy to get up and leave. I can't stand being here any longer, being with Dieter.

The music stopped.

I heard Dieter talking to his guest, laughing, and then footsteps and the door closing behind them. Going out to have some fun. Couldn't stand staying home with Madam Miserable.

Although I was so exhausted I could barely stand, I forced myself off the bed, took Dieter's pillow and a blanket, carried it into the living room, and threw it on the sofa. Then, I walked back into the bedroom, locked the door, undressed, and lied down again, feeling a little better. Before falling asleep, it dawned on me that this was what I had to do from now on—take the initiative, be the strong one, make decisions, and not let him walk all over me. This is my bed, my place of comfort and safety. I won't move out. If he can't stand living with me, he'll have to go.

By the end of January, summer was hot and humid. When I came home from work, the air inside my apartment was thick and had taken on the smell of rotting bananas. I opened the windows for ventilation, slipped into a light summer dress, settled on the sofa with a glass of chilled Chablis, and listened to the quiet evening. Only faint traffic noise reached our posh, upper-floor apartment, and I could hear some birds singing. Dieter wasn't home, a blessing after my hectic work day.

The phone on the small side table next to me stared at me. I ought to call Eva. It's been a few weeks since we got back from Lightning Ridge. How can I explain not returning any of her calls? But I didn't feel like—or couldn't—chat with her about my struggles to get through every single day when all she wanted to talk about was the new life growing inside her and how worried she was about her baby's future.

Living with Dieter had become a daily, and often nightly, obstacle course. Most days, I was the last one to leave the office so I could avoid spending time with him in the apartment. Luckily, he was out many evenings but when he was home, he did everything he could to annoy me, whining and complaining when I wanted peace and quiet or not speaking to me when I needed to discuss things. I never knew what to expect, but I never let on that he succeeded in driving me crazy. I didn't want to give him that satisfaction.

I found his presence revolting, even when he just sat there, noisily flipping through his overpriced art magazines. I stayed calm, withdrew into myself and pondered how I could get rid of him without having major financial difficulties. He made more money on one photo shoot than I earned in a whole month. He paid the exorbitant rent on our place and most of our living expenses. I helped myself to as much as I could but only from the checking account. He moved quite a bit of his earnings into a savings account, and I didn't dare touch that one. If I split now, I wouldn't be able to pay more than the security deposit for a dump of a place.

I lit a cigarette and grabbed an ashtray, overflowing with butts, from the kitchen sink. No wonder the apartment smelled so bad.

I cleaned the ashtray and took it back to my place on the sofa, next to the phone. I should call Eva. Instant guilt spread inside me. If she weren't pregnant, I wouldn't feel so bad about having ignored her for so long. Damn this. I don't have the energy to face her with a half-decent apology today. Tomorrow. I'll call her tomorrow.

I looked around. The place was a mess. How could Dieter live like this? How could I?

If I didn't want to live in a pigsty, I had to pull myself together soon. It would be years before I could put enough money aside to make it on my own, and this guy was like quicksand, dragging me down with him. Do something positive. Call Eva.

When I picked up the phone, I saw the note on it.

"Hi," it started. I immediately knew Dieter was about to insult me again. "I decided to leave Australia. And you. You can keep the furniture and my car. Do what you like with it. I cleared the bank account. That money is mine. Bye. Dieter."

I had to read the note three times. The furniture? Those

stupid uncomfortable designer pieces. The car? Just about ready to break down. Who cared about that? But the money. My hands started shaking. God Almighty, he wouldn't have taken it all. And what did he mean about leaving me? I wasn't ready for this. Where would he go? Why leave Australia? He had his business here. I was shaking so badly I had trouble stubbing my cigarette out. This couldn't be. I jumped up, went into the bedroom, and opened the wardrobe. On his side, a few forlorn hangers dangled in empty space. Everything was gone.

I opened the desk drawers. Empty. He really had left me.

I went back to my seat in the living room to think this through.

Dieter was gone. Although I wanted him out of my life, the way he'd cut me loose stung deeply. I deserved more than a casually written note. I'm his wife, goddamn it. I'm entitled to half of his money. He'd left me in an overpriced apartment with the next rent due in a week and no money in the bank. And God knows what other financial obligations he'd lumbered me with.

I had to get hold of him and talk some sense into him—convince him that he couldn't do that to me. He wrote in his note that he was leaving Australia, but he couldn't be on a plane yet or even on his way to the airport. Dieter wasn't capable of organizing a trip at a moment's notice. And then it struck me. Dieter might have planned this well in advance, and Uwe might know where he is.

I picked up the phone and dialled Eva's number without hesitation. It took only two rings.

"What a surprise," Eva said with pointed sharpness. "It's

been a while."

I wasn't in the mood to make apologies. "Do you know where Dieter is?"

"Why should I?"

"He spoke to Uwe quite a few times in the last weeks, didn't he?"

"Huh?"

"Does Uwe know where Dieter is?"

Eva finally noticed my growing agitation and her voice softened with concern. "What's wrong?"

"Dieter left me."

"What?"

Where did that come from? I hadn't meant to be so direct. Eva didn't need to know the embarrassing details. I paused and collected myself. "I mean, we decided to separate. He moved out today. We still have a few things to sort out I'd forgotten. You know Dieter has never been bothered with the trivial aspects of everyday life. I need to speak to him urgently, but I don't know where he is. I thought maybe Uwe knows. It's really important."

"I had no idea. You poor thing!" Eva paused, and when I didn't offer further explanation, she started to probe. "How did that happen? I always thought your marriage was working. You never hinted at problems."

"Why should I? You and I, we haven't spoken much lately." Had I really not called her since we'd come back from Lightning Ridge after Christmas?

Eva was quick to catch on. "So the crisis started after Christmas?"

"Dieter was like a different person after our fight in the

car." That sounded wrong again, so I corrected myself. "Truthfully, our problems started much earlier. He's always been superficial and arrogant. I just didn't want to see it. We never should have married."

"Could it be that you changed after what happened in Lightning Ridge, and that he couldn't deal with that?"

"Are you listening to me, Eva? It's not me who's the problem. I just told you he's always been the problem. But all that doesn't matter now, and I don't care. I just need to speak to him urgently. Can I talk to Uwe?"

Eva hesitated. "Uwe isn't home."

Is she stalling? Is she hiding something from me? "Can you please ask him to call me as soon as he gets in? He won't be late, will he?"

I could hear her swallow hard.

"No, he won't be," she said.

"All right then—"

"Wait a minute," Eva said. "I can hear the door. I think he's back."

She sounded relieved. I could hear her whisper, "It's Isabella. They separated. Dieter moved out already," while she handed him the phone.

"How are you, Isabella?" Uwe said, formal as ever.

"Not so good, as you can imagine, thank you." No need to go into further detail. "Have you heard from Dieter?"

"Not lately."

To be so vague was not like him. "Uwe, I need to know."

"A few days ago."

Really? Not lately? My blood was boiling. "What did he say when you spoke to him last? Did he mention that we were separating?"

Uwe cleared his throat and sounded a lot more confident when he said, "Yes, he did. He said you two had been talking about it for a while."

The bastard. He'd planned it. My heart sank. "Did he say what his plans were? Where he was going?"

Uwe hesitated, always Dieter's friend foremost.

I had to tread lightly. "Please. I'm not out to make trouble for Dieter. I just need him to arrange a few things we both forgot—important things. It's in his best interest that we take care of them."

"Like what?"

"A few appointments I'm not sure if I should cancel and I don't know where to send some payments from shoots."

"Dieter assured me everything was taken care of."

I let that slide, but I wanted to scream at Uwe what a two-faced bastard he was. He and Dieter had discussed the split in detail. Uwe must have known that Dieter sprung this on me, but in front of Eva, he pretended otherwise. I drew in a deep breath, trying to stay reasonable. "Uwe, you know Dieter. He always forgets something. Why won't you tell me where he is?"

"Because I don't know." He took in a deep breath. "He flew out today, but I don't know where to. I promised not to tell anybody about him leaving until he was gone."

"He didn't tell you?"

"He said it's nobody's business."

I couldn't control my anger any longer. "We've been married two years, and you think I don't have a right to know where he is?"

"I keep telling you," Uwe said, cold as ice, "this has nothing to do with me. This is between you and Dieter. Don't be unfair—"

"Unfair?" My voice trembled. "I'll tell you what's unfair. To throw me out of the car like you guys did. That's unfair. To make me walk through the bush all alone in that heat. That's unfair. To leave me with nothing, cleaning out our bank account. That's unfair.

"Isabella, get a grip on yourself. I have nothing to do with your quarrel," he said and hung up.

The line was dead but I kept screaming into the phone. "It's easy for the bastard. Pissing off and starting new again somewhere else, with my money. I worked harder than he did and degraded myself for him and his career, opening my legs for Hal like a cheap whore. And all so he could leave me with nothing—no money, no prospects, no future, not even family or friends—but a shit job in a shit country full of misogynistic racists."

I stopped ranting. Of course, that was it. I'd never make it here. I was a foreigner, a bloody migrant to most Australians, and, to top it off, a good-looking woman without a husband. I'd always be an outcast, a career threat to my male colleagues, and a danger to their spouses.

A wave of rationality lapped at my anger, slowly eroding it. I leaned back on the sofa, stretched my legs, and repeated silently in my head the core thought of my newfound rationality.

You'll never make it here. Leave this country.

Of course. All I had to do was leave—like Dieter. The two contract years were up, so the Australian government wouldn't stop me. Why did I not think of this sooner? Why wasn't I the one who cleaned out the account and did a disappearing act? That's what I should have done, but no point in crying over spilled milk now. I could still simply get up and go, without worrying about unpaid bills, without giving notice at work or cancelling the lease on the flat.

Bitter laughter bubbled up my throat like vomit. I coughed and swallowed it, together with any thought of running away. That wasn't me. I wasn't made like Dieter.

I gave myself three months to sort out my affairs.

As luck would have it, I found a tenant to take over my lease within a week. I moved to a cheap motel in Rosebery with a view of the airport so I could watch the jets take off while I counted what I could save. My boss was glad I gave him enough notice to train my replacement, and he gave me an excellent reference. As I had to type it out myself, I backdated my start of employment by a year and held my thumb over the date when he signed. That covered the year in Hal's employment that was undocumented. If I wanted to start over again in Munich, I needed an impeccable record.

My last day at work was also my last day in Australia. One of my colleagues had offered to take me to the airport, but when it was time to leave, my boss came into the office with a bottle of bubbles and enough glasses for all of us. "A quick one," he said when the phone rang.

It was Uwe, wanting to speak to me.

I couldn't refuse to take the call in front of everybody.

"Hi," Uwe said. "Eva is still in the hospital, but she asked me to invite you to the christening."

I felt guilty again, a permanent state it seemed when it came to Eva. "What is it, girl or boy?"

"A girl." Uwe sounded disappointed. "She wants to call her Nadja."

"Nice."

"Are you coming?"

"I'm flying back to Germany tonight. Tell Eva I'll contact her when I'm back. And, congratulations."

"Where are you—"

This time, I hung up on him. My boss handed me a glass filled with sweet, bubbly wine. I downed it in one gulp. Time to leave, never to return.

PART TWO

30 years later

25

JOHANNA

Distant barking woke me from yet another nightmare featuring my ex-husband. The dogs. The wind must have blown my house door open while I was asleep, and now those stupid dogs were both outside, fighting again.

Only five months ago I had picked one-year-old Tiger from the animal shelter after the vet had told me that old Ben was terminally ill and wouldn't make it much longer. Then, two weeks later, Ben got better. By the time I could take him home again, I already loved Tiger so much I couldn't give him back. Those two were jealous from the start, Ben going at the young one with everything he had.

I jumped up, caught myself from a brief dizzy spell, and rushed outside to separate the stubborn animals. On the way, I grabbed the broom and, as an afterthought, the bucket with dirty water I'd left there some days ago. When I reached them, they were one indistinguishable ball of muscles.

I dumped the bucket of water over them, and they let go of each other. I used the brief second of surprise to pull one of them by the tail and lunge at the other with the broom.

I dragged Tiger back to the house and yelled at Ben to go sit. He stayed where he was and barked back at me, but it sounded like he was telling me he'd won the fight.

I let go of Tiger only when we were inside the house.

"Sit," I said to him.

Tiger was still excited, but he obeyed.

I bent down to inspect his wounds. One of the bites was deep. I stroked his neck and told him gently what a fool he was while I stitched him up.

When I finished, I took my first aid kit and looked for Ben. He had settled next to the metal work shed, where he always rested, protecting me, when I was inside.

"Let me check you out, you old grump," I said. "Why can't you two get along? You don't have to be jealous of each other. I love you both."

Ben's tail drummed on the tin sheet. He relished the attention and only raised his head once, when he heard a ringing sound coming from the house.

I continued patting him. Let the phone ring. It's just one of the bored miners trying to persuade me to come to the pub. I looked up. The clouds hung so low I nearly stretched out my hand to see if I could touch them. A bad sign—more serious rain to come. The flatland around Lightning Ridge had already become a knee-deep lake as the hard, dry ground couldn't soak up the excessive precipitation fast enough.

Lightning Ridge was slightly elevated but this year, the town itself was in danger of flooding.

I moved Ben into the shed and told him to climb on the bench and lie on the blanket. "You'll be safe here if the water comes." I filled his bowls with water and dry food and went back inside.

The sky had darkened even more, and an ominous wall of charcoal gray clouds pushed in from the west. I planned to brew a pot of tea but changed my mind when I noticed the bar of chocolate in the cupboard. I took it with me to the old rattan chair by the window to watch the approaching onslaught of ugly weather.

The phone rang again. It could be John. I was tempted. I looked at the sweet treat in my hand. Chocolate or John? You can only have one.

The phone was still ringing. I went over to the phone and picked it up.

"Johanna, it's me, Eva."

"What?"

"Eva. From Sydney. You know."

My hand was shaking when I put the chocolate down next to the phone. Of course I knew. Eva. Dear, chatty Eva from my past. Another nightmare?

"Dear Lord, Johanna. I can't believe I got hold of you. I never thought you'd be at the same number or that you'd still live in Lightning Ridge."

Eva took a breath. I didn't say anything.

"Well, anyway. I called earlier but nobody answered. I thought I'd just keep trying until somebody picked up who hopefully knew where you'd moved to."

Silence.

"Are you still there?"

"Yes."

Eva hesitated again. "Well, as I said, I didn't expect to speak to you. How long has it been? Must be about twenty-five years."

"More like thirty," I said.

"Dear Lord, that long?" Eva seemed genuinely surprised. "Of course. Nadja was still a baby then."

"How is your daughter?" I asked.

"Nadja is fine. All grown up. She lives and works in Melbourne. Can you imagine? Me and Steve, all alone in the house—"

"Steve?"

"Oh, dear me," Eva said. "You don't know. How could you? Uwe and I separated a long time ago. Nadja was only three or four then. By the time I finally was ready to go back to Germany with Nadja, I'd met Steve and that changed everything. If anybody had told me I'd marry an Australian one day—"

"You're married?"

"Of course. I knew the moment I met Steve it would work. I'm very happy with him, Johanna."

"Good."

"We've got to meet, Johanna. As soon as possible."

"Why?"

"Isabella is coming back."

"When?"

"She's coming for the Commonwealth Games. I was a little surprised. I can't remember her being interested in sports, but well, I guess we all have changed. She asked me to arrange a time when we could come visit you."

I didn't say anything.

"What do you think?"

"I don't know," I said after a pause.

"Maybe you and I should meet before she arrives. I need to know what to say to her, how to react. Jesus Christ, I'm so confused. Isabella will stay at our house. Steve thought we couldn't let an old friend stay in a hotel, and I agree. She's so looking forward to her holiday. You know, we stayed in touch over the years, casually, but still."

"I figured that much," I said. "But I really need to think this over. Give me your number. I'll call you in a few days."

"Yeah, think about it."

"It's been raining here for weeks."

Eva drew in a breath. "So?"

"So, you can't visit me. It's impossible to get through. I'm sure you've seen the extent of the flooding on the news."

"Sure. But they said the rain will stop soon. Johanna, we wouldn't come until the middle of October, after the games. By then, the roads will be passable again."

"But you can't come earlier," I said.

I wrote down Eva's number and hung up with the promise to call soon. She was right. The rain would stop eventually. I went back to the window, picked up my chocolate bar again and ate one row after another until only the silver wrapping was left.

Outside, fat drops pounded against the window pane. Soon, the wall of water would be so thick I wouldn't be able to see the porch posts. Already, a gale force wind raged but my roof was solid. As long as the floodwater didn't rise to a level where everybody had to evacuate, I felt safe in this house and I wouldn't leave it. This was my home—this house and this god-awful hole of an opal miner's town. How I had hated it when Kurt decided to move here. The memory of living here with him was still so unbearable I pushed it aside.

Maybe I should go to the pub after all, but all the others would have gone before the rain started. I should sit the storm out in the comfort of my dry home—in the company of old friends like Eva and Uwe, Isabella and Dieter, and my dear, dead husband Kurt.

I shivered. The ugly nightmare from earlier was still looming in the corners of my mind.

To hell with it. Chocolate *and* John was called for. I patted Tiger's head on my way to the door and slipped into my oilskin coat.

When I arrived at the pub a few minutes later, I was soaked to the bone. The atmosphere in the packed saloon was electric—noisy, boisterous, and full of cheers. Why do we feel so alive when confronted with the powers of nature? Is it knowing that disaster can strike any second, and that we are helpless in the face of it? That we might be lucky this time, while our neighbour loses everything?

26

John must have felt my presence before he saw me. "Hey! Johanna!"

He tried to catch my attention over his patrons' heads. I pretended not to notice him, then steered in his direction and squeezed in between two drinking buddies who made space for me when they saw him glaring at them.

"Give me a pint of your best," I said.

He poured without letting me out of his sight and placed the filled glass in front of me.

"What brings you here, my lovely? On a Monday?" He gave me a big smile. "Scared of the storm?"

I smirked back. "Bored out of my mind, obviously."

He leaned over the counter. "Don't leave. Let me just take care of those unruly guests over there who are trying to kill each other with my good glasses, then I'm all yours."

Of course, he might not see me again all evening. I turned and scanned the room for acquaintances I wanted to talk to.

I knew just about everybody in the pub but didn't feel like joining any of the rowdy groups of miners trading dirty jokes and drinking like there was no tomorrow. I noticed Mira in a corner, a born and bred Australian with light-sensitive eyes and translucent skin, thanks to her Scottish ancestors. A damn nuisance in a hot country, she always said, but a great explanation, if not outright excuse, for her obsession with mining opals. Underground, she didn't have to worry about a sunburn.

Mira spent three months of every year in Lightning Ridge, and most of those way down in her mine. She always came alone. Her husband, a famous Brisbane plastic surgeon, despised getting his hands dirty.

I made eye contact while walking over to her.

"What the heck?" Mira said. "It's not Wednesday."

"In this weather," I said, "nothing is normal."

"I've never seen anything like it. It'll be days, no, weeks, before the mines dry out again—a fucking disaster, if you ask me."

"It was exactly the same three years ago."

"Granted, it rained as much, but after July, it stopped. I only lost five days then. No comparison to this year. Those useless meteorologists must have all gone on maternity leave."

I laughed. "They're all guys."

"So?" Mira pulled out a cigarette and lit it. "I bet those goddamn amateurs take daddy leave because they love changing diapers. That's all they're good for. My mine is full to the brim, and none of those fuckers ever sent out a warning. I'm sitting in this shithole—the bloody village, not this pub—and can do nothing but twiddle my thumbs. I got in the car yesterday when it stopped raining for a goddamn second, but I didn't get very far. The water has reached its highest mark on the fifty-five junction."

"That's bad." I emptied my glass with one gulp. "Really bad."

The fifty-five, as everybody called Castlereagh Highway, was the town's lifeline—the only road in and out. Red and white markers next to the elevated road indicated how deep the surrounding land was submerged, and with it, all lower portions of the road.

"I'm telling you, it's a nightmare. We're all stuck in here." Mira let out a heavy breath. "Trapped like bees in a honey jar."

I laughed. "What's the rush? Is hubby expecting you back in Brisbane?"

"Not fucking likely. He must be the happiest guy around. I bet he makes generous donations to the rain gods. With me gone, he and his receptionist can fuck their featherbrains out, in our marital bed, I bet, without risking me barging in unannounced."

"No other reason?"

"None other. I sure don't want to go back so I can listen to his boring bullshit over breakfast, trying to impress me with stories of how he's fixed another sixteen-year-old with plastic boobs."

I stared into my empty glass. "Why don't you divorce him if you dislike him so much?"

"I'll divorce him the day my mine yields the big bucks, not a day sooner."

Mira's mine had not been kind to her, and she was not here long enough to understand that you have to give a mine your heart and soul, not just a few months. Mira only used the mine as an excuse to hide and recharge for the ongoing fight with her provider husband.

"Even if you divorce him, he'll have to support you," I said.

"Are you kidding me? The creep has moved all his money

into shady investments I can't touch." Mira broke into a big smile. "Can't wait to see his face when he finds out the opal mine made me rich."

I didn't bother to ask why she assumed he wouldn't claim his share. We've had that conversation before. Mira inherited the mine from her uncle before she got married, and her husband had never set foot in it. She loved the mine, not only because she needed the thrill of chasing the big find, but also because she could be herself in Lightning Ridge—ripped jeans, messy hair and smudged makeup, if she put any on. Her uncle must have known her well.

"Another whiskey?" I asked.

"Twist my arm." Mira stubbed out her cigarette in the ashtray and followed me to the bar.

John immediately made room for us, took our order, and placed the two drinks in front of us with an apologetic shrug. "Sorry, no time for a chat," this gesture said, but I could see another message in his eyes. "I'll make time for you later."

I turned back to Mira. "Let's hope that magic day of revenge will come soon."

Mira lifted her left hand, a tiny space between her finger tips. "I'm this close. I can feel it in my bones. A few more yards of digging, and I'll hit the street. My new wishing rod went crazy the other day—before the goddamn rain stopped me dead."

Same as all the other hopefuls. I bit my lip to stop the thought from reaching my lips. "It'll stop raining eventually," I said instead. "Has to."

"It better," Mira said. "If it doesn't, we're all in deep shit. Nobody will come help us. The whole of Queensland is under water, and the government servants sit on their fat bums and wait it out. Have you heard that old Charlie is missing? He drove out to check his claim last week and nobody has seen him since."

"I'm sure he'll come back."

"Don't think so. I bet he's stuck somewhere and is starving to death. Maybe he's injured and can't move. Maybe he's dead already. I don't even want to think about the poor bugger, all alone out there. They'll never find him…" Mira stopped and took a deep breath. "Oh shit. Your husband. They never did find him, did they? Fuck, I'm so sorry. I didn't mean to…"

"Forget it," I said. "That was a long time ago." I drank my double shot in one gulp and waited for the familiar burn. After Mira followed my example, I lifted our empty glasses, motioning to John for a refill. Alcohol is one, but certainly not the worst, of the many tricks I'd used over the years to fight the shadows of the past.

27

EVA

Our house sits high on a hill, in a curve of the serpentine road running from Avalon to Bilgola Heights. The hill is so steep, some curves have a nearly ninety degree angle. To be surrounded by a road on three sides, as our house is, considerably lowers its value. Enough for Steve to be able to buy this lovely property soon after our wedding.

Steve earned good money as a computer company technician but not enough to splurge on a home with an ocean view in this classy northern beaches neighbourhood. While Nadja was still in school, I had only been able to work part-time, and after that, I was too old to start a new career, so I took on temp jobs to help with the monthly payments. The house was all we could afford, but what a lucky break that was. Even sitting on a busy road, it has a fabulous view of the ocean, and now that we'd finally managed to pay off our mortgage, we could start to enjoy our lives a bit more.

I checked my watch. It was already late afternoon. "Steve, are you ready?" I called. No reply. I lowered my reading glasses, closed my book, and heaved myself out of my chair.

I opened the window to the garden and saw Steve working on our car.

"Still not ready?" I yelled down.

He yelled back, without lifting his head from underneath

the open hood. "What time is it?"

"Already after four."

"When will she arrive?"

"The plane lands at seven."

"Great. Gives me a bit more time."

I closed the window, walked through the house, and checked every room. Isabella should be comfortable. Everything was clean and neat and pretty—fresh flowers, new candles, colourful pictures on the walls, and lots of pillows on the yellow sofa. The late afternoon sun rays shined through the high window panes and warmed the inner courtyard. Pity it would have set by the time we'd return.

I heard Steve wash his hands in the lower bathroom and take his shoes off before he came upstairs. He looked worn out and pale. All those overtime hours spent in preparation for the Commonwealth Games were taking their toll. After the games, he should take time off and get some colour back in his face.

"What shall I wear?" he asked.

"It's humid. The blue shirt has short sleeves and goes with the beige trousers I bought the other day."

"All righty." He disappeared into the bedroom.

I was ready. I just had to grab my wool jumper in case the airport was cold.

Should I call Johanna again? Two weeks had passed since my last call, and Johanna had not called back as promised. What should I tell Isabella? So typical of Johanna to withdraw into her shell, meaning her stupid opal mine. I won't let her off the hook this time.

I opened my small address book, looked up Johanna's

number, and dialled. When Steve came into the room, nicely dressed and shrouded in a cloud of aftershave, the phone had rung about ten times. I hung up. "Damn."

"Who were you calling?" Steve went into the kitchen to get a bottle of water from the fridge.

"Johanna. But she isn't home."

"Don't worry, Eva. You'll catch her later."

"Later is no good. She's supposed to tell me if we can meet while Isabella is here."

"So, what's the problem? Isabella will stay with us how long? Three weeks? Plenty of time to reach Johanna. She's probably in her mine."

"Haven't you seen the news? It's still raining cats and dogs up north. The mine will be closed."

"Got it," Steve said.

He didn't argue the point and didn't get upset. A simple "got it" calmed me instantly, and I didn't even have to apologize for snapping at him. He's never cross with me. That's one of the things I love about him.

Maybe Johanna has more pressing problems to deal with than calling me. "I hope she's okay. I'm getting worried about her."

"She's used to living alone. She'll manage. I'm sure that once the rain stops, everything will go back to normal and she'll contact you. The weather is supposed to be improving now."

"About time. Those poor farmers in Queensland got hit pretty hard. I bet some of them will have to start all over again. Dreadful. Johanna's mine will be okay, though. She just has to wait until the ground dries out. Still, how long does it take to make a phone call? I think she's avoiding me. She didn't seem overjoyed at meeting us. Maybe she really doesn't…oh, what the heck. I don't know what goes on in her head."

Steve locked the door behind us, and we got in the car and drove off. After a short silence, I picked up my train of thought again. "Would be nice if we'd get an improvement."

"Huh?"

"The weather," I explained. "With the games starting tomorrow, we have so many tourists visiting. I don't understand why they scheduled the games for the end of September. Everyone knows spring means big storms with heavy precipitation." I wondered briefly how long it had taken me to get used to our southern hemisphere seasons. Spring starting in September and Christmas at the height of summer had thrown me for years and made it so much harder to accept Australia as home. By now, of course, I cringed at the thought of shivering in the snow on the way to a New Year's party. Poor people back in Europe.

Steve turned onto Barrenjoey Road and we drove south along the ocean side until we reached Mona Vale. There, the road split and we took the main road, leading downtown. It was rush hour.

"Pretty bad today," I said. "I hope we'll make it in time."

"We will," Steve said.

28

Once we arrived at the terminal, I rushed to the display board. Isabella's flight had landed five minutes earlier. My nerves began to tingle as I positioned myself in front of the glass doors the passengers came through. Will I recognize her? Isabella had sent me a slightly blurred picture of herself, supposedly taken in Munich recently—a laughing, tanned woman with an indistinguishable hairstyle and eyes hidden behind huge sunglasses. It could have been anybody. I'd have to try and remember her as best as I could and mentally add thirty years.

I searched for a fresh, smiling face with a certain age-defying beauty, but only overly tired, long-distance travellers in rumpled clothes with pasty complexions and ruffled hair walked through the automatic doors.

I straightened my skirt and checked my earrings and necklace—pretty turquoise and silver jewelry Steve had given me last Christmas—and pulled at the ends of my white blouse to make sure it hung loose enough to hide the telltale bulges of our good life. I turned to Steve to ensure I looked okay, but he sat on one of the benches, absorbed in *The Sydney Morning Herald*.

I took a small mirror out of my handbag to check my makeup, nearly missing Isabella. Fleetingly, I became aware of a slim, elegant woman walking so energetically toward me that the large leather handbag she'd slung over her shoulder bounced with every step.

And then we were in each other's arms.

I moved a half step back. "You look marvelous. So fresh, not like the other passengers."

"Business class," Isabella said. "Can't do it any other way. Those poor guys, cramped back there in economy for so long. Dreadful."

"Still," I said. "It's a long flight. You haven't changed at all. Only your hair is shorter."

Isabella laughed. "A few wrinkles around the eyes."

"None I can see."

I grabbed Isabella's suitcase and wheeled it toward Steve to introduce him. Isabella nodded and extended her hand, but Steve pulled her into an embrace and kissed her on both cheeks.

I stopped biting my lips. Nothing to worry about. This was Steve, a guy who got along well with everybody. If Isabella had mellowed a bit with age, she'd be a delight to have around.

"You can't imagine how excited I am," Isabella said, "to be here again, after such a long time."

We walked to our car, a peach-coloured, second-hand Ford Explorer—Steve's pride and joy, although he wasn't keen on the colour. But the price had been right. As the salesman explained, no other colour reduced the value of a car faster, except maybe pink.

"This is our first longer drive with our new car," I said when we arrived at the parking area. "We only got it last week."

"But it's the older model," Isabella said.

"Well, well," Steve said. "A woman who knows about cars."

"That's part of my job," Isabella said.

She explained that, among other products, her import/export company purchased parts needed by the German automotive industry. "Not Ford, though. But we have contracts with Daimler Chrysler in Stuttgart and Audi in Ingolstadt, so I make myself knowledgeable on all makes and models. Otherwise, their managers won't take me seriously."

"Well, I've got plenty of reading material at home for you, then."

"Heavens, no. That's strictly business. I'm on a well-deserved holiday—the first in ages. I intend to enjoy every minute of it." She was sitting in the passenger seat and turned back to me. "You did take some leave, too, didn't you?"

I pushed my face between the front seat headrests. "The first week, yes, definitely. The second week—only if they find a replacement for me. Fingers crossed."

"Really? You've known for weeks I was coming."

"I've been in this job less than a year. I can't demand time off whenever it suits me. But the first week is for sure. The office is closed then."

"Totally closed?"

"Oh yeah. Many companies close their offices so their employees can enjoy the Commonwealth Games. It's a big thing here, nearly as big as when we hosted the Olympics."

"That's crazy." Isabella made a face. "But I remember what sports fanatics the Australians were and still are, obviously."

"That's why you came, isn't it?"

"I got tickets for every day in the Homebush Stadium. Didn't I write you that I bought two tickets for every event?"

I bit my lip. "You did."

"One ticket is for you."

"I know. I'm sorry. I just can't promise about next week."

Isabella shrugged it off. "Well, anyway. Let's hire a car and enjoy the games together as long as we can."

"You can use our car," Steve said.

"Don't you need it to get to work?"

"I can take the bus for a week."

"Wouldn't dream of it."

"That's the least we can do. You already got the tickets for Eva."

Isabella made a face again.

"Don't you like our car?" I asked.

"Forgive me, but I had something a bit racier in mind. As I said before, I want to enjoy this trip."

"But—"

"Forget it, Eva," Steve said. "It's okay."

"Look at this rain," Isabella said. "That'll mess up the opening ceremony."

"It'll get lighter, but it won't stop."

Isabella leaned back. "Who cares? That's the only event I couldn't get tickets for."

Half an hour later, we arrived in Bilgola, and Isabella took a hot shower, slipped into a designer-looking sweat suit, and joined us in front of the fireplace. We drank the French champagne she had brought and chatted until midnight.

Isabella didn't mention Johanna once.

The next morning, I woke with the fleeting memory of a dream about Isabella sitting on a cart pulled by a hippopotamus. Isabella had shouted orders I could not understand—or remember.

I looked at the alarm clock. Already eight. I sat up and slurped the coffee Steve had placed on my bedside table.

"Don't mind if I don't join you girls for breakfast," he said, coming out of the bathroom, towelling his hair. "We both overslept and I've got to rush."

"No problem."

Steve would get himself breakfast at the stadium's canteen. For the next ten days of the games, he would be there from ten in the morning until nearly midnight, just in case the computers messed up, and, if need be, he'd stay overnight.

"What's your plan for today?" he asked, splashing aftershave into his palms and rubbing it on his cheeks.

"I'll wait until she wakes up, then we'll see. I don't think we should overdo it on the first day. Maybe a walk along Bilgola beach and then dinner at home in front of the TV. Pity we can't watch the opening ceremony together."

"Just look at the screen carefully. You might see me there."

"You've got to wave. Otherwise, I won't see you."

He laughed. "I don't like your chances on that one. There will be over a hundred thousand spectators in the stadium tonight." He bent down and kissed my cheek. "Gotta dash." On the way out, he turned around. "I'll take a cab to work."

"But Isabella wanted to rent a car."

"Just tell her not to. She'll get used to ours."

I couldn't imagine and wrinkled my nose at the thought.

Steve stopped grinning. "Has she always been like that?"

"Like what?" I knew exactly like what.

"Shall we say, demanding?"

"You mean the expensive champagne?"

"I like champagne, especially when it's a gift from a guest. What I mean…" He searched for the right expression. "I mean, she seems to be a little spoiled and has certain expectations. I don't know…I may be wrong." He waved back at me. "Never mind. It's not important."

29

Isabella emerged from her room after ten, looking like she was ready for a day at the office—a long strand of pearls over a white blouse, freshly shampooed and blow-dried hair, and enough makeup to cover any signs of the long flight around the globe.

I sat, still draped in my good old faithful—baggy, flannel pajamas—at the kitchen table, a fresh pot of coffee in front of me.

"You look deep in thought," Isabella said. "Anything important?"

"Nothing specific," I said, although I'd been contemplating calling Johanna again. "I've been remembering the three of us—you and me and Johanna—how we met on the ship and how naive and enthusiastic about the future we'd been."

"That's normal when one is young." Isabella poured herself a cup of coffee. "What was her name?"

"Who's?"

"The ship, Eva."

"*Queen Frederica*."

"You've got a better memory than I have. I barely remember anything from the past." She drank a sip and made a face. Too hot. "What shall we do today?"

"Breakfast, first. You must be hungry."

Isabella shook her head and let her shoulder-length hair fly.

"I never have breakfast. Let's go to Manly and wander around, look for a restaurant by the ocean and have lunch there."

I decided to give breakfast a miss, too.

"Manly has changed a lot. The main drag is now a pedestrian shopping zone with really nice shops and plenty of restaurants along the beach. You'll be surprised how good they are. Maybe not as good as the ones you are used to in Europe, but still."

Why did I suddenly feel so defensive? Plenty of tourists come to Manly to enjoy their vacation. It should be good enough for Isabella, too.

"We can catch the ferry to Circular Quay after lunch and stroll around downtown." I got up. "Think about it while I get dressed."

I decided on my dark blue dress with the tiny white flowers because its clever cut showed off what was good and hid what was not so perfect.

When I returned, Isabella's glance slid down my dress until her eyes settled with a frown on my open sandals. She didn't comment, but I went back and changed into my suede loafers.

Twenty minutes later we arrived in Manly, parked the car, which Isabella had climbed into without the slightest hesitation, and strolled down Main Street until it was time for lunch at an Italian restaurant by the ocean. We ordered fresh scampi and white wine and sat back and looked out at the waves, holding our faces into the gentle breeze. The natural boundary thirty years of near silence had created kept our conversation casual.

Isabella talked mostly about her career—how she opened

her own company soon after returning to Germany and how quickly she'd become successful. "In the first year, my brothers helped me by forcing their friends to give me small orders, but soon enough, I found my own circle of clients. I visited all major corporations in South Germany, offering my services. I guess I went at the right time because just about all the product managers I approached accepted me with open arms, and after only a year, I was in the profit zone."

Isabella took a sip of her wine and carried on. "Thinking back on those years, I believe my main function was to cover up how poor the language skills of the German middle- and upper-management were, and still are, in some cases. They are glad to have a reliable partner handling their overseas purchases so efficiently."

"I bet," I said. "Do you still want to go to Central?"

"Huh?"

I could see jetlag on Isabella's face. No makeup could cover the tiredness in her eyes or the sudden breaks in concentration. "Let's finish our lunch and go home for a nap before the evening entertainment starts."

Isabella fell asleep in the car, a fine line of saliva dripping down her chin. The poor girl, human after all.

When I checked her room a little before seven, Isabella was fast asleep and had to be woken rather forcefully.

"What's up?" She looked confused and disoriented.

I shook her by the shoulders again. "The opening ceremony starts soon."

"All right. All right. I'm coming."

She showed up minutes later, dressed in her bright yellow

jumpsuit with smeared makeup and unkempt hair.

"I don't know how you do it," I said. "You must be dog-tired but you still look acceptable."

"Are you kidding? I look like an old rag." Isabella yawned without covering her mouth. "But it doesn't matter. We're alone."

"I see. You mean, you don't give a shit if I see you like this? Good old Eva doesn't matter."

"That's a compliment, you silly nilly. I am comfortable with you." Isabella grabbed a pillow and threw it in my direction.

I picked it up and threw it back with a bit more force and much better accuracy. "I wouldn't bother to dress up for you either."

"You never did."

"What's that supposed to mean?"

"All I'm saying is tent-dress and flip-flops."

"You mean this morning?" I asked. "I'm on holiday."

"Good to hear that this was only a temporary derailment of your otherwise impeccable taste."

"You, on the other hand, might consider to dress more holiday appropriate."

"Madam is giving me dress advice? Seriously?"

We stared at each other for a second, then we both broke into laughter.

"Let's get blitzed," Isabella said when we had recovered from our giggling fit.

We opened a bottle of Chablis and settled on the sofa to watch the ceremony. The weather god had been kind after all. This was the first night without rain and strong winds that would have cancelled the fireworks at the end of the spectacle.

30

JOHANNA

I woke to a sky with promising breaks in the dark cloud formations. The rain had stopped, and by noon, a strong breeze helped the sun take full control.

I sat with Mira on the local cafeteria's porch. She had ordered a blueberry muffin and was picking crumbs off her plate.

"I've got to risk it," she said. "The water is receding everywhere. They opened the road up north already and just sitting here will drive me nuts. I need to get back to Brisbane." She looked at me. "How the hell can you live here year-round?"

I made a face, leaned back, and crossed my arms. "What's eating you today? You always said you liked it here."

"I do—when the mine is open. I get up in the morning, go to the mine, dig until I'm spent, pack up the day's spoils, go home, and hammer and cut the rocks until my fingers bleed—always in anticipation of the big find and always hoping I will discover refractive properties with my black light, announcing the glorious chance of finally hitting that damned elusive street of opals the next day. At the end of yet another wasted day, I go to the pub to talk to people I can have a halfway decent conversation with. People who understand why I'm doing what I'm doing and don't ask stupid questions. People like you. Don't deny it. You work like a maniac for the same goddamn reason we all do—greedy for the big one—although you find as little as I do."

"Enough to live on," I said. "Most days."

"Oh fuck. We all find enough to carry on, but is it really worth spending your whole life in pursuit of this madness? I can always go back to Brisbane when I've had enough, to those fools in their offices and shops, to the traffic and the hectic, to the whole damn glorious civilization."

"Until you've had enough of that again."

"Exactly. I have a choice. But you? Even with the water going down, the mines won't open for a while. I can't understand how you can handle the monotony. What do you do day after day, year after year? Sit around and watch the days drift by?"

Mira always got belligerent toward the end of her stay in Lightning Ridge, and I was a reliable target for her frustrations. I knew what she really meant.

"You have to admit," I said, "things have improved over the years."

She chased a fly off her face. "Sure. John turned the pub into a cultural hotspot for this lovely community with bingo, happy hour, and darts tournaments. What more could you want?" She gave it a throaty laugh.

I kept my face blank. We had never spoken about my lusting after John.

"You have forgotten what civilization is like. When was the last time you went to a city?"

"I think about thirty years ago." The number shocked me when I said it.

Mira let out a shriek. "What? You're not serious?"

I started counting in my mind. "When we came to Australia, we lived in Sydney first. About two years later, Kurt decided to move up here. I've never been back, not even after his disappearance."

Mira stared at me, willing me to elaborate.

"It doesn't seem that long. In those days, I would have preferred to stay in Sydney. Living conditions here were disgusting—dirty, dusty, and primitive. We had no bathroom and no running water, not even in the kitchen, which was only a stove and a cupboard. I had to do the dishes outside, next to the well. Everything we had saved in Sydney was spent on shovels, picks, and buckets for mining, and on the place we lived in. We had to work really hard in the mine, and when we came home, I still had to do the household chores." I pressed my lips together but the words didn't stop coming. "Kurt insisted that everything be clean and neat, and food was the only pleasure he allowed himself. I cleaned, scrubbed, and cooked and was always tired, but I couldn't keep the place clean—not with all the dust, flies, and heat."

Mira bunched the last of her muffin crumbs to a ball and flicked it off the porch. Ants appeared from nowhere, and in seconds, the ball was black.

"The walls were not sealed. Dust came in everywhere and settled on everything, and because we had no fridge, I had to go grocery shopping every day while Kurt went to the pub and drank his beer…"

"Sounds like Kurt was a true-blue Aussie." Mira stuck a cigarette between her lips and lit it. "Damn machos they were in those days."

"He was German."

She took a long drag and blew out the smoke. "Honey, I know that. But all the Aussies come from somewhere. Kurt adapted to our habits pretty well from the sound of it."

"What else could he have done?" I asked. "The grocery shop was opposite the pub. He let me wait for him in the car, parked just outside the pub."

"How generous."

"I didn't mind waiting."

"Why didn't you go in the pub with him?"

No point in telling her that those precious minutes were the highlight of my day. "In case you don't remember, women were not welcome inside a pub then. And anyway, I didn't drink alcohol."

Mira burst out laughing. "What changed? If Kurt could have seen you the other night. You sure held your own at the bar. And by the way, I noticed John couldn't stop staring at you."

I tried to stay cool.

"Remember? That was the night the rain came down in buckets."

Did I remember? It was a night I tried hard to forget. After most patrons had gone home and Mira had fallen asleep on one of the benches, John had come over and slid in next to me, close enough for me to smell his skin. He'd put his arm over my shoulder, and for a second, I wanted to put my hand on his thigh between his legs, move my face closer to his, and kiss him, but he spoiled the moment by asking if something was bothering me since I was sitting all alone with an empty whiskey glass in front of me. I nearly told him of Eva's call, but I got up and left instead.

I cleared my throat. "John's a decent guy. He never mentioned me being drunk when I dropped by the next day to pay my bill."

"Why should he? It's none of his fucking business if you get hammered, but I think he actually enjoyed seeing you like that."

"Kurt wouldn't have. He would have had a fit," I said.

The late afternoon sun hit our table. Mira got her oversized sunglasses out of her handbag and put them on.

"When we came over on the ship, he never let me join the others when they were drinking, though alcohol was quite cheap."

Mira lowered her glasses and held my glance. "You weren't allowed?"

"Kurt said it's best not to start with it, not as a woman. I told him Eva and Isabella sometimes drank, but he said he was not married to them."

"Were those your friends?"

"Isabella brought a bottle of schnapps into our cabin once and let me have some. It didn't agree with me. Kurt was pretty mad at her when he found out. Alcohol was not permitted in the cabins. With such a lot of passengers confined in a tight space that rule was meant for our own protection." I took a last sip of my cold coffee. "I gotta dash."

"I was hoping you'd tell me more about your friends."

"Another time."

Mira got up. "I'm leaving early tomorrow morning."

"Well then," I said, "drop by my place tonight. I have a little farewell present for you."

31

My house has a concrete foundation. Its size and shape makes it look like a mobile home, but it is a proper house with insulated wooden walls, a tin roof and double-glazed windows, partitioned into two rooms, a kitchen nook and a bathroom. Best of all, I own the two-acre parcel it sits on. I have cultivated this land, creating a blooming garden with fruit trees and vegetable patches. Everything grows in this climate if you give it enough water and love.

Sitting on my wooden porch, looking beyond the colourful yard speckled with nature's abundance, I can see the vast sky above the desert, spreading from my wire fence to the horizon. After so many years of toiling underground, my soul enjoys drifting into this infinite space, this beautiful place—my own space.

I've transformed this land into a valuable property. It must be worth nearly as much as the new homes around the inner village—those belonging to the rich mining companies who have settled in Lightning Ridge over the past twenty years, once word got out we have the most lucrative opal mines on the continent. Those houses are too close together for my taste. None border on the bush at our doorstep. 'It's all about location,' they say. Fact is, my house must be worth more than my mine by now.

Ben trotted up to me and settled at my feet. I gave him a quick scratch behind his ears and got up and went inside, careful to close the outer door before I opened the mosquito screen. Tiger was inside, and both dogs respected this flimsy plastic mesh as if it were made of metal.

I poured myself a glass of water, stood by the sink, and looked at the grassless area in front of the window where I planned to prepare a new vegetable patch. No time like now—after the rain, when the earth is easier to handle than in summer. I had to take my mind off the mine. The useless bloody mine never gave me enough to make me proud. I should get rid of it.

Only one more year, I'd promised myself in January, like I did at the beginning of every new year. This time, though, I would stick to it. When the mine was operational again, I'd give it until the end of November, and if the fickle monster didn't give back more than the pittance I'd survived on the past thirty years, I'd close it for good, sell everything and move away.

Move to where, you fool? The mine holds you ransom, don't you know that?

I am a prisoner of the mine, and yet, I am its warden as well. My duty is to look after the mine, keeping it secure and secluded. For me, there is no escape, no mercy, and no amnesty. Nothing will ever change this miserable routine for me.

I can't explain why I haven't packed my bags and run a long time ago. I just know I never could.

Beyond my regularly occurring doubts, sometimes hope enters my thoughts—hope that things might change without my doing. Like every time I see John. I yearn for a life outside my confinement, a life with a man like John, but then I remember the man from my past and why I'm not allowed to have hope for a better future. In those bitter and lonely moments, I sometimes get so depressed I want to end my life, but I have no right to kill myself. The mine doesn't give me much, but I have enough to live on and I have my dogs, the garden and the house. I've always felt secure in the house, knowing I could make my own decisions and come and go and do as I like. No pressure. No force. No fear.

Loneliness is a small price to pay for freedom.

And what is the best remedy for loneliness? Hard work.

I got the shovel and started digging a patch for the vegetable garden. An hour later, I felt better. Sweat ran down my back. I straightened to wipe my forehead and heard the phone ring. *Must be Mira.*

I stuck the shovel into the loosened earth and went to the house. I needed to wrap the picture John had taken in front of the pub that I'd had framed for her. We both looked like such fun people in this picture, the way we smiled at each other, holding each other close. I like that picture a lot, and Mira will, too.

Maybe I could convince her to stay one more day.

But it was John on the phone, not Mira. "Hey," he said, sounding quite excited. "Guess what? While they were out in the bush looking for Charlie, the guy that's missing, they found a human skull and some bones not far from your mine. They think the rising water washed them out of a collapsed mine shaft."

I listened to him without understanding much beyond his first words. *Skull. Bones. My mine.* All the blood rushed from my head and the light in my eyes flickered. It wouldn't be long before I'd pass out. I held onto the phone and concentrated on my breathing while John finished. I mumbled a thank you and disconnected the call before my body gave way, then the phone slipped out of my hand, and I sank to the ground.

Lying on the floor, I could feel the blood leaving my head. Drifting into the shadowland, I felt a shape bend over me. Large. Dark. Kurt. He looked like a boxer, raising his right fist and swinging it down. I tried to protect my head but his fist hit my forearm with such force that my arm was thrown back, exposing my face. Another blow. Blood spurted from my nose onto my blouse. Oh God, I'll never get rid of the spots. He'll truly be mad now that I spoiled the good blouse. I drifted into blackness.

When I came to, I noticed the phone still dangling next to my head. I lifted myself up and got a tissue from my pocket to wipe the blood off my face, but there was no blood on the tissue and my arm didn't hurt either. There was no Kurt.

I put the phone back on the hook and tried to remember what John had told me before I passed out, but the image of Kurt's brutal attack lingered in my mind. I suddenly knew it had been him who'd hit me thirty years ago on the *Queen Frederica*. The knowledge I had suppressed for so long was so powerful my knees buckled again and my lungs tightened. Unexplainable fear gripped me.

I steadied myself, drew a few deep breaths, went to the sink, and poured a glass of water. I nearly dropped it when the phone rang again. I had to force myself to pick up the receiver and put it to my ear.

Only Mira, thank God.

My voice was shaking but she didn't notice. She'd be

over in about an hour to collect her present. One hour to get myself together and push Kurt back into the prison I had built for him thirty years ago. I had hoped he'd waste away in there, over time losing colour and contour, but my hatred must have kept him alive and made him strong enough to manifest himself in such dynamic glory that he could literally knock me down. Damn him.

I got a bottle of white wine and put it in the freezer. Chill. Pull yourself together. Mira won't understand. She'll make a joke of me seeing ghosts.

But a ghost isn't easy to shake. He followed me as dark matter, behind my back. I could feel him, felt his cold fingers in the breeze from the open window. He refused to go back where he belonged. He'd escaped and was here to torment me again.

If I let him.

The time had come. I dialled Eva's number.

32

EVA

Isabella and I went to the Homebush Station every day the first week of the Commonwealth Games, watching all the preliminaries, but on day five, the afternoon heat on the spectator stands got to us. We left early, bought chicken legs and salad on the way home, and made ourselves comfortable on the porch. A fine early evening breeze cooled the air but the porch tiles still burned our naked soles, so we put our feet up and relaxed.

Isabella drank more wine than water, but I was careful, never having been one for excessive alcohol consumption.

The phone ringing broke our comfortable silence. I picked it up and heard a female voice.

I covered the mouthpiece and whispered, "My God, it's Johanna," to Isabella. "Hi, Johanna."

"You sound surprised, Eva."

"I didn't expect to hear from you. Isabella arrived a week ago already."

Pause.

"She is sitting right next to me," I said. "Do you want to speak with her?"

"No."

Pause again.

"Well, did you think about, uh…?" I wasn't sure how

to phrase my question with Isabella sitting there. What if Johanna didn't want to see her? What if she said something rude? Isabella was watching me with a frown, and Johanna wasn't making it easier for me. She kept quiet, waiting for me to speak. This was getting ridiculous.

"Do you want to see us," I asked, "or don't you?"

"Not really," Johanna said. "I want to forget about the past, but I'm afraid what I want is irrelevant. We will have to meet. Soon. Best you come to Lightning Ridge."

"Oh, good. I'm sure Isabella will come visit you." I threw a side glance at Isabella. She put her feet on the ground and straightened in her chair. "I may not be able to come along. It all depends if I can take leave next week. Don't know until I've spoken to my boss."

"You both have to come. I can't meet her alone."

"Why not?"

"Listen to me." Johanna sped up her words. "The three of us need to have a talk. It's important, trust me, and it has to happen fast. You need to come this week. Leave tomorrow. The highway is passable again, and most of the water has receded."

I shook my head and tapped my right temple with my forefinger. Isabella grinned.

"Isabella got tickets for all of next week. She doesn't want to miss that."

"You have to come this week."

"What's the sudden rush? First, you don't call back, making me think you don't want to see us, and now, when it suits you, we're supposed to hop in the car at a moment's notice."

"Shut up and listen, Eva. You're right. I didn't call. I saw no reason for it. But now, unfortunately, the situation here has changed, forcing me to discuss with you, *both of you*, how to handle it."

She lowered her voice, and I had to concentrate to hear her, but the meaning of what she said was clear. An involuntary cry escaped my mouth, and I pressed my hand over my lips. Isabella jumped up when she heard me.

"What is it?"

I motioned for her to sit down again while I listened intently as Johanna explained.

"All right," I said when she finished. "I understand. I will inform Isabella. I'll call you tomorrow morning. Yes, for sure. Bye."

"What is it?" Isabella asked again as soon as I had hung up.

I coughed to steady my voice. "Johanna got a call today from a guy called John, the local pub owner, who seems to know all the latest gossip in town. What he told her, though, isn't idle gossip." I reiterated what Johanna had explained about the search for a local man, the excessive rain, and what it had spit out from a collapsed shaft next to her mine. "With the rising water level, a skeleton—or part of one—was washed out of the ground," I concluded with a deep breath. "They found human bones and a skull."

Isabella slumped back in her chair and we stared at each other.

"Do they know who it is?" she asked after a long moment.

I sat down. "Not yet. The neighbouring mine was abandoned ages ago, after the owner ran out of money and patience, and the next claim holder didn't work the land, either, after hearing it was useless, so it's been dormant for a long time. Anyway, the search party that discovered the remains reported the find to Bill Wiseman—the policeman who recorded Kurt's disappearance. He, of all people, is now head of the station in Dubbo, and he stopped at John's pub for a beer when he picked up the bones."

"And told him what?"

"Bill didn't say he suspected any wrongdoing, and it's not that unusual to find skeletons in the bush. You know all those crazy illegal unregistered diggers. Some have accidents and nobody ever misses them, and then, if their remains are found, they are buried in an unmarked grave at the local cemetery."

Isabella's back straightened again. "Well, that's good, isn't it?"

"Maybe not, according to Johanna. Bill told John the skull has a hole in it—a big one, like it was crushed by a heavy object, and he needs to investigate this further. Johanna thinks that after such a long time, they may not connect the find with Kurt, but Bill may put two and two together once he's had some time to think about it."

"Damn. That doesn't sound good at all."

"Johanna is worried."

"You think it could be Kurt?"

I hesitated. Johanna's reaction had scared me. "Could be."

Isabella got up. "Then we better leave tomorrow."

"And the games?"

"Oh, for God's sake, Eva. What do I care about the stupid games? We only went there because I thought Johanna refused to meet with us. I was upset about it, thinking all week that I'd have to fly home without…without figuring out… Well, I should have insisted you arrange this meeting the moment I got here."

"But I did call her."

Isabella waved it off. "Forget it."

"No, I won't. You snapped at me for no reason. If meeting Johanna was so important to you, you should have called her yourself."

Isabella's eyes grew large and dark before softening. "You're right. Sorry. We're both stressed out. Let's calm down and think about what we have to do next." She filled my glass. "You will come with me, won't you? I can't face Johanna on my own."

I bit my lip. The last thing I needed was to lose my job over a few days in the bush that wouldn't achieve anything.

"You were there, too," Isabella pleaded with me. "It affected your life, too."

"Why don't we just wait and see what this find means? Maybe nothing will come of it."

"Please."

"Why is it so important to you to meet Johanna?"

"There is something in the back of my mind. All these years, I haven't been able to pinpoint what it is, and it's driving me crazy. I need to figure it out, and maybe you and Johanna can help me with it."

33

Half of Sydney's residents had taken their annual leave to join the celebrations surrounding the Commonwealth Games. Because business was down for those two weeks, my boss sounded pleased when I asked for unpaid leave until the games were over, and Steve was all for it, too. "With you guys out of the way," he said, "I can concentrate on the games." Who could blame him? His work load was huge and he wanted to do a good job.

We got a late start the day after Johanna's call. Isabella drove the first leg of the trip, and I let her concentrate on Sydney's heavy traffic before I asked, "What shall we do if it is Kurt?"

She shrugged. "I don't see any point in speculating."

"I'm just saying—"

"I'd rather you wouldn't." Her tone was sharp. "You've always been one for over-talking things, always worried about what might not be."

"How can you say that? You know it's a possibility."

"Very remote."

"Not remote at all. I feel it in my guts that it's him."

"Oh, please." Isabella stiffened in her seat. "Can't you just be quiet for a second? This constant chattering drives me crazy."

A little hurt, I bit my lip and stared ahead, same as her. I'd to prove to her that I could very well keep my mouth shut.

She'd have to apologize to me before I'd say more than what was absolutely necessary. We arrived in Gunnedah at eleven at night, worn out and still not talking about what lay ahead of us. We stopped at a plain but well-kept motel next to the highway and woke the manager. He had only one room left. We paid the thirty-five dollars, went to our room, undressed, and fell asleep next to each other.

The next morning, Isabella was awake when I opened my eyes. She stared at the ceiling.

"Shall I get us coffee?" I had seen a coffee machine in the lobby when checking in.

She kept staring. "Hot coffee would be good."

I got up, slipped into my shorts and T-shirt, and made my way to the lobby. Isabella was already dressed when I returned balancing the hot paper cups. She had pulled her hair back with a rubber band, exposing a perfect neckline—not a single sagging line in her glowing skin. Nature had favoured her beyond fairness. What I would have given for a Mediterranean complexion like hers. Only the area around her eyes was still slightly swollen from sleep.

"I'm not taking a shower in this filthy bathroom."

I put a cup on her bedside table and shook my hand to cool my fingertips. "It's lovely outside. The birds are singing and the sun is up. It's going to be a gorgeous day."

Isabella took a sip of her coffee and made a face. "Yikes! What's that supposed to be?" She jumped up. "We better get going. This motel is depressing me. What a dump. I haven't slept all night. The mattress is too soft, my back hurts like hell, and my skin is itchy. I'm sure I got flea bites."

"If you say so."

"And the coffee tastes like dishwater."

"Leave it."

She pointed to the ceiling. "Did you notice this lamp and the furniture? Why do motels in this country have to be so ugly? It doesn't cost more to make it pleasant. These people have no taste."

Her words made me remember how she'd been. Best not say anything when she was in one of her moods, but she noticed my silence.

"What's the matter with you?"

"Nothing."

"Come on."

"Leave me alone. I'm going to take a shower."

Isabella waited until I came out, towelling my hair. "So, what's eating you?"

Before I could think, it bubbled out of me. "We're on this trip not only to visit an old friend but to find out a few things about our past that affect all three of us. Instead of preparing ourselves for what lies ahead, you refuse to discuss it with me. Since you arrived in Australia, you've constantly bitched about everything, as if you are trying to avoid an honest conversation. Our car is not good enough. It's too hot. The people in the stadium are too noisy. I should risk my job to accommodate you. This motel is crap. The coffee is disgusting. From day one, you made sure we all understand what a hardship it is for you to be here. I can't help it if you don't like it here. I didn't ask you to come back." My voice went up a notch. "Our car is all we can afford. You upset Steve with your insensitive comment. You expect a palace for a motel that charges only a few lousy dollars. And the coffee is fresh and hot."

"Wow, Eva, I didn't mean it like that. I'm sorry if I've upset you."

"Why did you come here if you hate it so much?"

"I came to see you and Johanna."

"Why?"

She looked me straight in the eyes and I thought I detected tears in hers. "I honestly don't know. I can't explain it. Can't we just drive to Lightning Ridge and see what happens?"

Considering the horrible secret hidden in our past, I thought that might be for the best. And if anything was to be gained from this trip, she'd need to figure it out herself.

"I'm really sorry if I upset Steve," she said. "Didn't mean to."

I softened. Steve was my frontman. I had used him to make a point. He didn't care if Isabella liked our car or not, and I shouldn't either. My life was as good as Isabella's, if not better. I had a good man by my side, something I don't think she'd ever had.

"You never married again when you went back to Germany?"

She caught my change of tone right away. I've never been one to keep things bottled up, and once they're out, I never hold a grudge.

"After Dieter?" she said. "Lord, no. Him leaving me was such a shock I was numb for a long time after."

We sat and sipped our coffees.

"I thought you held up really well after the split. I figured you hadn't lost much. Dieter was weak, and him cheating on you surprised me. I didn't think he had it in him."

"He didn't," she said.

"Come on, don't deny it. You told me when you called after he left."

"No. I called him a cheating bastard and you assumed he had another woman."

"You didn't correct me."

"I was hurt."

"Why did he leave you if he hadn't found somebody else? And why did he leave Australia in such a hurry?"

Isabella searched my face as if I knew the answer. "He had no reason. At least he didn't give me one."

"I had no idea."

"You should have asked me how I felt."

She put her finger on my guilt. "I'm sorry. I never thought about it. We were different then." I paused to think back. "I depended on Uwe to organize our lives, Johanna obeyed Kurt to the point that it was freaky, and you never openly stood up to Dieter although you seemed so strong. We were all unknowingly oppressed."

She looked lost in memories, too.

"Is that why you went back to Munich? You thought you couldn't handle life on your own in Australia?"

"I wasn't lacking courage. I was being sensible. To stay would have meant to fight a losing battle. Single women in business had a very low glass ceiling then. I enjoyed my work but I couldn't have survived on my salary alone."

"You got paid more than me as a secretary."

Isabella got up abruptly. "We better get going."

"I never understood that."

She ignored me. We walked to our car, stowed our two

bags on the back seat, and drove north. Isabella let me drive, put her seat back and pretended to sleep. For a while, I concentrated on getting into the rhythm of driving again. Few cars passed us coming from the other direction, and very rarely did one overtake us.

She must have felt my brain ticking and picked up our conversation without prompting.

"Once I had been kicked out of the ad agency, my career prospects were in the cellar. If I had known then that Dieter was going to leave me soon after, I wouldn't have bothered to find a new job."

"What did he do to disappoint you so much if it wasn't another woman?"

"He cleaned out our joint bank account, cheating me out of my own money. I wish I would have taken my share and gone back home before he got his grubby fingers on it."

"Did you never think about leaving?" Isabella asked with a quick side glance.

"I've been homesick at times," I said

34

JOHANNA

At dawn, I'd made up my mind to go back to the mine. The earth above ground had dried up sufficiently for me to inspect the area surrounding my mine. Maybe I'd find the spot where the skeleton, or at least parts of it, was discovered.

Eva and Isabella wouldn't arrive until late afternoon, which would give me plenty of time for my search. I got up as soon as the first silver stripe of dawn twinkled on the horizon, put on my old sweat suit, slipped into my solid work boots, and left the house without waking Ben.

Outside, Tiger greeted me with enthusiastic tail wagging, and I decided to take him along. Just outside the town limits, I turned onto a completely dried out gravel road. A dust cloud so thick nobody would believe we had just experienced serious flooding followed us.

I drove past sunflower fields, already covered with tall, green stems, took another turn, and drove through an open area, deeper into the bush. The landscape changed from generous vegetation to barren, rocky fields, covered with low, dry bush interspersed with brown mountains of dirt. The land looked as if gigantic moles had worked it.

Those dreary-looking hills were the remnants of a once-busy mining area. Every time I drove past them, I thought about all the disappointments they'd brought upon the miners, and about all the enormous energy wasted on them.

Ten minutes later, I arrived at the million dollar mines where Japanese companies had settled with their heavy mining equipment a few years back when news of a major opal find got out. Some lucky bastard had discovered a large opal street and sold out to an overseas mining investment company. After that, things got embarrassing for us old established diggers. I drove past machinery small independent miners could only dream of. If multinationals kept coming, our old, overused drills and conveyor belts soon won't be sufficient any more, and we'll have to kiss our beloved profession goodbye.

Deadline looming. I reminded myself of my promise to give up by the end of the year.

I left the amazing display of engineering behind me and drove on until I reached my claim. I parked my truck close to the manhole, got out, and looked around. It was eerily quiet. None of the mines around my claim had reopened yet. I tried to remember where we had buried Kurt.

I went back to the car, let Tiger out, opened the toolbox, and took out a plastic bag containing Kurt's pocketknife. I didn't know why I had kept it for so long, considering that I had dumped everything else that even remotely reminded me of him. Like a maniac, I had torn his clothes to shreds, burned his notebooks with drawings of claims and maps of potential opal finds, had thrown his hair brush, coffee mug, and lunchbox out. Nothing got past my compulsive need to eliminate him from my life—nothing except this small knife in its leather cover.

I held it under Tiger's nose, and he sniffed it. Then, I rubbed it around his wet nose until he lifted his head as if he had taken the scent. I followed his lead when he lowered his head to the ground and started trotting. He stopped occasionally, changed direction, and crisscrossed my claim until we came to the border of the neighbouring one.

The claim covered nearly two hundred parcels of fifty by fifty meters each. Dirt and rock hills of various sizes dominated the barren landscape around me.

What was I thinking? A dog and a piece of leather so old it couldn't possibly hold any scent were supposed to lead me to where the bones had washed up? How could I be so stupid?

I would have to look for the rest of the skeleton myself. I searched for the old path I hadn't walked since that dreadful day so long ago. Although it was nearly overgrown, I made good progress. Tiger followed me, overtaking occasionally, sniffing like an expert hound.

Suddenly, walking around a sharp bend in the path, I came across a red and white marker with a flag on it—not far from my side of the claim and not far from an old, deserted manhole, secured with a corrugated tin sheet. The flag had a number written on it and looked clean. This must be where the bones were found. Why on earth had somebody looked here? Then I remembered John telling me about a search party for good old Charlie.

I looked around. Where exactly was I? As far as I could see, scrawny bush covered the land evenly with a few trees sticking out in between. There was nothing to give me any bearings. I searched my memory but couldn't find any recollection of the exact location Eva and I were at when we'd buried Kurt. All I remembered was our concentrated effort to get the heavy body on the wheelbarrow and pushing it as far away from my claim as possible. But how far?

Tiger's sudden rough bark pulled me out of my reflections. He buried his nose deep into a hole not far from the flag, looked up at me and then down again, scratching the ground with his claws. My heart began pounding, although his behaviour was no proof that the find coming out of this hole had anything to do with the scent Tiger might have in his nose.

"Good dog," I said anyway. "Enough now. Come, we're going home."

I chose a shortcut through the bush toward my claim. This path was a lot more overgrown, and I was careful not to disturb the vegetation too much. Nobody needed to know I'd been there.

Just before I reached the border to my land, I bent down to move a broken branch and saw something gleaming out of the corner of my eye. I looked closer at the shiny metal stuck halfway in the earth and carefully pulled it out. The round metal disc was a medallion with a chain attached to it. Several links of the chain were rusty, but the medallion itself must have been made of better material because it was only dirty. I wiped over it until I could see the engraving of a man carrying a child on his shoulders. I turned it over but couldn't decipher the wording engraved due to the hardened dirt in its fine lines.

I slipped it into my pocket. It didn't look valuable, but it was a sign that my trip today had not been in vain. If nothing else, I had a piece of forgotten jewelry brought back to life.

35

Around 11:00 a.m., I was back in Lightning Ridge at John's pub. He stood behind the counter and prepared for a busy lunch crowd, polishing glasses while humming a popular melody. I used the back entrance, which was always open, snuck up on him, and tapped him on the shoulder.

He spun around defensively, lifting his hands until he recognized me. Immediately, his posture and expression softened. "Jesus, Johanna," he said, "don't do that."

"You scared of me?" I asked.

He pulled me to him and gave me a casual peck on my cheek as he always did when we met, but this time, he didn't let go right away. "I'm scared of anybody who smells as delicious as you."

I could still feel the soft touch of his lips on my skin and pushed away from him. To get some distance between us, I moved around the counter and sat on a barstool opposite him.

He squared his shoulders and let out a long breath, disapproving of my standoffish nature. How often have we played this game before? Then he smiled at me. "What would you like to drink?"

"Mineral water. The largest glass you got."

"I noticed your elegant footwear," he said. "Boots in this temperature. You must be hot."

"Dying of thirst. I've been to the mine."

"And? Everything okay there?" He handed me the glass of water.

"Yep," I said. "Looks like I can open up again soon."

"You miners are crazy."

I took a large gulp. "Not all of us. Mira is one of the rare, sensible specimen—or should I say speciwomen—who show some restraint? She's gone back to Brisbane." She'd been delighted with the picture I gave her, promising she'd look at it every time she needed a reminder of what was important in life.

John took up polishing glasses again. "Actually, she called here this morning when she couldn't reach you at your place. She asked me to tell you that she got back all right." He leaned closer to me, still polishing. "Apparently, all hell broke loose when she got back. Her husband—can you believe this creep—sent her divorce papers via his lawyer. But he's still living in the house. Didn't tell her himself, the coward. Mira is so mad she wants to finish him off."

"Jeez, that's crazy. I thought he didn't want a divorce."

"I don't know. Maybe his girlfriend is pregnant."

"Could be," I said. "I think Mira is better off without him. She can straighten out her life and move on."

"Like you did?" John asked.

I didn't bother to reply. My life was none of John's business. But he didn't let go.

"Don't tell me I'm wrong," he said, leaning even closer to me, forgetting to polish the glass in his hand. "If I can believe local gossip, you had a good marriage before your husband died. So how come an attractive woman like you still lives alone?"

Obviously, in the memory of the townsfolk my beloved husband had been a decent miner, and I was still his grieving widow. I lifted my glass and drank slowly.

"Admit it. You are scared of a new relationship. I can only imagine how scared you'd be to lose another partner."

Did he really have to bring up Kurt on a day like today? I slid my empty glass over to him. "You are wrong. My husband has been dead for so long now I can barely remember him."

"So why are you still alone?"

He had no right to ask such questions. I got up, ready to leave.

"Sorry. Forget it. Let me get you another drink." While he poured, he changed the subject. "By the way, remember the skeleton I told you about?"

I felt the change of subject might take me from bad to worse but couldn't stop him now. "What about it?"

"They've taken it to Sydney for forensic analysis."

I sat down again. "They did?"

"It's a pointless exercise, but it's the law, according to Bill. They need to establish the approximate date of death, which they can do pretty accurately nowadays."

I held my breath. "What happens then?"

"Then, Bill and his team of country sheriffs will check the records for missing persons around that date, but he thinks the checks will only prove it was a stranger travelling through our area—one who wanted to save himself the fee for registering a claim. You know those types. They come and go and are nothing but a gigantic nuisance for us townspeople."

I drew a deep breath again. "I guess Bill is right," I said, trying to keeping my voice noncommittal. "He'll know how to handle it."

My heart raced. Please let Bill stop looking after the description of the first missing stranger matches the approximate period of Kurt's disappearance. I slipped from the stool again. "Gotta go. Tiger is in the truck."

"In any case, it'll be fun," John called after me. "When they are done with the skeleton, they'll bring it back here and display it in town."

I stopped in my tracks and turned back toward him, unable to hide my shock. "They'll what?"

He grinned. "I didn't know you were so squeamish."

I took a step toward him. "What did you just say?"

"They plan to put it in our opal museum as the unknown miner who died in search of the great find. It's supposed to deter other crazies from going into the bush and mining illegally. Should go over well with the tourists. I think it's a great idea."

"I think it stinks to high heaven." I hit the counter with my fist. "Who the hell came up with such an idiotic idea?"

"Calm down." John looked a bit startled by my outburst. "All of us did, last night, after a few drinks. I don't remember who started it, but Bill was there, too, and he agreed that it's doable. The authorities will give permission if the skeleton ends up in a museum, so long as the display is tasteful."

"Tasteful, my ass. A bunch of drunken miners. How dare you. I will not allow it. You understand? Never."

I turned and ran. Behind me, I could hear him calling, "But Johanna…?" Luckily, I reached the door and slammed it shut behind me before he could finish. My God. They are going to bring Kurt back to this town.

I made it into the truck before I lost control. Tears of anger and helplessness, suppressed for so many years, flooded up and out, making me double over. Bit by bit, my inner wall, the one I had so diligently erected, crumbled. I was shaking, gripping the steering wheel in an effort to get myself under control again, leaning my hot forehead on it. But the broken pieces of the wall could not be put together again. I felt exposed, defeated, destroyed.

When I lifted my head again, I saw the first patrons walking toward the pub. I turned on the engine, wiped my eyes so I could see, and focused on the drive home. As soon as I had reached the safety of my house, I stumbled inside, threw myself on the sofa, and started to cry in earnest again—loud, hard, and desperate.

Ben came up to me and licked my wet, limp hand. I lifted my head to see if I had closed the door so Tiger wouldn't come in, and that small moment of worry, together with my dog's sweet gesture, brought me back from the precipice of hopelessness. I had responsibilities—to my dogs, to my opal mine, and to me. Not all was lost.

It's just a dumb idea by a silly crowd of pub-goers. Nothing was decided, and the bones may not even be Kurt's. I gasped with the deep-seated conviction of how foolish it was to think so. Of course it was Kurt. The location of the find pointed to it. Besides, how likely was it that a stranger died in the same vicinity as Kurt's final resting place? Final? Ha! Dry laughter burst out of my parched throat.

I couldn't let this happen. I had to fight it—come up with an argument the town would understand. John would understand. If I told him the truth about me and Kurt, would he understand or will he despise me? How will he feel about me if I tell him how Kurt had treated me? Me, the level-headed, no-nonsense woman he's come to appreciate. Will he lose all respect for me?

The outburst left me drained, but I forced myself into an upright position. Ben's tail began to wag when he realized I was back in this world. I patted his head and was rewarded with even faster tail wagging. "You poor thing," I said to him. "You must be so confused. You don't know me like this, do you? Shall I tell you what I had to go through to make me into the strong person I'm today?" Everything I wanted to but couldn't tell John was safe with Ben. The dog sat with pointed ears in front of me, seemingly listening. "After Kurt was gone, I finally had my peace."

Ben put his head on my lap. Thinking back to those days, I had to laugh, this time with a twinge of honest joy.

"You know, after Kurt died, I felt so good I had to force myself to play the grieving widow. All the townspeople thought how hard it was for me without a husband. Working the mine by myself was unheard of. They felt so openly sorry for me—the young woman who'd lost this strapping guy, this tireless miner with the big shoulders who was always so courteous and polite. How they'd misjudged him. Do you want to know how he really was, Ben? He was only pleasant when somebody was close by. Once we were alone, out in the bush, down in the mine, he bossed me around to his heart's content. Johanna this, Johanna that. Go up the ladder. Fetch me a drink. No, Johanna, you stupid cow, not the water. Up you go again. Get the Coke. What takes you so long, Johanna? Are you being lazy? Do I need to teach you a lesson again? Christ, if you didn't have me, you'd never learn anything. You are useless without me. Nothing but a piece of garbage."

I stopped to think about it. Why did I allow him to treat me like that?

"You know, Ben, in those days, I believed I couldn't survive in the bush without him. I didn't know how to mine for opals. He knew it all, and I didn't dare question his word. Only after his death did I realize I could manage very well on my own. It wasn't easy, but my life had been so much harder with him around, and his constant harassment. He tormented me day and night. Johanna, you can't do this. Johanna, that's how you have to do that. I could still scream when I think about it. And now they want to display him in my town, all because they don't know that those bones are Kurt's. If they find out the truth, they won't make a tourist attraction out of him."

The terrible consequence of that thought hit me. "But then they find out the truth about me, too."

36

EVA

After we left the motel, I drove nearly two hundred kilometers before Isabella took over. The constant hum of our tires on the hot asphalt was soothing, and with hardly any traffic to keep me awake, I drifted off. Images of Isabella and me, all of them from days long gone, floated through my mind.

"Where the heck is this damn turnoff?" Isabella suddenly said, startling me. "Did we miss it?"

"Don't think so," I said, although I had no idea where we were. I stared through the windshield, caked with dead insects, hoping we hadn't missed the road leading to Lightning Ridge. How flat the land next to road had become, with only sparse vegetation along its sides. How long had I been out?

"Sweet dreams?" Isabella asked.

"I've been remembering the past, the time we spent together here in Sydney. For years, I didn't waste a single thought on it, and now, I have one flashback after another."

"That's understandable. We haven't seen each other for so long, and each of us leads her own, quite different, life. Now, we are being confronted with the past and our minds need to process it. I bet it'll get even worse when we meet Johanna."

The thought scared me. "I'm remembering stuff that's irrelevant now, and it stops me from concentrating on how we can help Johanna solve her dilemma."

"You make it sound like she's got a problem when you know as well as I do she's panicking for no reason. They found a few bones in the bush. So what?"

"What if those are Kurt's bones?"

Isabella glanced at me. "Maybe they're not."

"But what if?"

"Who gives a damn? No one but Johanna cares whose bones they are, and the police will never connect them to Kurt. He's been officially declared dead, so he may not even show up in any missing persons' report."

We fell silent again.

"What if we missed the sign?" Isabella asked after a while. "I don't know if I should drive on or turn around. Goddamn stupid countryside."

She was right. We had no idea where we were. I said a silent prayer that was instantly answered when a turnoff sign appeared farther down the road. Hallelujah. I relaxed in my seat but made sure I didn't fall into my passenger trance again.

Isabella relaxed behind the wheel, too. We were only fifty kilometers from Lightning Ridge.

"Maybe we better start thinking about how we can calm Johanna down."

Isabella squinted in the bright sun. "There's nothing we can do if Johanna wants to be upset. She was the one who went to the police and reported the accident to begin with. We've got nothing to do with it."

"Oh, really?" I frowned at her but she didn't look at me. "I went with her to the police station and confirmed she drove Kurt into the bush to go on a hunt he never returned from. My signature is on that statement, but I never saw him leave. I lied, Isabella, for you, and for Johanna. How can you say we have nothing to do with it?"

She hit the brakes, glared at me, and said, "I never said we've got nothing to do with it." She accelerated again, back to our normal cruising speed.

"You just did. You said—"

"Okay, okay. What I meant was we don't have anything to do with it *anymore*. You weren't there and didn't see the accident. You don't know how it happened, and neither does Johanna. Officially nobody is accusing her of anything. If she feels the need to justify herself now, without any provocation, she probably has her reasons, and there's nothing we can do about it."

"What reasons?"

"No idea," Isabella said. "Johanna is the one who last saw him alive. Whatever she said in her statement stands, even today, and if she insists that's all she knows, then who's to contradict her?"

"But if she loses it and says something different, we're all implicated."

"In a roundabout way, maybe, but so what? If she starts to talk nonsense, we'll pack up and leave."

"I see. You wouldn't just leave Lightning Ridge, you'd leave Australia—fly out and forget about the mess Johanna and I might be in."

She hit the steering wheel. "Jesus, Eva, don't twist my

words. I didn't say *I'd* leave. I said *we'd* leave, meaning you and I would leave Lightning Ridge. If Bill Wiseman does indeed remember Kurt's disappearance and gets suspicious, we'll drive back to Sydney. Do you really think this old case is important enough to order us back to Lightning Ridge? To ask us what?"

"Why this skull has a hole in it?"

"I can think of a number of reasons. Maybe he shot himself or maybe he tripped and hurt his head. They might determine what caused the hole, but they'll never know how it happened."

"They'll wonder about the location."

"Where the skeleton was found? God, we don't know if they found the whole skeleton. They were talking about a skull and a few bones only."

"Flushed out of a hollow mine shaft close to Johanna's mine?" I asked, determined to prove the seriousness of the situation to Isabella.

Isabella drew in a sharp breath. "Maybe it's Johanna who should disappear for a while. Then, nobody can ask her questions and all will be forgotten in due course."

A sign displaying the town's name appeared. Immediately behind it, rows of plain white houses with red and green roofs and chicken wire fences popped up. "Poor Johanna," I said. "This is her home. Where else would she go?"

37

ISABELLA

Eva stopped the car at the metal gate with 253 on it, and we watched Johanna walk down her driveway with heavy steps, wiping her hands on her oversized jeans. She gestured for us to wait and dragged a madly barking dog by its collar from the gate, locking him in a shed close by.

"Jesus, she's a mess," I said.

Johanna opened the gate and pointed to a space between the house and the shed for me to park. Eva jumped out and ran toward Johanna.

"How wonderful to see you again." Johanna stiffened under Eva's awkward hug but that didn't seem to bother Eva. "Look at you, slim like the last time I saw you. How on earth do you two do it? Isabella hasn't put on an ounce either."

Johanna gave us a sad smile. "Glad you could make it." She gave me the quick once-over, making me slightly uncomfortable. My designer T-shirt with the shiny appliques seemed a touch out of place, as did my large leather tote and high heel sandals.

"How was the drive?"

"Uneventful," I said, "except for Eva's constant chatter."

Eva laughed. "Not true. I slept most of the time."

"You must be thirsty. Come on in." Johanna walked ahead of us to the house. "Don't mind the dog. He's harmless."

Eva immediately stiffened and we both remembered her fear of large dogs. "Wait a sec. I'll move him to the other shed," Johanna said.

We went inside while she pulled the dog past Eva, who visibly relaxed once he was gone. I sat down on the sofa, which was surprisingly comfortable, and Eva stood and looked around.

"She's got it nice here," Eva said.

That was a bit of an exaggeration for a green sofa, a brown and a blue easy chair, and a multicolored rug on the wooden floor planks. Nothing matched, but the room felt cozy. The white bookshelf on the wall was overflowing with books, periodicals, and a few framed pictures. None of the pictures were of Kurt, but I did notice one of the three of us from thirty years ago.

Johanna came back in and got a bottle of mineral water from her fridge and three glasses.

Soft light filtered in through the window and fell on our faces. Even Johanna looked better in this forgiving afternoon light.

"I owe you an explanation," she began. "I must have sounded quite confusing on the phone but the situation we're in developed so suddenly, I didn't know what to do. We need to talk it through."

"Of course," Eva said. "That's why we're here. Isn't it a wonderful coincidence that Isabella happened to visit Australia right when you wanted to talk to us?"

"It's no coincidence."

"What do you mean?"

Johanna took a deep breath. "Kurt has pushed himself out

of the ground to force us to tell the truth. We have to face the past. He won't rest until we do."

I sat up straight and stared at her. "Now I've heard just about everything. You can't be serious. He's come out of the ground to haunt us like one of those skeletons at a fun fair?" I stretched my arms sideways and let them shake as if I could rattle them while making a low whistling sound, partly to demonstrate what I meant and partly to mock her insanity.

Eva laughed but Johanna only stared back at me.

"Exactly like that," she said.

I dropped my arms. "How the hell did you get such nonsense into your brain? You've never been superstitious before."

"Let me repeat. It is exactly like that. When I heard about the skeleton find, my first reaction was thinking that we could get past it, but now I know Kurt is chasing us like the monster in a haunted house."

I leaned toward her. "What kind of drugs are you on?"

"It's very simple, Isabella. Once they analyze the skull and bones, they'll know this person did not die of natural causes. The hole in the skull indicates blunt force trauma and with today's forensic analysis, they'll quickly establish sex, age, height, and other physical attributes of the victim. They will figure out the approximate time of death and everything will point to Kurt. Then, they'll treat it like a murder investigation because they will check the records and suspect that I lied thirty years ago. They will want to know why we didn't tell the truth." She kept her stare fixed on my face. "You understand, Isabella? We have to tell the truth now."

I didn't waver under her stare. "Why the hell are you looking at me like that? You are blowing this thing totally out of proportion. You are beside yourself with worry and can't think straight. I told Eva on the way up here that we have no cause for concern. We don't know anything. It may not even be Kurt."

"But it is," Johanna said. "I checked the site where they found the skeleton. I couldn't remember exactly where we buried Kurt, but I looked at the maps of the old mines when I came back, and you know what I discovered? All the deserted mines in that area were connected in the early days. Eva, remember the hole we dug to bury Kurt partially collapsed on us?"

Eva nodded.

"That's how it must have happened. The rainwater flooded the mine and carried Kurt's bones along a shaft until they were pushed above ground. It can't be too far from where we dumped Kurt."

"Don't talk like that," Eva said. "Don't say we dumped him."

Johanna smirked. "You think he should rest in peace? Ha! That won't happen. When they finish with him in Sydney, they're bringing him up here to display him at the opal museum. Then I'll have my very own private freak show and can lay down flowers at his feet every day."

"Oh no! They can't do that," Eva said.

"Who's to stop them?" Johanna asked. "Me, the grieving widow?"

I imagined how I would feel if Dieter were on display in my hometown. I had to giggle. "If it were Dieter, I'd make a scarecrow out of his skeleton and display him in my front yard. I'd place a funny hat on his skull and wrap his favourite scarf around his wobbly neck—the one with the psychedelic patterns. Remember that one?"

Eva stopped looking so shocked. "The one with the weird colours? He was so proud of that one. He threw it over his shoulder with this grand gesture every time it slipped down. Like that…" She copied Dieter's movement so exaggerated, both Johanna and I burst out laughing.

"But he only did that when he was nervous," Johanna said.

"Which was practically all the time," I said between laughing fits. "The guy was so insecure he must have been close to a nervous breakdown constantly."

We were all giggling uncontrollably. It felt so good to laugh together, and it certainly took away a lot of the tension we all felt.

"Anybody for a beer?" Johanna asked when we calmed down a little. She retrieved and handed us beer cans without waiting for an answer. "And when we finish these, I suggest we go for some food."

"You mean they have a decent restaurant in town now?" I smirked.

"Stop being so negative," Eva said.

Johanna shrugged her shoulders. "The same old local pub but with new management. They serve decent burgers and fries nowadays. Even you might like it, Isabella."

38

JOHANNA

I guided Eva and Isabella to their motel so they could check in, shower and change after the long drive, pointing out the pub on the way. Then, I went there ahead of them to pick out a quiet table before the boisterous crowd of thirsty miners, still bored from doing nothing, descended.

John looked up when I came in, lifting an eyebrow.

"Save your breath," I said.

His blue eyes took on a darker shade. "Why did you storm off like that this morning? I've been wracking my brain since what might have upset you so much. Was it me?"

"No."

He studied my face. "You've been crying."

I turned away from him. "It's nothing."

"Do you want to talk about it?"

"I'm kind of busy. I'm waiting for my girlfriends to arrive."

Both his eyebrows shot up. "You and girlfriends? What's the world coming to?"

"Friends from my early days, when I was still in Sydney."

"Oh, I see. Did they come alone or with their husbands?"

His question gave me tiny stitch inside. "Just them. One couldn't bring her husband—he's too busy—and the other is divorced. You can try your luck with her."

"I'd rather try with you," he said with such intensity I couldn't doubt he really meant it. I savoured the quiet pleasure it gave me, taking the edge off the dread I'd felt all day.

I sipped my whiskey, promising myself this would be the only one tonight, while I tried to prepare myself for the meeting with Eva and Isabella. I must have been so deep in thought I didn't notice them arriving until they were right behind me.

"Woo-hoo! That's some eye candy," Isabella said.

I turned around. "What?"

"The question is not what, but who. Who the hell is that dishy guy behind the bar?"

I ignored her comment. "Sit down. We have to make a plan for the coming days. How long can you stay?"

Isabella glanced back at John. "With the right motivation, forever."

"For three days max," Eva said. "I need to be back in the office by Monday. If it's any longer, I'll need to check with my boss to see if I can extend my unpaid leave."

"Three days should be plenty," Isabella said.

I looked into my empty glass. Why did this stuff have to evaporate so quickly? On cue, John appeared, carrying a tray with three generously filled whiskey glasses. "I hope I'm not disturbing you, ladies." He put the tray on our table. "On the house. Johanna's friends are my friends."

Eva thanked him, and Isabella added an offer for him to sit down.

"Get lost," I said. "We've got things to discuss."

"Wouldn't dream of disturbing you," John said. His eyes were brighter than before, but I detected a hurt look in them before he disappeared.

Eva and Isabella raised their glasses with a queried expression on their faces.

"He's just a friend."

"The vibes I get point to more," Isabella said, leaning closer to me.

"Not interested."

"In him, or having sex with him?"

When I didn't reply, she pushed further. "That can't be. You're a healthy, single woman. Isn't there somebody in your life?" She paused. "You didn't spend the past thirty years all by yourself, did you? You must have had a relationship, or two, or three."

"None of your business."

"I'm curious. What's wrong with a little gossip?"

"If you ask me—" Eva started.

"Nobody did," Isabella interrupted.

Eva seemed undeterred. "We should catch up. So much has happened since we lost touch with each other. Getting to know each other again might help us sort through our current situation."

I had no desire to open up what I had locked away so successfully, but Eva had a point. I needed their help, and I had to give a little to get it. "Who starts?"

"The one who likes to talk the most," Isabella said.

"Sorry to disappoint you," Eva said to Isabella, "but my story is probably the shortest. With you back in Germany and Johanna here in Lighting Ridge, I felt alone and forgotten. I hadn't made any new friends since our arrival, relying on both of you to be there when I needed somebody." Then, she addressed me. "Although you weren't exactly a huge support, Johanna, it helped that you listened to me. I suddenly had nobody who'd understand my frustrations and inability to adapt to the new country we lived in. Uwe never had the time, or the inclination, to console me. If you remember, soon after the, uh, the tragedy, he left his firm and became self-employed. When was that again, Johanna?"

"About two years after Kurt and I moved here." I swallowed the lump in my throat. Two years I had survived in this hellhole.

Eva turned to Isabella. "And then, about a year after the, uh, the accident, you left Australia."

"Correct," Isabella said. "Darling Dieter disappeared in January, a few months after the, uh, the terrible—"

I couldn't hold back any longer. "Oh Jesus Christ, you two! Call a spade a spade. You mean after Kurt's death, not the tragedy, the accident, or the terrible whatever. You mean the day he died, so that's what you should call it."

"All right, then," Isabella said, unperturbed. "About three months after Kurt died, Dieter did his disappearing act."

Eva took a sip of her whiskey and made a face. "And about the same time, Uwe resigned to go independent. When he opened his own carpentry shop, I was flabbergasted. Until then, he'd always been so conservative, so careful. I expected him to stay with the company he worked for until they made him a partner. He'd been expecting it, and his boss had talked to him about it already. For Uwe to throw that chance away when I was pregnant was a hard blow for me, but he emptied our bank account and put all our savings into the new venture. God, I was so mad at him. I didn't know it was even an option until it was done, as if it was none of my business."

"He'd always been a weird guy," I said. "Boring like pea soup."

Isabella giggled. "He really was a bit of a wimp."

"Hey," Eva said, "show some respect. You're talking about my ex-husband."

"As boring as a Sunday school teacher," Isabella said.

I joined in the banter. "And pedantic like a tax collector."

Eva lifted her half-full glass against the window. "I guess yours are empty?"

"Let's have another." I signalled John for another round.

Isabella covered her mouth with her hand in a mocking gesture. "For somebody who never drank a drop of alcohol, you're holding your own quite well."

"So what?"

"She means we are not used to see you drink, Johanna." Eva's explanation earned her an eye roll from Isabella. "Where was I? You're confusing me. Uwe wasn't that bad, was he?"

We both rolled our eyes, and Isabella went as far as sticking her finger in her throat, accompanied by retching sounds.

"All right, all right. He was boring. I admit that," Eva said. "The years with him were the most boring of my life. Unfortunately, I thought I had no way out. I had willingly chosen this life with him, and we were so far from home. What options did I have?"

"Get a divorce, cut him off, and go back home. You'd been so homesick and miserable, I don't know why you didn't go back to Germany without him."

Eva stuck her chin out. "I'm not as stupid as you think. My plan was to wait until Nadja was ready to go to school. That would have been my grand excuse—to give her a better education. People back home would think the schooling system here wasn't as good and they'd understand, maybe even congratulate me on my decision to put the child ahead of my own wishes. I wouldn't feel like such a loser, then. I helped Uwe build up his business for those first years, without pay, of course. The business did well, but money was always tight. Uwe said we had to save as much as possible for a down payment on a house, and I didn't mind skimping because half the savings would be mine, which would come in handy when Nadja and I went back to Germany."

John appeared with another tray. "Listen," I said but he placed his finger on his lips and winked at me. He wasn't upset with me, thank God. I couldn't handle too many emotions at once. I felt drained from having to confront the past with these two but at the same time exhilarated about filling in the gaps of our joined history. "What happened then?" I asked with John out of earshot again. "You never did go back."

"Uwe bought the house much sooner than I thought, only two years after he started his own company. One day, he said, 'Come along, I have to show you something.' With that, I wasn't just a married mother of a small child, I was one with a huge mortgage on a house and no money in the bank, totally dependent on my husband to provide for Nadja and me. I felt my life was over."

"And you were still plagued by homesickness," I said.

"Yes."

"What a tragedy."

Eva shrugged. "To me, homesickness was more like a chronic illness, one that is not very painful until it flares up occasionally, but those moments were brutal. I was so depressed I could barely function, but I had to take care of Nadja. She was my salvation. Uwe ignored her because she was a girl, not suitable to groom for his business."

"The creep," I said.

"He spoke of another child, but how could we, with me feeling so low and him working so much? Four years later, he surprised me again. He came home one morning, after being out all night, and woke me up, all flushed and excited, to tell me that his lover had borne him a son."

Isabella and I gasped.

"That's right. He'd started an affair with another woman years earlier, and I was too stupid to catch on, believing his stories about seeing clients and suppliers and travelling to trade shows. He waited until the child was born to tell me— had to make sure it was a son, I guess."

"Now that's super creepy," I said.

"He told me I could keep the house if I agreed to a quick divorce. He'd bought another house for his new family already and would move out as soon as I signed the papers."

"I hope you didn't," Isabella said.

"Of course she did," I said.

Isabella boxed me on my upper arm. "God, you and Eva. Cut from the same cloth."

I wanted to point out to her that she hadn't been a model of emancipation in those days, either, but Eva carried on telling her story.

"I signed the divorce agreement, which specified that I'd get the house and a small sum of money and that I'd waive any current or future rights to his company. The monetary payment was a bonus. Uwe said he didn't have to give me anything since the business was in his name only, but he wanted to be generous. I believed him, not realizing he left me with a mortgage much higher than the one-time payment."

"He screwed you," Isabella said. "Why didn't you ever tell me? In your letters, you only mentioned the two of you had drifted apart and separated amicably."

"What else could I say? I was angry with myself for being so naive. I still get angry when I hear how well his company is doing. His carpentry shop is now a huge furniture manufacturing company with branch offices and outlets in all major Australian and several Asian cities. When I signed the agreement, his company was worth a hundred times what he paid me, and by now, I'd be a very rich woman if I owned half of it. But what's done is done, and Steve and I are happy and lead a good life. And Nadja has turned into a true treasure. Guess what she's been studying?"

"Law, I hope," I said. "So she can sue her father if he tries to cheat her out of what she's entitled to."

"Nadja doesn't know anything about her father. He's as good as dead to her. First, she studied design at art school and then she was an apprentice at a carpentry shop so she could become a furniture designer. Seriously, I never told her what Uwe did, and she takes up furniture design. Isn't that hilarious?"

Her laughter was contagious.

"And it gets even better. Uwe's new wife left him a few years later. She met a new guy and took off to New Zealand with the boy to live in some kind of a cult."

Isabella slapped her thighs in delight. "I'm picturing Uwe miserable and lonely, finding out that his precious heir is singing the Hare Krishna mantra while Nadja works for his strongest competitor, raking in one order after another, slowly ruining his business."

"Cheers to that." I raised my glass toward Eva. "I hope he will die bitter and lonely."

"And poor as a church mouse," Isabella said.

We toasted to Uwe's miserable future. "Goes down like honey. Shall we have another?"

"Only if you tell your story next," Eva said.

I waved at John, who nodded back at me. "Not much to tell. After Kurt's death, I stayed in Lightning Ridge. The mine gave me enough to live on. Some years were better than others, but I can't complain. It's hard work, but the ever-present hope to hit the jackpot makes me toil on. Once you start mining, it's hard to stop."

"I always hoped you'd come back to Sydney," Eva said. "Especially after my divorce."

"You never asked me to." I waved the hurtful memory off. "Never mind. We had so little contact by then and our lives were so different. You were so distant, I didn't want to burden you with my troubles. And, from what I can gather, you had your own load to carry."

John came back, this time with a whiskey bottle in his hand. He placed it on our table. "Looks like the ladies are settled in for the evening. Enjoy." He went back to the bar.

I stared at his back and wondered again if I had offended him. "After all we've been through together," Isabella said, "how could we drift apart like that?"

Eva exchanged a queried glance with me. How could Isabella make such a statement? I crossed my arms. "How can you think nothing has changed between us after that dreadful night, Isabella?"

Isabella looked at me with empty eyes.

"Everything changed," I said. "You went back to Germany, and I never heard from you again. Eva was trying to get her life in order after her divorce, so calls and letters from her became more and more infrequent. And I had my own problems to deal with, which took priority over staying in touch with both of you. I didn't need anybody in those days." I paused and thought briefly about the time after Kurt was gone. "Actually, I was better prepared for widowhood than most people here thought. Thanks to my deceased better half, I was familiar with the mining process, so I rolled up my sleeves and went to work. I could do nearly everything by myself. It didn't faze me when a machine broke down because I could usually fix it myself, and if not, one of the other miners helped me. I hired part-time help when extra hands were needed. I had everything under control, and above all, I had my peace—no Kurt forcing me into the mine every day without a break. Sometimes I didn't see the sun for weeks. I was in the mine before dawn broke and not back up again till dark. I even ate lunch in the mine."

"How terrible," Eva said. "I couldn't have done that. I was scared of that dreadful manhole. Remember when we were visiting you? I refused to step on that narrow, shaky ladder leading into the horrible dark. I admired your courage."

"I was scared, too," I admitted.

"Honestly? You were? How did you overcome your fear?"

I pondered Eva's question. Could I tell them how I did it? Will Isabella and Eva believe me? Will I regret my confession tomorrow? Maybe it was the whiskey talking, but I couldn't resist unloading the memories flooding back with such force.

"The first time Kurt took me into the mine, I told him I couldn't breathe. I felt like I was buried alive. He burst out laughing, and his laughter scared me more than the mine did. 'You better get used to it,' he said. 'That's our life now. You'll go down every day and work, and if you're scared, I'll help you lose your fear.' He bought a chain long enough to reach from the bottom of the manhole to the side tunnel he was working with his jackhammer. I had to fill buckets with the detritus and carry them to the manhole, where he would later heave them above ground to sift through. My duties kept me down there while he spent most hours above ground. Even when I had filled enough buckets for a whole afternoon's work, I couldn't go up, not until he unlocked the chain around my ankle. For hours, I sat in the small circle of light falling in from the manhole, on constant lookout for poisonous snakes seeking the moist coolness of a mine."

My voice faltered when I came to this part of his inhumane treatment, and I fell silent. I could not tell them the biggest humiliation I suffered. Even when my spirit was broken, when I didn't cry or beg anymore, or feel anything inside, he didn't let me off the chain until it was time to go home. Then, he came down the ladder and took me on the dirt floor, rough and hard. Only there, never at home on our mattress, did he use my body, and that degradation insulted me more than anything. I was a piece of dirt to him, and he enjoyed getting filthy.

After a brief silence, I hurried to finish my account. "I had no strength to fight him. To try and break free of him would have been the end of me."

Eva and Isabella stared at me with horror in their bloodless faces.

"That is the most horrific story I have ever heard," Eva whispered.

Isabella only nodded. It took her a few minutes before she could speak. "I'm glad he's dead. If he were still alive, I would have to kill him."

But you already did, rushed through my mind, and I read the same message in Eva's expression.

"You're doing it again," Isabella said, puzzled. "Stop looking at me like that."

We quickly broke our stare. Now was not the time to confront Isabella with what she'd done. Now was the time to renew our shaky friendship by getting thoroughly drunk together.

We did our best, and eventually I lost track of time. Our conversation got sillier by the minute until it didn't even make sense to us.

Next thing I knew, John was getting me out of his car and guiding me up my driveway. Luckily, my door was unlocked. I had no idea where my keys were. I walked straight through to my bedroom, fell on the mattress, and waved for John to join me. My eyes were too heavy to keep them open. I heard a door close and a car start. Then I passed out.

39

EVA

I carefully turned my head on the pillow to look at the clock. It was nine already, and bright daylight was shining through the flimsy motel curtains. The pounding behind my temples increased, and I fell back and pulled the cover over my eyes.

Isabella was in the bed next to mine. "Dear Lord, forgive my sins. I'm dying."

"Don't be so theatrical," I said. "You don't die from a hangover."

We fell quiet again. Thoughts about last night crept into my mind, and I wondered how Johanna was feeling.

"I bet Johanna feels just as rotten. Boy, did she knock them down," Isabella said.

Quiet again.

"That guy behind the bar drove her home."

I felt for the water bottle next to my bed and drank half of it. The fluid helped only briefly, then my stomach objected and I rushed into the bathroom. I came back exhausted and stretched out on the bed again, hoping Isabella would let me suffer in peace.

"I can't remember the last time I was that drunk," she ruminated, more to herself than to me. "It must have been that evening ages ago when Dieter invited Hal and his wife to our party. What a nightmare that was. In those days, I was having an affair with my boss and totally lost it when he showed up. I humiliated him in front of his wife, and Dieter, the fool, didn't even catch on."

Isabella's bombshell admission shocked me to the core. I raced back into the bathroom and retched until nothing was left inside me.

"Did I hear you right?" I said when I reached my bed again. "Did you say you were sleeping with your boss?"

"With Hal. Yes."

This wasn't just juicy gossip. This was a serious confession. However, her wickedness dated back nearly thirty years, which made its sordid details less despicable. I briefly contemplated asking her to delay any details my stomach might not be able to handle but then my curiosity got the better of me. "Tell," I said. "Everything."

"Not much to tell. Hal and his wife came to our party. Must have been the Saturday before Easter, if I remember correctly. I blew my top and he took swift action and fired me the next day. I wasn't allowed to show up at the agency the following Monday."

"Oh boy. I had no idea."

"Not even Dieter knew the real reason behind the dismissal."

"Why did you cheat on him?"

Isabella turned onto her side, so she could look at me. "You need to ask? Don't you remember how shallow and unemotional he was? He used me to get into the advertising world."

"I thought you liked helping Dieter," I said.

"I was damn good at it." She sat up and shook her arms to improve her circulation. We both started to feel better. "By the time I got fired, Dieter had established himself as a talented photographer and could build on that reputation. He managed quite well on his own, but he still made me feel like shit for losing my job. He never asked why, but I'm sure he suspected something was going on."

I couldn't picture Isabella being as calculating as she made herself out to be. "Were you attracted to Hal?"

"In a way," she said. "He was no Adonis, but he wasn't bad looking, and he was my boss. Power can be an aphrodisiac."

That sounded more like her. "And we all believed you resigned because you were fed up with that job."

"Leaving, for whatever reason, was ultimately the best thing that could have happened to me. I wasn't keen on the new job but I discovered that I liked import/export." She looked at the clock and sighed. "Enough reminiscing. Let's catch a few more hours of sleep. We told Johanna we'd be at her place later in the afternoon." The hang-over must have mellowed her usual judgemental attitude. She closed her eyes and mumbled, "At least, that's a decent motel. Nothing like the one Dieter put me in last time. Lightning Ridge has come a long way", before she drifted off.

I followed her into dreamland soon after.

When we came to, it was nearly three, and although we felt a lot better we decided to walk over to Johanna's—slowly, to give our weak bodies time to recuperate. After a long, hot shower, we went our way.

"Do you think Kurt really put her on a chain?" I asked,

once we had found our walking rhythm. "Or do you think she lied to us?"

"If she lied," Isabella said, "it was subconsciously—more like telling her version of the truth." She pondered this statement for a while, then continued. "Kurt was an asshole. I never liked him, you know that, but what she said yesterday…that's hard to swallow. He would have had to be a psychopath and a total sadist to degrade her like that. And what does that make her? A normal woman would never endure such treatment. One has to be deranged—"

"You think Johanna is mentally unstable or delusional?" I asked, considering it.

"It's possible."

"But that would mean that she…in the night…"

"What?"

I shivered in the bright afternoon sun. "I remember how resolutely and firmly she'd handled herself that night. If she is crazy now, she might have been crazy then. No, I can't believe this. Johanna is telling the truth. Kurt was a sadist. He always had a mean, dangerous streak in him."

We arrived at Johanna's, and Isabella opened the gate. "I'll ask her for more details."

When I didn't see any dogs in the yard, I rushed after her, quickly closing the gate behind us. "No, please, don't. We don't want to embarrass her."

"I have to know. She was drunk last night. I want to hear it again when she's sober. I have to know."

She walked so fast ahead of me I could barely keep up. "Why's that suddenly so important? Kurt is dead. It's over."

"Wrong." Isabella stopped, and I nearly ran into her. "If

Kurt was such a sadistic monster, it's plausible Johanna killed him unpremeditated, acting out of despair. This could be an important element for her defense, should she need one."

I gasped. We stood in the driveway and stared at each other.

"I mean," Isabella said, "if they find out that the skeleton is Kurt and then accuse her of faking the hunting accident to cover her tracks, then at least we have an explanation. It was self defense. We can attest that Kurt was a really bad number, but to do that convincingly, we have to hear the truth from her."

I couldn't believe my ears. Isabella was constructing a scenario in which Johanna could justify a crime she had not committed.

Isabella was calling out to Johanna, but then we realized her car wasn't there.

"Maybe she drove to our motel," I suggested. "A different way than we walked. Maybe she had to do some shopping."

"Okay, let's go back to the motel, and if she isn't there, we go to the pub and have a cold beer."

"Are you mad? It's only afternoon."

"We'll find Johanna there," Isabella said. "Don't underestimate that guy behind the bar. Something is in the air with those two. I bet Johanna will show up this afternoon if she isn't there already."

40

JOHANNA

The pub was empty when I got there. The lunch crowd had gone, but John was still behind the counter, cleaning up. I could barely hold it together until I reached one of the small, round pub tables. I sat down, slumped forward, put my face in my crossed arms, and cried my heart out. Within seconds, John came over, sat down next to me, placed his arm over my back and patted my shoulders.

"Hangover can't be that bad," he said.

I sniffled into my elbow.

"Do you want to tell me what's wrong?"

"It's Ben," I said between sobs. "I had to put him down. He was in bad shape this morning—didn't eat and could hardly get up, so I took him to the vet, and then…and now…now he's gone."

"I'm so sorry."

John kept talking in a soothing voice, stroking my back until I calmed down enough to straighten up. His hand lingered on my body, and I could feel his warmth through my thin T-shirt.

"I have Tiger in the car," I said. "Can you take care of him?"

"Sure. Take as long as you need."

He thought I needed to be without a dog for a few hours

or days, but that wasn't what I meant. "It might be forever. I'm going to Sydney, and I may never come back."

He dropped his hand.

"It's a long story," I said.

"I have time."

I finally opened up to him and told him about Kurt and my life with my sadistic husband. I didn't hold back on any of the sordid details. I described the dreadful night he raped Isabella and all that followed after that. John let me talk, not interrupting me once. I was just about ready to explain my decision to go to Sydney when we were startled by a loud bang at the door.

"Damn it." John got up and went to the entrance. "I know my customers. They won't go away if they see my car parked outside."

He opened the door, and I saw Eva and Isabella standing outside in the afternoon sun. "Let them in," I said.

The three of them came back to the table.

"We've been looking all over for you," Isabella said with an accusing undertone.

"You've been crying," Eva said. "What's wrong?"

That set me off again.

"It's Ben, her dog," John said. "He's dead."

"How sad," Eva said. "We are sorry for your loss."

Isabella nodded quickly. "Yes. Right. But you've still got the other one."

I felt like throttling her and bawled again.

"That's just it," John said to her. "She's here to drop Tiger off. She has to go down to Sydney."

"What the hell do you want there?" Isabella asked sharply.

I still couldn't speak. John gave her a stern look and said, "Take it easy, Isabella. Johanna told me everything. I know your secret." When he saw the shock in Eva and Isabella's faces, he toned down his voice. "Don't worry, it is safe with me, but I still don't know why she needs to go to Sydney."

Eva stumbled over her own words. "What has she...I mean, did she really tell you everything? Like, everything?"

"I know how Kurt died and I know you're afraid your lies might surface now that he's been found."

Isabella jumped at me, clawing her hands into my shoulders and shaking me. "Are you mad? What on earth drove you to tell him?"

Her violent reaction got me out of my stupor. "We can trust John." My voice was still laden with misery.

"Oh, really?"

"Calm down," Eva said to her. "I'm sure Johanna is right."

"Like hell we can." Isabella glared at John. "Trust a pub owner? That's hilarious. At the next raunchy night he won't be able to resist spreading such a juicy secret. You must be out of your mind, Johanna. How can you be so naive?"

John didn't seem to mind her insult, but I got angry. "Shut up, Isabella. You are the naive one. You think you know better, and you open your big mouth about things you don't comprehend at all. You've always been pretentious and arrogant. Get off your ego trip and understand that you know nothing. You're trying to make me shut up, but it's you who should shut up and listen."

Isabella drew in a sharp breath. "What shall I listen to? To you insisting that we blab to all your friends? We might as well book a newspaper announcement, here and in Sydney, titled 'Johanna Strobel lied'. She never drove her husband to his hunt. He was already dead when she and her German friend supposedly said goodbye to him. Aren't you the one who asked Eva to confirm your statement to the police? Whatever game you're playing now and whomever you want to draw into it, I'm not playing. Leave me out of that shit you're stirring up."

I gasped. What did Isabella store in her memory? Did she really not recall how Kurt had died?

"Things have changed," I said. "We are past protecting each other."

"All you're after is to protect yourself," Isabella said, calmer now. "Eva, can't you talk some sense into her?"

Eva's eyes grew large. "Me? What can I do?"

"Ask her why she wants to go to Sydney."

I didn't wait for Eva to ask me. "Ben is dead."

John understood faster than my friends. "Do you need help burying him?"

"No, I'll do that later today, before I pack up. I need to do it alone."

"What's that got to do with you going to Sydney?" Isabella asked.

"I'm planning to bring Kurt's remains back. Ben's passing made me realize I won't find peace until they are buried."

"But why now?" Eva asked. "After so many years?"

"I never found any peace in all those years," I said. "Did you?"

I didn't expect an answer. Eva and Isabella suddenly looked very glum. It proved to me that neither had been able to lead a carefree, untroubled life. How many hours have I lain awake, searching the wall for the shadowy presence of Kurt? How often has Kurt visited me in a recurring nightmare in the depth of the night?

John tried to bring us back from brooding over what had been. "I think it wouldn't hurt to go back to Sydney to find out what the police know and what they plan to do with the skeleton. The three of you should do that together. There's no point in speculating what this case is all about."

Isabella smirked. "This case? Really? What do you know about this case? Do you expect us to walk into the Sydney police station and say, 'Hi guys, here we are. We only came to check up on this skull with a hole in it. You see, somebody told you a little lie thirty years ago. We need to tweak our story a little but before we do so, we want to hear what you've discovered.' That's what you're suggesting, right, John?"

Although Isabella stared at John, I felt compelled to answer. "And what exactly are we keeping a secret, Isabella? What happened to Kurt? What should we hide from the police?"

The air stood still. Everybody stopped breathing. How will she reply to that?

Isabella hesitated only briefly. "Johanna, I have no idea. And I don't want to know. I don't even know what made me want to visit you. Why the hell did I come back to Australia after all these years?"

That hit me hard. She looked so confused. I couldn't confront her with the truth. Not now. Not yet. "Maybe John is right. We should go to Sydney together and find out what we can, but without barging into the police station and demanding answers, Isabella. Somebody must know something. I'm from Lightning Ridge. I could pretend I'm representing the miner's museum."

Eva cheered up. "We'll be together when the truth comes out. We can deal with it together."

Both of us looked at Isabella.

"All right," she said. "If it makes you happy. Eva and I need to go back anyway, so no harm if you come along, Johanna, but we can't leave today. I don't know about you, but Eva and I had a hell of a hangover this morning, and we're not up to driving."

"That seals it." John stood. "Four beers coming up."

"I better make room, then," Isabella said and went to the toilet.

Eva and I were alone. I whispered to make sure only she could hear me. "It's a long drive. We should use it to make Isabella understand what she did."

John came back and placed the bottles in front of us before Eva could answer. "Johanna, you don't have to worry about Tiger. I'll take good care of him."

"I know you will. He would be so happy now that he doesn't have to compete with Ben."

"He'll enjoy it when you get back."

"It could be a long time."

"It won't be," he said.

I wished I could share his conviction.

41

I had to lean on my shovel until I got my breathing under control. Sweat, mixed with tears, ran down my face. Standing next to the open grave, I stared down at the lifeless gray bundle that used to be Ben. I couldn't quite bring myself to throw earth on it.

Ben had been by my side for so many years, loyal as only a dog can be—the only true companion I'd ever known. To lose him brought me to my knees, literally. I sank onto the dirt heap, overcome by a wave of pain. The finality of saying goodbye to this wonderful creature was more than I could handle. My whole body shut down, and even my tears stopped flowing. How could grief be so excruciating? I couldn't remember ever mourning a human being with such intensity. Have I ever loved a human being as totally and unconditionally as I loved Ben? Kurt? Didn't I love him like this, at least in the beginning?

All blood left my head, making me dizzy. I put my head between my knees. Everything twirled around inside my brain. The grave below me. He was in there. Ben. Or was it Kurt beckoning me to join him in the hole? *Don't go. Look up.* The sky twirled above me, then tipped upside down. I slipped into the mud or into the sky. Time shifted. I was in the grave, or was it the mine? Kurt was there. Panic gripped me. I was alone with Kurt. No, no, it couldn't be. I wasn't alone. I could hear a voice.

Eva looked down on me and extended her hand to help me up, pulling me back into the present. My knees were shaking and I had to sit down on the dirt. Eva sat down next to me, and we both looked into Ben's grave.

"I know what's going through your mind," she said. "You're wondering if we did the right thing. Stop punishing yourself. We knew the moment Isabella came back from the mine, so distraught and covered in blood, that she had killed him. He tried to rape her and she fought back and killed him. It was an accident. Our decision to protect her was the right one."

I lifted myself off the ground and wiped my hands on my jeans. "It was right then, but is it right now?"

Eva took my elbow. "Come back to the house. We can think about it there."

"Is that why you came?"

"Isabella is still at the motel. She wanted to take another nap and will come over later. I didn't want you to be alone."

She tried to pull me along but I stiffened. "Let me fill in Ben's grave first."

"I'll help you."

Together, we worked in the afternoon heat, shovelling dirt into a hole, same as thirty years ago. When our task was completed, I decorated the mound with a potted plant. We stood in silence until Eva was compelled to express her own doubts. "In years past, I often wondered if it would have been better to tell the truth, but then I thought about the consequences and how terribly embarrassing it would have been for her, and for you, considering he was your husband."

"Kurt deserved to die," I said.

Eva put her arm around my waist, and we walked back to the house. We sat with our tea mugs at the kitchen table. I pondered over the doubts she had expressed. "You said it was embarrassing for her and for me, and you are right. We were ashamed to tell the truth. We felt guilty, like what happened was our fault. Deep inside, we were worried how it would look and how Uwe or Dieter would react."

"Uwe would have sided with Kurt. He would have assumed Isabella seduced him and then rejected him."

"And Dieter would have thought exactly the same. He would never have forgiven her and would have treated her with a mixture of pity, curiosity and blame, turning their marriage into a living hell. And both men, along with the rest of the world, would have considered me guilty, too. What kind of guy needs to lay hands on another man's wife if he gets what he needs at home?"

"I guess so." Eva poured us more tea.

"No question about it," I said. "The funny thing is, once we came to Lightning Ridge, I never refused Kurt. I always had this fear in the back of my mind that he would defile other women. I truly tried to be a wife to him, but his needs became more and more complicated and degrading. No humiliation was enough to satisfy him. I was terrified of what he would do to me and to others if I objected. Once you are in that cycle of pain and shame, you can't find your way out."

Eva exhaled slowly. She must have held her breath listening to me. "Did he hurt you badly?" she asked.

"Not so much physically. He didn't have to beat me into submission. I was terrified of what he would do if I didn't obey. He enjoyed playing with my fears, though. He kept me tied up in dark places and made me work until I broke down from exhaustion. Down in the mine, I was his slave. He played out his sick fantasies there but never above ground."

I drank some tea and tried to push the memories back into their old locked-up place, but I had opened the gate.

"I could never escape him because he didn't let me out of his sight for longer than the time it took him to drink his beer in the pub, and even then, he watched me through the window. That was his real reason to live in Lightning Ridge. Of course, he was intrigued by the idea of getting rich by mining opals, but mostly, he craved the power he felt when he dominated me. He would not have been able to hide such cravings in a city—not forever, anyway. He needed the solitude of country life, and preferably a location where nobody checked up on me. A mine. It was like a revelation to him. I saw it in his eyes the first time we went underground. I just didn't know how bad it would get. I was already broken when he brought me here, but in Sydney I might have found the courage one day to stand up to him. Here, he controlled me so completely that I lived in constant fear of dying an unimaginably horrible death in the mine. I knew he had it in him."

Eva seemed to remember our passage to Australia. "It was him who beat you up so badly on that ship, wasn't it? When we found you on deck, you said you had fallen."

"I believed that myself for a long time," I said.

Eva's expression reflected her confusion. "If I had known how cruel Kurt really was..."

"Then what?"

"Then I would have felt a lot less remorse when we buried him like an animal."

"Nonsense," I said. "You felt all sorts of emotions, but empathy for Kurt wasn't one of them."

"I felt so sorry for Isabella."

"And here, we have the reason why we decided to protect her. What Kurt had done to her was bad enough, but to then report it and expose her to the media and the whole nasty circus of a court case seemed like additional punishment, and it wouldn't have changed anything."

"What has changed now? Why do you want to go to Sydney?"

"Because times have changed and I have changed, Eva." I hesitated briefly. "I'm not ashamed anymore."

"But Isabella hasn't changed." Eva leaned into me. "She still doesn't remember. Aren't you worried she won't be able to handle the truth? It's not just about us."

"No, it isn't," I said. "It's all about Isabella. About me protecting her."

"I don't get it."

Looking for the right words to explain the burden of my thirty-year-old guilt, I thought back to when Kurt had mumbled about seeing Isabella kissing a stranger. "Kurt tried to blackmail Isabella. I knew why and should have warned her, but I did nothing to stop it."

Eva looked puzzled. "You knew what?"

"She had an affair with her boss, and Kurt found out about it."

"So she didn't lie," Eva said. "She told me only this morning."

Somehow that made me feel better. "So it's true. I was never one hundred percent sure."

"Forgive me, but I don't follow."

I took a deep breath. "Kurt bragged that he would take advantage of his knowledge, meaning he'd use her like he used me. By then, I was more than familiar with his perversions, and I feared for Isabella. I should have warned her, but I was too much of a coward. Kurt was able to rape her only because she didn't know what he was capable of. She went to the mine totally oblivious of the danger Kurt posed. He wasn't exactly her friend, but she trusted him enough to take care of her. I spent a large part of my life in this godforsaken mine because of that."

Eva's expression was full of compassion, but I didn't want to be pitied. "To carry on living here after Kurt was gone was my choice. The mine didn't let go of me. To keep working down there was my punishment and my reward, my prison and my freedom. We buried Kurt on the abandoned claim next to my mine. When I realized the danger of him being found by somebody who would take out a new claim on this mine, I paid the annual fee for it. Just for a year, I thought. Then his body would have rotted away, and I could leave my mine, and him, for good. But that year, I found enough to make a living, so I stayed another year, and paid for another year. And another. The damn mine didn't want to let me go. I got used to living in this place and could afford to buy this house and tend the garden. I had Ben, my weekly pub visits, and the occasional excitement of finding a decent crop of stones. Mining is a drug. You can't stop as long as the mine yields something. And my mine does—not much, but enough to keep me going."

"Like an addict?"

"That wasn't the only thing that kept me going. To be honest, I wanted to prove a point. Imagine the satisfaction I would have felt if I'd struck it rich in Kurt's mine." I let my scorn out with a deep breath. "But ultimately, the mine was the same mistake as my marriage—what she gave me wasn't worth the effort I put in. It cost me the best years of my life. I'm done, Eva. There is nothing left for me but to go to Sydney and confess that I killed Kurt. I will tell them it was self defense. Maybe they'll believe me, and maybe they won't. I will take responsibility for all my mistakes."

"You want to do that? For Isabella?"

I shrugged. For Isabella. For myself. What did it matter?

Eva was shocked. "You can't do that. You shouldn't. You can't just give up everything."

"Look around you. What do I have to lose? The house is worth a bit of money, but I still have a mortgage to service. I have no savings to fall back on. The mine has been worked over to the point it won't support me any longer, and I'm too long out of my profession to get a job as a nurse. I have no partner in life, no insurance, and no pension." My laughter came up dry and dark. "Three warm meals and a bed is the best I can hope for. I hear they don't charge lodging in prison."

Eva started to cry. "There must be another way. You are depressed because of Ben. You can't make decisions in this condition. Isabella will show up soon. We'll talk it over then."

I hit the tabletop with my fist. "Don't you dare mention

my decision to her."

"But why not?"

Why not? Didn't she remember the condition Isabella was in the morning after the rape? I had to protect her then, and I needed to protect her now. Without me, she would not have been in that condition. "Enough. My decision is final. I will go to the police in Sydney."

"What about us?"

"Make sure Isabella flies back to Germany as soon as we get to Sydney. She'll never know."

"And me? What am I supposed to do?" Eva wiped the tears off her cheeks. "I helped you bury him. I covered for you. They will book me as an accessory to whatever they charge you with."

I hadn't thought all consequences through until now but my course of action became clearer with every argument Eva brought forward. "I will not incriminate you. I will not say that you were there when we buried him."

"But I said in my statement that I saw Kurt before you drove him into the bush to go hunting."

"Of course you did. When I came back, you never suspected I had killed my husband."

She mulled over it. "It doesn't make sense. He wasn't killed on the hunt. He was found in a mining area. Nobody hunts there. They will know I lied."

"I lied to you. I needed an alibi. We were young and we were close friends, so you never questioned what I told you."

She bit her lip. "One thing will derail your plan."

"And that is?"

"Isabella. She won't allow you to sacrifice yourself for

her."

"What did I tell you? She'll fly back home and will never know." Eva didn't seem convinced. "Even if she finds out what I said, she'll believe every word of it. It'll make sense to her. She has so totally repressed all memory of beating Kurt to death."

Eva gasped. "Are you sure she doesn't remember?"

"Stop it. She doesn't remember. Me taking responsibility for his death is the best thing for all of us." I could see the future clearly now. I would do a few years for something I had not done to pay for the mistakes I had made in my life. This balance of guilt and penance made me light-headed in its simplicity. "Go back to the motel. Tell Isabella not to bother to come over later. We leave tomorrow, and I need to take care of a few things to get ready for our trip."

I was preparing to finally change the course of my miserable life.

42

By nine o'clock, I had cleaned out the fridge, defrosted the freezer, given the rest of my groceries to my neighbour, tidied up so the realtor could show the house to potential buyers, and packed my bags for my one-way journey to Sydney.

My few personal belongings were stowed in a cardboard box which I planned to leave at John's doorstep before leaving the town that had been my home for so many years. It would make him think I might come back until he figured out its contents meant nothing and could be chucked away. I sealed the box and prepared instructions for him to have my water and telephone disconnected. I placed the note together with my last invoices for his reference in an envelope. The next morning, I'd add my house key and the rest of my meager savings I got from the bank earlier today. I didn't want to owe him anything. Tiger was still young. John would have to look after him for a long time.

To disappear at dawn without seeing him or Tiger again was the coward's way out, but I couldn't handle the farewell.

Ben's death had collapsed my carefully constructed life. Without my old companion, I could see the emptiness of my existence. I had made a terrible mistake staying for so long in this town, working the mine. I should have gone back to Germany like Isabella or back to Sydney like Eva after Kurt's death and built a new life for myself with a new partner, a new meaning, and a new chance.

I heard a knock on the door. My heart rate increased. John? Please, don't let it be him. I wanted to see him, but I dreaded the inevitable pain of saying goodbye.

"Surprise." Mira stood in front of the door, a six-pack dangling from her left hand. She noticed my consternation. "Aren't you happy to see me?"

"I thought you were in Brisbane?" I stepped aside to let her in.

Mira noticed the packed box and my luggage. "Going somewhere?"

"How much time do you have?"

"All night." She sat down, opened two beer cans, and handed me one. "I just got back from Brisbane and went straight to the pub. John told me you wouldn't be coming tonight, and he was kind enough to give me these." She lifted her can. "Said you might be thirsty. A very wise man."

I ignored her last remark. "Who starts?"

"With what?"

"With our exchange of news," I said. "My story will be a bit longer, so you start. John told me your husband wants a divorce."

Mira beamed. If this life change upset her, it didn't show. "The miserable little toad has officially entered his third spring. Blinded by love for his child bride, he paid me half of his hidden investment fund to make sure I wouldn't cause any trouble that might delay the wedding. I did pressure him a touch, pointing out that I knew all about his stash and that I would inform the tax department if he didn't bribe me. The whole situation was so ridiculous and embarrassing I decided to leave Brisbane as soon as he paid up." She took a long sip, emptying her can. "And here I am."

"And here you are. Congratulations." I opened another can for her. "What will you do now? Go on to Sydney or back to Brisbane?"

"Neither. I'm staying here until the divorce is final, which could be in a few weeks' time already. Then I'll go back, but only long enough to pack up and come to Lightning Ridge for good."

I gasped.

Mira grinned. "I knew that would blow your mind. But hold on. It gets even better. I will invest my hard-earned share of his illicit wealth in one of those giant monster machines, and we will start mining in earnest. Yes, you heard me right, I said we. You and me—we will finally belong to the big league! We've got two decent mines, and we'll suck them dry until there isn't a tiny nobby left in them."

"How can you…why me…what made you…?" I couldn't formulate the storm of emotions running through me.

"I've thought it through very carefully. You know everything about mining, you are tough and persevering, and you love digging. You are the ideal partner for my endeavor." Mira stopped talking when she saw my tears. "Oh please, don't. I can't handle crying women."

I wiped over my moist eyes. This was more than I could bear. Why did fate have to be so cruel and kick me in the gut when I was already lying on the floor?

Mira interpreted my tears wrongly. "There is no need for misplaced gratitude. I need you more than you need me. We'll have such fun together, and we'll strike it rich. I can feel it in my bones."

"Stop it." I couldn't take any more. "I'm so sorry, but you can't include me in your plans. It's over for me."

Mira gave me a moment. She knew I had to collect myself before I could explain.

I admitted everything, beginning with the day I met Kurt—how I fell in love, emigrated with him, met our friends on the ship, and shared our first years in Sydney. I told her how the abuse escalated after we arrived in Lightning Ridge and how I didn't warn Isabella. I told her about him raping her and how she accidentally killed him while defending herself. I told Mira everything, even how I went with Eva to the mine to bury his body and how Isabella had lost her memory.

Aside from John, Mira was only the second person who had heard the whole story. I was surprised how easy it was for me to tell her. I felt light as never before.

"Do you understand now why I have to go to Sydney and confess?" I asked.

"You think the truth will destroy Isabella and you believe this penance will free you from your horrible past."

I nodded, overcome with gratitude.

"Are you sure? This sacrifice would be a shame if you are wrong."

"Until a few moments ago, I didn't think it was a sacrifice at all. I was convinced my future wasn't worth much. Your offer makes me so sad because I would have loved to dig for opals with you, but it's too late now."

43

ISABELLA

We picked up Johanna at six in the morning. Eva was still not fully awake, so I took the wheel for the first leg of our journey. We loaded Johanna's suitcase and a large box into Eva's Explorer, and drove through the deserted streets of Lightning Ridge to the pub.

The sun came up, painting the town in a soft, warm light. Birds were singing in the trees lining the main drag. Such a damn idyllic setting.

Johanna placed the box in front of the pub's locked door, got back in the car, and off we went. I watched her in the rear view mirror settle in the back seat, looking forlorn and distant. She stared out the window until we were past the town's border, then she closed her eyes and seemed to drift off. Eva dozed next to me.

About fifty kilometers later, I decided to wake them. "I checked the route this morning. We can go south, the direct way via Bathurst, over the Blue Mountains, or we can go north first, via Brisbane, up to Surfers Paradise, and then down south again."

"That's a huge detour," Eva mumbled.

"It'll take us longer but it's a much nicer route. If we keep driving, we can make it to the coast today. Then, we'll drive south along the coast and check out Byron Bay, Ballina, and

Coffs Harbour along the way."

"Sounds great, but won't it take forever?"

"Three days should do it," I said, glancing back at Johanna. She was listening, I could tell. "We're not in a hurry, are we?"

"I'm not. I've still got this week off." Eva straightened in her seat and turned back to look at Johanna. "What about you?"

"Time is not the issue," Johanna said without opening her eyes. "Three days of driving means three nights in hotels. Those tourist hot spots you mentioned are pricey, and I can't afford that."

We arrived at the junction. Decision time. I stopped the car. "I'm inviting both of you. My treat."

"We couldn't—" Eva started.

"Once we get to Sydney, I'm staying at your place until I leave. It's only fair I pay for you now."

Johanna's head moved higher. I could see her face, calm and indifferent. "But you didn't stay at my place in Lightning Ridge. You don't owe me anything."

"Who cares? You can invite me for a drink whenever you want."

"I don't know," Eva said. "Do you really want that?"

"Sure," I said.

"I don't mean you. I mean Johanna." Eva leaned over her headrest. "Johanna, don't you think you should tell Isabella what you're planning to do once we get to Sydney?"

"Hold that thought," I said. "I don't want to know anything that will disturb our perfect little holiday." God. Those two. Can't they just relax and enjoy themselves? "Johanna, have you ever been to Surfers Paradise?"

"I've never been farther than Moree."

"And you, Eva?"

"I'm ashamed to say never farther north than Newcastle."

I put the car in first gear. "It's settled then. The weather is great, traffic is next to zero, we've got a decent car"—I winked at Eva—"and we are three attractive ladies taking a well-deserved excursion. Agreed?"

Eva threw a look at Johanna and said, "I guess a few days won't matter."

Johanna shrugged. "Sydney can wait. Let's do these last days together."

We reached Surfers Paradise at dusk. I saw a Marriott Hotel sign down the highway and turned into the rather impressive, perfectly manicured driveway. I told the others to wait and went to check if the hotel had three rooms available.

Ten minutes later, I opened the driver door again. "Final stop for today, ladies. I got us three rooms, all of them with an ocean view."

"Was it expensive?" Eva asked.

I grinned. "Cost me a fortune, but I figure I've got enough left on my credit card to treat you guys to the sea-dream buffet in their dining room. I suggest we all go to our rooms, freshen up, and meet there in an hour."

The bellboy was waiting to unload our luggage. Johanna got out of the car, grabbed her suitcase, and thanked him. "Don't count me in," she said to me. "I have nothing to wear for such a fancy place."

"You packed fresh jeans?"

"Yep."

"And a clean blouse. Maybe a white one?"

"Light blue."

"Done. Come to my room after your shower. I've got enough earrings, necklaces, and scarves to doll you up."

I slipped the head waiter twenty dollars, and we got a wonderful table next to the floor to ceiling glass front separating us from the swell of the ocean at our feet. Johanna looked nice. Eva had insisted she put a touch of pink on her lips to accentuate the blue blouse, and my bold necklace of lapis pearls and gold strands with matching dangling earrings detracted from her jeans and sneakers.

Eva was dressed in her usual, pretty, homely way. I looked around. Even though all three of us were decently dressed and good-looking, we were still underdressed for this posh restaurant. I suddenly missed my crowd of Munich friends who shared my desire for the little luxuries in life. Time to go home soon.

Another waiter appeared out of nowhere, opened the bottle of white wine I had ordered, and poured it for us. I raised my glass, feeling instantly serene. "To the future."

Eva looked at Johanna as if she needed reassurance. Only when Johanna raised her glass, too, did Eva sip on hers.

We picked our food from the spectacular buffet and chatted throughout dinner, making several trips to the buffet table. Finally, it was time for dessert and we sat in front of our plates, picking at the pretty offerings the pastry chef had come up with.

"I've had it," Eva said, pushing her plate away.

"Then let's stick to drinking." I waved to the waiter for another bottle of wine. "It's too early to go to bed."

Johanna had hardly contributed to our lighthearted dinner conversation. I remembered that she'd never been one for long, drawn out storytelling like Eva, so it surprised me when she said, "It may not be much fun, but I agree. We should stay and talk." She cocked her head, looking at me.

"What exactly do you want to know?" I asked.

"Did you ever regret going back to Germany?"

The waiter came with the second bottle. When my glass was filled again, I leaned back. "No, not really. In the beginning, maybe. Everything seemed so small and provincial after my Australian adventure. My Italian super-macho brothers were the biggest problem. They wanted me to remarry as quickly as possible. They had been hopping mad when Dieter took me to Australia, but that he then kicked me out and sent me back home was unacceptable. Damaged goods, you know. Their little sister needed protection from a second Dieter disaster. I couldn't even go to the market without brotherly supervision. God, you have no idea what suitors they came up with!"

Eva laughed. "How did you escape them?"

Even Johanna smiled. "I bet you gave them all a hard time."

"Not the first few months. I was too upset by the failure of my marriage and my life and had to find my balance again. I considered myself a total loser."

"I can understand that," Eva said, all serious again. "I wanted to leave Uwe and go back home, but to do so would have been admitting defeat." She let the thought drift. "So, how did you get out from under your family's protective wings?"

"Through hard work. Once I functioned reasonably well again, I applied for a job at a Munich import/export company. With my language skills and previous experience, I had no problem getting employment."

"And I bet this time without the unwanted assistance of a touchy-feely boss," Eva said.

I remembered telling Eva about Hal and nodded. "I had learned my lesson. I should be grateful to those slimy bastards, Dieter and Hal. Nobody would ever fool around with me again. My tough attitude towards being bossed around went over well with our company's clients. They liked me fighting for them to get fast deliveries and efficient service, and my salary soon reflected my hard work. As soon as I could afford a small apartment, I moved out. Finally, I was a free, happy and single." I took a long, gratifying sip. "Australia had been a tough lesson, but an important one for me."

Johanna stared at me like she couldn't quite fathom me in an independent situation. I couldn't blame her. "Did you ever meet up with Dieter again?"

"Never. One of my brothers checked up on him and told me he lives in America now. That's all I know."

"What's he doing there?"

"No idea. I told my brother to stop looking."

I saw doubt in Johanna's expression. "Dieter never contacted you after your divorce?"

I croaked out a laugh. "No, and I didn't contact him either. Too proud, you know, although I still have a few bones to pick with him. He owes me an answer to why he ran off without an explanation, leaving me with nothing."

"Maybe he found out about Hal," Eva mused.

"If he had known, he'd have used it to his advantage. I bet he would have tolerated me sleeping with my boss if that would have given him better paying assignments."

"You could be wrong," Johanna said. "You didn't know him as well as you thought, or you would know why he left you."

Her tone must have been a touch too cold for Eva. As always, she tried to smooth things over. "Isn't that a little unfair to Isabella?"

"Not at all," Johanna said. "Think about it. If Dieter didn't have an inkling of Isabella's affair with Hal, he must have had another reason—one she isn't aware of. We all got blindsided by our precious husbands. Kurt turned out to be very different from the man I met, and you, Eva, got royally cheated by Uwe."

On this subject, Eva's diplomatic streak vanished. "The creep. I still get hopping mad when I think about his rotten lousy two-timing."

I didn't like the serious tone our discussion was taking. Didn't we come here to enjoy a few days as travelling companions? "What's the matter with us? Can't we simply enjoy ourselves, without allowing those shitheads to still ruin our lives after all this time?" When they both nodded at me, I raised my glass for a toast. "Let them have no more power over us."

44

The following day, we continued to drive south after an early breakfast. I hadn't slept well and was feeling a bit low, so I let Johanna drive. None of us seemed to have the energy to start a conversation.

A few quiet hours later, we stopped at an ice cream shop on the beach. The small beach hut with tables and plastic chairs in front stood no more than a few meters back from the ocean at high tide. The sun was already blazing, melting the ice cream in our glass cups but I liked it mushy and milky, so I let it sit for a bit while Eva and Johanna spooned the delicious mix of vanilla and strawberry topped with chocolate sauce into their mouths.

"I had a dream last night," Johanna said, scraping the bottom of her cup. "I was playing with puppies in a green field dotted with buttercups."

"I've never seen those in Australia," Eva said, looking into the distance. "Meadows like we had in Bavaria just don't exist here." She watched a few clouds roll in. "Pity. It's going to rain soon."

I suddenly remembered why I had been so down when I woke up this morning. "You were lucky, Johanna. Flowers and dogs—just what the soul needs, right? I dreamt, too, but my dream was a chaotic muddle of nonsense—nasty, scary stuff."

"Maybe we are on one of those aboriginal dream paths

I read about," Eva said. "Your dream may have a deeper meaning. What did you dream about, Isabella?"

"Come to think of it, I've had the same dream before, several times, way back in Germany, but I haven't dreamt it for so long, I thought I had finally beat it."

"The dream path brought it back?"

"Then we better get off that path. I hate that dream. It takes me all day to shake it."

Johanna didn't seem interested, but Eva was. "Tell us about it."

I stirred my ice cream—it had the right consistency now—and began eating it.

"Oh, come on. You have to tell us."

With rain coming, this could be the last stop for a while where we could sit outdoors. Might as well make the most of it. Plus, I really had to fight the lingering anxiety the dream had evoked in me. Talking about it might help push it into non-memory limbo. "The dream always starts with the fight Dieter and I had when we left Lightning Ridge."

Johanna straightened in her seat and placed the spoon she was holding in her hand back on the table.

"I dream about making my way back to the mine, and I feel the effort it takes so intensely and realistically, as if I were living through it again. Suddenly, there is this dark, winged angel swooping down on me, pressing me into a tight hug. I feel his black feathers turn to lead and tighten around me as I try to escape what I know is a dream. I will myself to alter the dream but this devilish angel keeps me in his grip." I remembered the fear of the dream so well I had to take a deep breath to keep the horror at bay.

"What happens then?" Eva asked.

I tried to collect myself. "Somehow, I manage to wriggle free of the embrace. I fight for air and movement, rotate my arms, and hit something, again and again. With every hit, I wake up more, knowing it is over and I'm safe—until the next time."

Eva leaned forward and stared at me. "And then?"

"Then, nothing. I'm glad I've escaped that stupid nightmare, and I go back to sleep."

Eva turned to Johanna. "What do you make of this?"

Johanna studied her cracked thumbnail. "Well," she said without looking up, "why should Isabella be scared of this dream? She has everything under control, doesn't she? Isn't that what matters to you most, Isabella? You know how to defend yourself, and you are victorious in the end."

I found this response rather weird. "It sounds like you are talking about me rather than my dream, Johanna. Portraying me as a cold-hearted victor. Is that what you mean?"

"Forget it." Johanna stood and looked up. "The rain won't be long now. We should move on."

One hundred kilometers south, we reached Byron Bay in bright sunshine. All the clouds had moved north, taking our subdued mood with them. We saw a sign directing traffic to the lighthouse on the edge of Australia's most eastern point.

"Let's go look," I suggested as I turned.

We parked the car below the cliff where the lighthouse stood and walked the path up to the top of the hill. The cliff became narrower with each step, until the promontory had only enough space for the lighthouse bordered by a white picket fence. The quaint tower was clouded in fine spray rising from the violent waves slamming against the rocks on three sides.

I walked to the edge of the fence and climbed on its lower beam. Strong winds, loaded with water spray, hit my face. When I looked ahead and saw nothing but ocean and sky, I couldn't stop myself from playing out the bow scene in Titanic, opening my arms and yelling into the open space, "I'm the queen of the world."

Eva came up behind me and grabbed my arms when a sudden gust shook the fence.

Her body pressed me against the railing, and I could see the sharp drop in front of me.

"Let her go," Johanna yelled, jumping behind us, grabbing both of us around our waists and jerking us backward so forcefully we all fell on the ground a safe distance from the fence.

I looked at Johanna as we sat up and collected ourselves. She was breathing hard, her face ashen.

"I didn't mean to scare you," Eva said to me.

"You didn't," I said.

Johanna's hands were still shaking. "But it scared me," she said. "It reminded me of a moment on the *Queen Frederica* when Kurt scared me really bad—so bad I thought I'd die." She shivered, locked glances with me, and scrutinized me with eyes so cold I shivered. I thought she wanted to say more, but she pressed her lips together.

"What is it, Johanna?" I asked.

She rolled on her knees and got up with a moan. "This was a bad idea. I want to go on to Sydney."

Eva got up, too, and put her arm around Johanna's

shoulder. "I understand."

I didn't. Why were those two suddenly acting so weird? They'd been secretive ever since we left, and I was getting tired of it. I got up, straightened my clothes, and walked ahead of them to the car.

Five hours later, we arrived in Port Macquarie. Exhausted from the long drive, we checked into the first hotel we could see from the highway—a place called Sails. We hadn't booked, but luckily, they still had one suite available for three guests.

After we showered, we relaxed in the easy chairs by the window, dressed in the white bathrobes the hotel provided, and sipped the champagne I had ordered on arrival.

"I could get used to this," Eva said after the first tiny sip. "But I feel guilty for you spending so much money on us, Isabella. If we keep this up, it'll be a very expensive holiday by the time you go back to Germany."

"It's my first long break in twenty years, so what the hell," I said.

"You couldn't afford one," Eva said, matter-of-factly.

"I could have, but somehow, I never gave myself time off. Too many things to take care of, even in the week between Christmas and New Year's. The office and clients always took priority."

"What made you change your mind this time?" Johanna asked. "Why come to Australia now?"

"It wasn't a conscious decision, more of a gut feeling. One morning, I read in the papers about the Commonwealth Games in Sydney, and an hour later, I had booked my trip.

Until then, I had never thought about my Australian past, but after that, I couldn't get this nagging feeling out of my mind that the trip was important."

"Maybe you realized you have to face old demons?" Eva said.

"I beg your pardon?" What was that supposed to mean? I stared at Eva until she broke her gaze and concentrated on her champagne.

"Uh, I'm not sure," she mumbled into her glass.

"Eva is being kind," Johanna said. "She wants you to think back to that night thirty years ago when you came back from the mine, but she doesn't dare say so."

"Why? I remember that night very well."

Eva took a quick breath. "But only parts of it."

Eva and Johanna exchanged another deep glance. I'd had enough. "What on earth are you two talking about? You've been acting like conspirators since we left Lightning Ridge. Do you think I haven't noticed your sideways glances, and the hints and insinuations directed at me? And the coldness you've shown toward me, Johanna. I'm getting really tired of all this nonsense. Come on. Out with it. Don't hold back on account of upsetting my tender soul."

The room grew quiet. A weird foreboding of doom gripped me. I shook it off. "I insist. I want to know."

Johanna leaned back in her easy chair and studied the ceiling for a long minute. I didn't interrupt her effort to collect her thoughts. "You are right, Isabella," she said after a long moment of silence. "I am cold toward you. And you are also right to think it isn't fair. I begrudge you something that isn't your fault, but it is easier for me to secretly accuse you than to admit my own wrongdoing."

"Exactly," Eva said. "Johanna has to tell you something."

Johanna looked at her watch, then back at me. "It's past eight already. Let's go to the bar before dinner and continue our conversation there."

I shook my head. "I normally never say no to a bar, but this is ridiculous. Just come out with whatever is bugging you, and then we'll go drinking."

Johanna stood. "Trust me, what I have to say is best said with people around us."

"Because we risk getting into a heated argument if we stay in this room? You prefer to keep your emotions in check, as always, which is easier in a public surrounding?"

"Correct."

"So be it. I'll go to the bathroom to put my makeup on and give you two a chance to coordinate your stories."

The glance they exchanged when I said this told me I had hit the bull's-eye.

45

JOHANNA

After the bathroom door closed, Eva whispered to me. "Are you serious? Will you finally confront her with the truth?"

I lowered my voice, too, just in case Isabella tried to listen. "No, I'm after something different."

"You have to tell her she killed Kurt and that you are going to Sydney to ruin your life on her account. She has to know. She cannot agree to this."

"Not a chance. My decision stands."

"Then why bother? What is this talk supposed to achieve?"

"I want to find out what she remembers. I need to know."

"Why?"

"I need to know if she has lied to us all these years."

Eva put her hand on her breast and took a long breath. "A few days ago, you were convinced she didn't know anything."

I hesitated and collected my thoughts. "Since then, I have developed doubts—serious doubts. I'll have a lot of time on my hands when I'm in that small prison cell, and I don't want to wonder if I'm there because she tricked me."

Isabella had been so eager to pressure me for clarification, I didn't want to give her time to reconsider. When we were settled in our rattan chairs on the fully enclosed glass patio bar and had ordered our drinks, I asked, "How about you tell us everything you remember?"

Eva drew in a sharp breath but didn't say anything.

Isabella's expression spoke volumes about what she thought of my request. "God knows what good that will do, but I shall humor you. Where do you want me to start?"

"Begin with the morning you, Dieter, and Uwe left."

She described the drive out of town, the fight in the car, her walk through the bush, and her arrival at the mine—everything we already knew.

"And what happened after that," she said when she reached the crucial moment I was interested in, "doesn't need to be repeated. It's too painful for you."

"Go on anyway," I urged.

"If you insist," she continued. "Kurt attacked me, tried to…well, you know…and then I escaped—managed to get into his truck and drive back to you guys. You calmed me down and then I slept. I think I slept the whole next day, and some more. I was so tired I lost track of time. That's all there is to it."

"That's it?" Eva asked. "That's all you remember?"

Isabella squirmed in her seat. "I could elaborate on it, but what for?"

"Let me be the judge of that," I said. "What else do you remember?"

"That I was cold. I remember thinking how cold the mornings in Lightning Ridge could be. I remember my legs and arms getting scratched by the dry bush and being worried about stepping on snakes and getting stung by insects. I remember how scared I was to be alone in the bush, but most of all, I remember how angry I was with Dieter."

"And with Kurt?" Eva probed quietly.

Isabella didn't seem to find this question odd. "I focused all my anger on Dieter. He was the reason I was in this predicament. I still haven't forgiven him for throwing me out of the car. I'm still upset about it, probably because I never had the chance to punish him for his reckless behaviour. I could never show him how truly mad I was at him." Suddenly, she was grinning. "Maybe I should rectify this. I should fly to America and beat the living daylights out of him."

"I'm sure that would help you process the hurt Dieter caused you," I said, "but what about Kurt? Were you never angry with him?"

She looked out at the marina. "So many sailing ships," she said. "Not a single mooring free. I wonder what happens if a storm hits the bay."

"Isabella."

She swung her head back to me. "All right, all right. If you must know—no. No, I can't remember being angry with him. Good Lord, what's the big deal? I was used to men making advances. Kurt's groping was no different."

"Groping is different from rape," Eva said.

"Why? Both are a violation of privacy. In those days, I just shook it off when a guy went a step too far. I'm sure that's how I treated Kurt's attempt to exploit my vulnerability. He tried. He failed. I got away."

"You are still trying to fool yourself." Eva ignored my warning glance. "What exactly happened in the time between your arrival at the mine and your escape?"

Isabella picked at her lower lip. "I told you. Nothing much."

I couldn't hold back any longer. "Did he, or didn't he?"

"What?"

"Rape you."

"Maybe."

"Isabella," Eva said, "there is no maybe. We took care of you when you came back."

"Damn it, Isabella, tell the truth," I said.

She twitched. "Well…it could be that he did…kind of…we were fighting…hard…it could have been that he…injured me. I don't know. It was over so fast. It's not important."

"Do you remember that he raped you?" I asked.

She raised her voice, too. "Yes. Yes. All right. He did. Happy? Now, can we change the subject please?"

I put my hand on her arm and spoke in softer tones again. "I want to know what he did. Give me the details."

"Are you nuts?"

"You can't give me details?"

"Of course I can, but I don't want to talk about it. You are—were—his wife, damn it. I've had it with this conversation."

I smiled at her. "Don't be upset. I know nothing that happened was your fault."

She reacted to my change of tone with immediate curiosity. "Are you saying—"

"I'm saying you don't have a clue what Kurt did to you, and I believe you."

"You thought I was lying?"

"Until you told us that it was over very quickly."

"Sure. It happened so fast, he couldn't do much to me."

I straightened in my seat and could feel Eva doing the same. "No, Isabella," I said. "It was not over quickly. You arrived before lunchtime at the mine, and when you came to my house, it was evening. You spent the whole afternoon at the mine, and you don't recall a single minute of it. If you wanted to lie to me, you would have said you waited for Kurt, you were bored, you went for a walk, or whatever. But you said you arrived there, got attacked, fled, and came to my house."

Isabella picked at her lower lip again. "So?"

"You are missing a few hours, Isabella. You truly don't know what happened in those hours."

46

EVA

The waiter came over and told us our table was ready, so we got our handbags and followed him into the dining room. When he turned to leave after seating us, Isabella, unwilling to wait another second to continue our interrupted conversation, asked for the catch of the day and ordered for the three of us without bothering to consult us, including a bottle of white wine.

She looked over her shoulder to check if anybody was in eavesdropping range and moved her chair a touch closer to the table. "I can't believe I forgot a whole afternoon," she said in a low voice. "You can't tell me I erased several hours from my memory, Johanna. That's impossible."

"You were in shock. It's not only possible, it's very likely. What you experienced at the mine was so traumatic you couldn't process it, so you pushed it away."

Isabella looked so miserable, I felt sorry for her. "You must have gone over that day many times since then," I said. "Did it never occur to you that the whole afternoon between the time you reached the mine and the time you showed up at Johanna's house was unaccounted for?"

"Never." She moved her head gently from side to side, a bewildered expression on her face. "I never thought about the whole incident. Not until today."

"You can't be serious," Johanna burst out. I quickly squeezed her thigh under the table. She got the message and let Isabella carry on.

"Thinking about it now," Isabella said, "and hearing you talk like that gives me a weird feeling. It's hard to describe. It's like my brain is empty, and as much as I try, I can't think of anything to fill it with. I hear your words and it makes sense, but at the same time, I don't know what I'm supposed to do with the information. Do you understand what I'm saying? It's like it's another person, not me, you are talking about."

"You need time," I said. "I can imagine how confusing this must be."

"Did you always suspect that I was at the mine all afternoon?" Isabella asked.

"Of course," Johanna said.

"Why?"

"I knew you had left with the guys in the morning, and you didn't get to my place until evening. When you arrived there, your dress was covered in blood, especially the skirt portion, while the top was torn to shreds. You were all messed up, shaking and shivering. Between sobs, you kept saying stuff like, 'He came after me. I took a hammer. I hit him.' What other conclusion could I draw but that you'd been raped, repeatedly and brutally by Kurt? And I knew from experience that he liked to take his time."

Isabella gasped, as did I. Why couldn't Johanna choose her words more carefully? I stared at her and detected a tiny twitch of her lips. A smile? What was there to smile about? Luckily, the waiter came with our food and gave us all a chance to recover. He asked if he should pour the wine and when Isabella didn't react, I told him to fill our glasses. When he was gone, Isabella grabbed hers as if it were a lifeline and downed it in one gulp, then filled it again. I caught the waiter's surprised look from the corner of my eye but he quickly turned when he noticed I'd seen him.

"Why did you never tell me? Why keep it so secret?" Isabella said.

"Because we wanted to protect you," I said. "We felt sorry for what you had to endure and didn't want to add to your pain." I cleared my throat. "I know now that was wrong. You never got a chance to process what happened to you and that's not healthy and can lead to all sorts of problems."

Isabella lifted her head and looked at me sharply. "Are you implying I've turned into a nutcase because I had no idea what supposedly happened to me?"

"Supposedly?" Johanna asked. I wished she wouldn't sound so sarcastic.

"You never had a chance to work through the trauma," I said.

Isabella bit on her lower lip and shook her head. "No need to go on about this," she said. "I'm not stupid. I understand what you mean, and I appreciate your concern for my well-being, but honestly, I'm fine. No mental breakdown here. I'm perfectly normal."

"That's classic denial," Johanna said.

"And what you are saying is classic bullshit." Isabella's grin was joyless. "Maybe you guys have a problem—with your conscience. Maybe you feel guilty about not reporting the rape. Stop beating yourselves up over it. I don't care. I'll need some time to get used to the idea, but it was so long ago, it's kind of surreal. Just think, you might have done me a favour by keeping it from me."

I was shocked about the degree of her denial. I couldn't let her carry on like this. "You still don't understand the full implications of what we told you."

Isabella's grin froze. "Of course I understand. I was raped. It wasn't my fault and can't be changed. I haven't done anything wrong and I'm not blaming Johanna for doing what she had to do, so stop poking into a wound to make it better. Best to bury the past and get on with our lives."

"We can't bury it." The frustration made my voice loud enough for some heads to turn. I quickly lowered it again. "If you refuse to face the truth, you will ruin Johanna's life."

"Let it be," Johanna said.

"No, I will not." I couldn't let Isabella put the blame on Johanna. "Isabella needs to understand."

"You are not making any sense." Isabella said. "Understand what?"

I took a deep breath. "You are not blaming Johanna for what? For covering up the rape? God Almighty, she's covering up a murder. When Johanna drove to the mine to confront Kurt, he was already dead. After he raped you, you got a hammer and beat him to death, and then you ran away."

All three of us were as white as a sheet. The waiter came to our table and asked if everything was to our liking. None of us had eaten a bite, but we instinctively took our knives and forks and pretended to eat while mumbling that everything was fine.

Isabella was the first to put the cutlery down again as soon as he'd left. She looked at me with pity in her eyes. "Did you really think it was me? All those years, you thought I had killed him?"

"Of course," I said.

Isabella looked at Johanna. "Tell her."

"What?"

"That it wasn't me." When Johanna didn't reply, Isabella carried on. "Truth be told, I don't remember if I was raped or not, but I always knew Kurt ran after me and I ran away from him. That's what I told you, correct?"

"Correct," I said.

"I vaguely remember hitting Kurt with something. I told you it was a hammer?"

I nodded.

"So be it, but I didn't kill him. I hit his arm or his hand, hard enough that he let go so I could escape, but I didn't smash his skull. No way. I didn't kill him."

"How can you be so sure?"

"Because I remember the moment I ran away from him very vividly. He nearly caught up with me. He reached the truck door and tried to open it, so I grabbed something from the passenger seat—I guess that hammer you mentioned—and hit his hand while I pressed the gas pedal down. The truck made a leap forward, and he couldn't hold on to the door handle. I saw him running after me, getting smaller in the rear view mirror. He was very much alive then."

"If that is the case," Johanna said, "you must have been very surprised the next morning when you woke up in my house and I told you he was dead."

"Not at all. I knew immediately what had happened."

"And what was that?" Johanna asked.

"Please, Johanna," Isabella said, "don't act all innocent. You killed him when you went to the mine to look for him. You were mad as hell. You were outraged, insulted, deeply hurt, and humiliated by your husband defiling your close friend. You were so full of hatred and contempt for him, I dare say you had more reasons than my rape to be out for revenge. Living with a macho like Kurt couldn't have been easy. A lot of anger must have built up inside of you, but I always assumed it was an accident. You two had an argument, you lost control of yourself, and boom, you hit him. Unfortunate for him, but he deserved it for the way he treated you on the ship and later." Isabella paused for a second and drank another sip of wine. "That morning, when I woke up, I didn't remember that he had succeeded in raping me, but I did know he was alive when I left him. Because I had reason to run away from him was enough for me to assume you went back to the mine to make him pay for whatever he'd done—to me and to you. I always considered it very noble of you to jump to my defense, even if your underlying reasons had little to with me. I have kept quiet about this unfortunate accident until now, and I can promise you, that's how it will stay."

The waiter arrived again and studied our full plates with a puzzled look.

"All is good," I said quickly, "but we're dealing with a private emergency here, and that ruined our appetite. Please give our apologies to the cook."

He cleared our table without a comment.

Isabella leaned forward and patted Johanna's arm. "You

have nothing to worry about."

Johanna pulled her arm away. "How do you explain the missing hours, Isabella?"

"I can't. And I don't care. I knew Kurt was alive when I left. That's the only thing that matters to me. I'm certain you didn't plan to kill him, but you did. Why don't you admit it? You, and Eva." She turned to me. "You know it, too, right?"

I returned her intense stare. "I should know that Johanna killed him? Don't be ridiculous, Isabella. I know she didn't."

"Excuse me?"

"He was already dead when we got there."

"What kind of proof is that? You weren't there when Johanna went to the mine. You didn't go with her, did you?"

"Of course not. Somebody had to stay with you. You were in bad shape, but Johanna told me…" I hesitated, suddenly aware of the weak link in this explanation. "Johanna, you didn't, did you?"

Johanna put her hand over her heart. "I swear by God, and by everything that is dear to me, that Kurt was dead when I got there."

"But that's not possible," I said. "How could he have died if neither of you did it?"

For a while, we each considered different scenarios.

Johanna kept staring at the tabletop when she broke our silence. "When you came back to the house, Isabella, you admitted you hit him."

"How many times do I have to tell you? I hit his hand on the car door."

"Maybe so, but that's not proof that you didn't hit him again. You must have blocked out this memory, together with the assault and the missing hours. You could have hit him on the head when you realized he hadn't let go."

I thought I detected a moment of doubt flitting over Isabella's face before she said, "Think about it. How could I remember seeing him alive, running after the car, if I had killed him?"

"You can't prove that," Johanna said, and I noticed the same expression of doubt in her face.

"I don't have to prove anything," Isabella said. "You are saying Kurt was dead when you got there, and you can't prove that either."

"So, we don't believe each other," Johanna said. "But humor me and explain one thing. If you thought I killed him, why did you never mention it to me?"

"There was nothing further to discuss, was there? You told me he was dead and that it was an accident. Good enough for me."

Suddenly, I remembered. "She is right," I said to Johanna. "Your exact words were, 'Kurt is dead. It was an accident.' And then, Isabella said to you, 'Then it's better you bury him quickly. Nobody needs to know what happened.'"

Johanna's eyes grew large. "Eva, don't you believe me anymore?"

I felt like bursting into tears. "Damn this. I don't know what to believe. Johanna, think about it. Is it possible that you…I mean, when you rushed out to the mine, full of rage, hurt…let's face it, those are powerful emotions…"

Johanna's shoulders slumped. "I see. It is me now who has to take on the role of angel of revenge. I killed him in a fit of madness?"

"That's exactly what you're accusing me of," Isabella said.

"True," Johanna said.

"Why the hell do you insist on making me the culprit?" Isabella said. "Are you so worried that the truth will come out now that they found the skeleton? Do you need a scapegoat? Are you planning to denounce me once we get to Sydney?"

Johanna withdrew visibly. I could see the hurt Isabella's callous remark caused her and had to interfere. "Quite the opposite, Isabella. Johanna is planning to plead guilty. That's why she came with us. I tried to talk her out of it, but she is adamant. She wants to protect you, Isabella, because she believes that her life is worth a lot less than yours—that she has no future."

47

I didn't get much sleep that night. At 7:00 a.m., I gave up and went to the breakfast room to help myself to more coffee since I had used both coffee filter packs in my room already.

I wasn't overly surprised to see Johanna and Isabella sitting by the window table already, full cups of coffee and no plates in front of them. Their pale faces reflected the condition I was in—overtired, disheveled, and confused. Outside, a brilliant blue sky was mocking us.

"Let's skip breakfast and head on to Sydney," Isabella said after a brief, tense exchange of greetings. What a miserable lot we were.

Half an hour later, we had checked out, stowed out luggage in the car, and driven off. I took the first leg. We only had three hundred seventy kilometers to go, but I was sure I wouldn't last that long.

Isabella fell asleep on the back seat soon after we hit the monotonous drive along Pacific Highway.

"Dead to the world?" I asked after we hadn't heard a sound from her in about ten minutes.

Johanna looked back. "I'd say so," she said in a low tone.

I matched the level of her voice. "Do you think she truly believes you are the guilty one?"

"I'm pretty sure that's what she thinks," whispered Johanna. "She made her point so convincingly I spent half the night wondering if she might be right."

"Same here," I said.

"Terrific."

"I'm sorry."

"Never mind. Your mistrust hurts, but I can understand it. I'm confused myself."

We fell silent again, driving through one of the most spectacular landscapes on earth. Beaches with shiny white sand stretched along the coastal region, embedded in promontories covered with light green reeds.

Sometime later, Isabella sat up and leaned forward, placing her arms on Johanna's seat. "I've been thinking," she said.

I gave it a half-hearted giggle. "Could have fooled me."

"What if you are right?" she asked. "What if I killed Kurt and don't remember? Maybe I fooled myself all those years. How come I never realized that several hours were missing? Where the hell was I in those hours, and what did I do?"

"Don't think about it," Johanna said. "Give yourself some time. Let the memory come back naturally."

"I don't have time." She hesitated. "Johanna, can't you wait before you go to the police? A few more days won't matter."

I loved her suggestion. "Great idea. We can stay at my house and think things over. Steve is still busy with the Commonwealth Games."

That reminded me to call him. We stopped an hour later so Johanna could take over the driver's seat. I went for a little walk and dialled Steve's number. He picked up right away, and I gave him a hurried rundown of the events, finishing with, "Kurt didn't have an accident. Isabella killed him—at least, that's what I always thought—but Isabella thinks Johanna beat him to death, and now they're blaming each other and I don't know what to think."

"Relax," he said. "From what I've heard about this guy so far, he was quite a piece of work—a misogynistic piece of shit. It's usually the wife who kills those guys, so, my money is on Johanna."

"Very helpful," I said.

"Look, I'm pushed for time. We'll discuss it Wednesday when I'm back home."

"What if Johanna goes to the police before then?"

"I can't come home any sooner than that. We are preparing for the closing parade through the city Tuesday." He thought for a second. "Why don't you persuade the girls to come to the parade with you? That might distract Johanna, and we can meet up for dinner afterwards and try and solve the mystery."

Steve always made me feel better. He never thought in problems, only in solutions. I just had to keep Johanna and Isabella at peace with each other for the next two days.

48

JOHANNA

We'd finished a subdued breakfast when John called on Eva's landline. I knew right away who it was and wanted to decline the call but she dropped the phone in my lap and went into the kitchen.

"Hi, Johanna," John said.

I couldn't speak. All I could do was trying to stop the lump in my throat from turning into a flood of tears.

He could feel my sorrow but didn't ask questions and simply kept talking—about Mira taking him into her confidence about my plan, about him understanding what I was trying to do, and even about me leaving without a goodbye. He understood that, he said, because he hated goodbyes, too. All the chances I'd missed and all the things I'd lost made me so unbelievably sad. He ended his loving, tormenting monolog with a promise that he would call again.

I hung up, hoping and dreading that he meant it.

On Tuesday, the three of us left before lunchtime to catch the afternoon ferry from Manly to downtown Sydney. I didn't tell them that I wouldn't join them until we parked Eva's car at the ferry pier.

"Why's that?" Eva asked. "Don't you want to see the parade through downtown?"

"I prefer to spend the day on my own. I need some quiet time."

"Are you sure? What will you do?"

"I'll wander around Manly until I get tired, then I'll take the bus back to Bilgola. I know where you hide your spare key for the house."

Eva dug in her bag and produced her car key. "Here, take the car. We can take a cab back. I don't want you to take the bus, and I feel better when the car isn't parked at the pier all day."

I waited until the ferry docked and gave them a quick wave before I turned and walked along the promenade. I had no desire to do any shopping and had no eye for the beauty of the ocean side. Nothing mattered anymore. My heart felt like a solid rock. I couldn't feel it pumping and couldn't even feel my feet on the pavement, carrying me along without a plan. *This is my last day of freedom. What should I do with it?* What joy was there to sit on a restaurant patio and watch other peoples' purposeful lives? Busy, happy, stressed, sad, bored even—but always full of expectation for what the next day would bring.

My appetite had diminished with the loss of my life's prospects, but I decided to visit one of the street cafes for a final freedom cup, so to speak. After I had ordered, I noticed I was still holding Eva's car key, playing with it subconsciously. When it slipped from my hand and fell on the floor, I picked it up and deposited in my handbag. In it I noticed the St. Christopher medallion I had found only two weeks ago on my claim, and without thinking much, I attached the key to its rusty chain and put it back in my handbag.

An hour later, I was back at the house. A heavy mood had taken hold of my whole body, making me tired. I stretched out on the sofa and tried to slip into a merciful sleep.

The phone rang and I let it ring, but the damn thing wouldn't stop. Suddenly, the thought that something had happened to Eva and Isabella crossed my mind, so I rushed to it, hoping it would continue to ring until I got there.

John answered my breathless hello with a similarly excited, "Thank God, it's you."

I was immediately alarmed. He didn't sound like he wanted to have a gentle chat. This was serious.

"What is it?"

"Bill came to the pub yesterday with Mira. The two of them seemed to have hooked up. They got pretty drunk together, but before Bill was a goner, he told Mira that he got the coroner's report back from Sydney."

"The forensic analysis?"

"That's the one. Mira was holding up like the trooper she is and could remember large chunks of what Bill told her when she came to see me just now."

"And?"

"And, it's much worse than I thought. I was hoping the report would be inconclusive. Johanna, I'm begging you, don't mention Kurt to anybody in Sydney."

I could see the direction this conversation was taking. "So, it's official that the skeleton is a murder victim?"

"It doesn't look like it was an accident. Bill thinks there will be an inquiry into the case, but he also told Mira that it will be extremely difficult to prove anything after such a long time." John took a deep breath. I had been holding my breath, too, and needed to release some of the tension he had projected onto me. After a few seconds, he carried on in a lower, calmer voice. "Mira said they established that the cause of death was a blow to the back of the head, administered by a pointed object. And there is more. They've recovered most of the skeleton. The coroner's report noted the clavicle, several ribs, and the bones in his left hand were smashed, too. Bill assumes your husband didn't stand a chance."

Him calling Kurt my husband hurt like hellfire.

"Sorry," he said. "I mean, Kurt."

I gasped. "Bill mentioned Kurt's name?"

"No, no. So far, nobody has made the connection to him. Bill only spoke of *the victim*. But listen, Johanna, the way it looks, the perpetrator must have attacked the…uh, the victim, from behind. It's not like you assumed. Isabella didn't fight for her life and kill him accidentally. She deliberately battered him with a pointed object until he didn't move anymore. Do you understand what I'm saying?"

"That Isabella is a cold-blooded killer and that she doesn't deserve me going to prison for her?"

"Exactly. She is crazy and dangerous. You never know what such people will do next."

My hand was shaking so badly I had to stabilize it with my other hand. "What kind of pointed object?"

"Huh?"

"You said he was hit with a pointed object."

"A hammer, I guess."

"A hammer is not pointed."

"Who cares?"

"I do."

"Well, Mira might know. She is standing right next to me, insisting with some frantic gestures that I shouldn't hang up. I guess she wants to talk to you."

I waited until he had handed her the phone.

"Hello sweetie, how are you holding up?"

"Can you get me a copy of this report?"

She was taken aback by my abrupt tone. "How the hell would I do that?"

"Please. Can you? It's important."

"Why?"

"Usually, forensics can determine what kind of weapon was used, and I want to know what the coroner means when he calls the weapon a pointed object. A hammer?"

Mira's response came fast enough to make me realize she had pondered the same question. "Bill never specifically mentioned a hammer. Are you thinking that if it wasn't a hammer it couldn't have been Isabella?"

"When she came to the house, she mentioned she used a hammer to defend herself. Even in the state she was in, confused and agitated, she was adamant about that. She couldn't have made up a story. If she had used a pick, she would have said so."

"Oh my God," Mira said, "you believe it could have been you after all."

Mira sure was fast. "A hammer could have been in Kurt's truck. He was always repairing something. But a pick is a valuable mining tool. Kurt never left those lying around, but I knew exactly where he stored them and how to use them."

Mira let a moment of silence pass. I could feel her reluctance to join my blame game.

"I can handle a pick very well," I said, desperate not to lose her. "I have used one a million times. Maybe I went to the mine filled with so much rage I couldn't act rationally. Maybe I saw him lying on the ground, injured from the hammer blow and unable to defend himself. Maybe I could see him recovering, feared he'd go after me, and my mind went blank. I rushed to the storage shed, got the pick, and hit him from behind until he didn't move anymore."

"Jesus, Johanna."

"I liked to believe that it was Isabella, and that she doesn't remember, but now I fear it is me who doesn't remember. I need to know what's in that report—hammer or pick. It'll reveal the truth."

Mira's voice was shaky. "Can't you just forget it? Nothing may come of this inquiry and they won't connect you to it as long as they don't know who the victim is."

"They will find out as soon as they dig into the old files."

"Can't you just leave Australia?"

The thought raced through my mind. Why not disappear? Before they arrest me, I could be God knows where. Back in Germany. Somewhere in Asia. They'd never find me.

"Would you rather end your days in prison?" Mira asked.

"I cannot carry on like this. Thirty years of not allowing myself to think of the past, of burying it so deep, pushing it so far away that I lost myself. I need to face the truth with all its consequences."

49

EVA

The Commonwealth Games' closing parade was a joyful celebration of another successful presentation by my hometown. Yes, home. I had so fully integrated myself into the land Down Under that I was bursting with pride as one decorated parade float after another, filled with waving athletes and volunteers, passed us. All the while, I kept looking for Steve until I finally spotted him near the end of the parade. When he saw me, he jumped off his wagon, rushed over, and gave me a hug and a kiss. I could feel his relief that his hard work was over and his gratitude that I had put up with his absence so patiently.

After he greeted Isabella, he grabbed our hands and dragged us both away from the crowd. We turned off Grosvener Street onto George Street. "Let's go to the Rocks," Steve said. "Stay close to me. If we get separated, we'll meet at the Waterfront restaurant there."

It took us over half an hour to make our way down to the Rocks. We were lucky enough to get the last table on the restaurant's patio, positioned nearly underneath the Harbour Bridge. We had a spectacular view of the Opera House, and both landmarks were lit up in honour of the closing of the games.

Steve ordered and told the waiter we'd start with cocktails.

We didn't want to rush our three course meal and planned to occupy this wonderful table until the ten o'clock ferry at the close by pier would take us back to Manly.

"Now, tell me everything," Steve said when we were served our drinks and could start to relax. "What on earth happened in Lightning Ridge, and why is Johanna not with you?"

I knew I hadn't made much sense on our last phone conversation, so I started to explain but got stuck on some details because Isabella was sitting right there.

"Don't mind me," she said when I stumbled over my words. "I don't care if you think I did it. I'm doubting my own version of events. Johanna got me pretty confused. Those missing hours drive me crazy." Her voice and her glance lost focus, drifting over the heads of restaurant guests around us.

By then, Steve understood most of what I was trying to explain. "You have no memory of the afternoon?" he asked Isabella.

"All that comes to my mind is a dreamlike picture of a dark pipe, made of angel wings."

"Meaning that you were down in the mine?"

"My last memory is of arriving at the mine after a long, hot walk and bending over the manhole and yelling down to see if Kurt was there. Next, I see myself running to his truck, knowing that he is following me. Then, when I reach the truck, I realize full of panic that he's there, too. I start the truck, hit his hand through the open window, and speed off. I have no idea what happened between my arrival at the mine and the scene by the truck."

"Could it be that you went down the manhole to look for Kurt?" I asked.

That startled Isabella. "I remember looking down and calling him, and I think he answered back. Then, I climbed—" She paused for a second, a baffled expression on her face. "Wait a minute. I was gonna say, I climbed *up* the ladder when I realized he was behind me, but that can't be, can it?"

"You remember him chasing you to the truck."

She nodded. "I heard him puffing and grunting behind me like a dangerous animal, but I was faster."

Steve placed his hand over Isabella's. "Don't you think the angel pipe is the manhole?"

"Seems to be," Isabella said. "But it still doesn't make sense to me. I feel a bit like waking up from a dream and knowing what I dreamt, but not being able to describe it. Just now, when you said I was in the mine, I had a vision of it... and that somebody...oh, I don't know. All I remember now is that it was dark."

I placed my hand over hers and Steve's and gave both a gentle squeeze. "Don't try too hard. The answer will come to you eventually."

Steve withdrew his hand. "I don't think so."

Isabella's head shot up, and I tried to stare him into silence.

"Isabella experienced a trauma. She can't deal with it by herself. She needs professional help."

Isabella laughed. "Thanks a bloody lot. I've been to a top notch psychiatrist in Munich every week for years, and where did it get me? He never even asked me about the missing hours. Didn't notice them, I guess."

"Maybe you never gave him an exact timeline?" I asked.

Isabella pondered this, then shook her head. "Didn't interest him. He was much more interested in figuring out why Dieter never asked me about my injuries when I got home from Lightning Ridge."

"To be honest, I'd like to know that, too," Steve said, looking at me. "Didn't he contact you guys to find out where Isabella was?"

"Johanna had no phone. Dieter could have called the pub, but when he didn't, we assumed he was still mad at her and didn't care if she stayed with Johanna for a while," I said. Then, I looked at Isabella. "We kept you in the house for a week, and Johanna took care of your wounds as best as she could. Most scratches were gone by the time we took the train back to Sydney, and you did a good job covering the bruises on your face."

"I can't recall that I was in pain."

"Only because Johanna gave you this strong medication. You were drugged up to your eyeballs."

Steve scratched his chin. "That still doesn't explain why you didn't tell Dieter about the whole mess once you got home. He must have seen what condition you were in."

Isabella gave one of her dry cough laughs again. "No secret there. I didn't get a chance to tell him. The creep ignored me when I came home, never asking me a single question."

Steve and I started to talk at the same time. "That must have hurt you even more," I said, while Steve put it more bluntly. "Why didn't you tell him anyway?"

"I was still mad at him and wanted him to apologize without me prompting. We hardly spoke the following weeks, and then he was gone. He threw away our life together—our marriage—over a fight about the noise of a car radio. At least that's what I thought then."

"But now you suspect that was only a pretext?" Steve asked.

She shrugged her shoulders. "My therapist said I suffer from dissociative amnesia."

"Meaning?" I asked.

"Meaning that a traumatic experience can lead to selective memory loss in an effort to cope with it." She paused. "An experience like a rape, for example."

"I'm afraid we don't have time to wait for your memory to come back," Steve said. "If I understand correctly, Johanna wants to go to the police tomorrow and admit to murdering Kurt."

"And we can't convince her otherwise," I said.

Isabella bit her lip. "They will ask all of us a lot of questions."

"I'm not afraid," I said. "We can only get to the truth if we tell our individual truths, and let them piece it together."

Steve picked up a menu. "Until then, let's enjoy our dinner. I'm starving."

50

ISABELLA

By the time we finally got dessert, we only had fifteen minutes to spare to catch the ten o'clock ferry. I wanted to pay but Steve wouldn't let me and there was no time to argue.

We made a mad dash to the pier, but by the time we got there, they had closed the gate.

"The last one leaves at eleven. We better get that one," Eva said between laboured breaths.

I was a little winded, too. "Stand here for an hour?"

Steve turned away from the gate. "Let's head over to the bar at Bennelong Restaurant. We can see the next ferry come in from there and get back to the dock in time."

That sounded like a good plan. "But only if you let me pay for the drinks."

He laughed. "You'll regret this. They charge an arm and a leg for champagne."

I didn't care about the cost, not on a night when I had to cope with such torn feelings. I still didn't know how we all got ourselves into a situation where Johanna wanted to go to prison for something I might have done but for which I didn't feel any remorse. While every fiber of my being fought the idea that I could have killed Kurt, I also rejected the idea of Johanna being the guilty one.

I signalled to the waiter to pour our champagne and raised my glass. "Steve, Eva, cheers to whatever may come tomorrow," I toasted them, before I downed my glass in one gulp.

Their faces looked instantly sober and I regretted my flippant remark. "It'll work itself out," I said, slipping off the barstool. "Got to go to the loo. Don't let the champagne get warm."

"The ladies room is on the second floor," the waiter called after me. I saw the lift next to the staircase and opted to take it. My legs weren't very steady after all the wine and champagne.

On the way back from the washroom my head was spinning when I got into the lift again. Inside, I had to move close to the row of buttons to see which one to press. As soon as I figured it out, the doors closed. My finger was still on the button when the lights began to flicker. I pressed the button in quick succession. The lift vibrated with a few shakes, like it was trying to set itself in motion, and I moved back to the wall, but then the movement stopped and the lights went out. The space around me went pitch-black. The metal cubicle was sealed like a strong room.

I instantly panicked. I couldn't breathe. My legs gave out under me and I slipped to the floor with my back to the wall. My heart hammered like crazy and I slung my arms around my knees to steady the shake.

I couldn't see or hear and could only feel terror take over my whole being. The nightmare was back. I was back at the mine, at the manhole.

Kurt called up to me. "Come on down. Quickly. I have to show you something. I need your help."

Relief. *He is there. He'll be able to drive me back to Johanna. Damn Dieter.* I placed my foot on the ladder and carefully made my way down, one step at a time. *This damn thing is making a noise like a baby rattle. How old are those anchors that secure it to the earthen wall of the manhole anyway? Can't be trusted.* Going back up crossed my mind but then Kurt called again, reassuring me. "I really need a hand down here," he yelled. The deeper I went, the narrower the space around me got, with the light from above fading fast. *What am I doing climbing into this hellhole right into Satan's maw?* And there he was, standing at the last rung, holding the ladder for me, shining the lamp above his helmet right into my face.

"What do you need me for?" I asked.

He ignored my question. "Where are Uwe and Dieter?"

I began to explain why I was alone but only got as far as telling him that Dieter threw me out of the car.

"You came here all on your own?" His voice was harsh. "Come, I made a sensational find."

To stay where I was would leave me in total darkness, and there were snakes around, for sure. He took a larger flashlight from his pocket and switched it on. I followed his light deeper into the mine, close behind his massive shoulders, which threw a shadow on most parts of the narrow passage. I nearly touched his body.

He turned a corner and stopped. I took a small step back, but he pounced on me with such force he knocked me to the ground. He was on top of me, smelling of sweat, his T-shirt filthy with grease and clay. The air around us was stale and putrid. *I can't breathe. I can't move.* He is too heavy. His hand forced my legs open and I begged, "Don't do this. Please, think of Johanna," until I felt more than his hand. I screamed while he forced me into his frenzied rhythm. No reason left, I choked, then retched. The monster above me panted and spittle dripped on my face.

"Isn't that what you want, you slut? You fuck anybody. I know that. Dieter never gave it to you like that. You need a real man."

His face contorted, he threw his head back and roared with a final rush of brutal shoves. Then, he went limp. *I will suffocate under him.* His wet body covered every inch of me, my face firmly pressed into his arm pit. Before I lost consciousness, he rolled off me, still panting, leaving me lying in a puddle filled with tiny rocks that scratched my back. My dress was soaked in his bodily fluids, the top part torn to shreds.

"To hell with you, you cold bitch," he said, getting up and walking away.

The world went dark around me. My lungs didn't burn anymore and my heart slowed. He was gone. *He left me here to die. I don't want to die.*

Then, I saw a faint glow around the corner and could hear him coming back. Then he was there, a chain in his hand.

"I'll teach you some manners. I'll train you good. Teach you how to treat a real guy, you stuck-up bitch."

Panic swept through me. I lifted my body off the ground but he kicked me down with his boot again.

Oh God, no! He wants to chain me down here, to the peg

next to me, way back from the manhole. Please, dear Lord, no.

He fastened the chain around my left ankle. I could hear the lock closing. He stepped back, threw the key into the darkness behind him, and looked at me wriggling, moaning and crying.

"Please, please, don't do this." I didn't even know if he heard me. He walked away again. That time, I welcomed the darkness, but it didn't last. He came back with a small brown snake in his hand.

"I'll teach you," he said, spreading my legs with his free hand. He knelt between them and started playing with the snake, letting it glide over my naked skin. I tried to scream but only horrified gasps came out. While he dangled the snake over my mouth to force me to close it, he was turned on again. He loved my repulsion and laughed like the madman he was when I tried to twist away from the animal's pointed head.

His stamina was fed by the sadistic nature of this game. I thought it would never end. My body followed my mind into a catatonic state. *I will be stuck in this hell forever, punished for things I have done. I deserve this for cheating on Dieter, sleeping with Hal. I deserve to die for it.*

A voice broke my thoughts. A voice. Far away, but still. *I must yell for help.* "Please. Rescue me." My own voice came out as a faint whisper.

Quickly, Kurt threw the snake away and got up. "Shut up, you bitch," he said and hit me hard on my head. I lost my vision and could hear only muffled sounds. "I'm coming," he called, walking away from me. Then, he was on the ladder. I heard it creaking and imagined feeling the earth move slightly. A sliver of light. I could see light, getting stronger and brighter.

The light flickered a few times and blinded me when I opened my eyes. The vibration was caused by the lift starting up again.

I got off the floor and straightened my skirt. No blood on it. In an instant, I was transported from the mine, wondering how I could have managed to stay sane all those years. Precious seconds passed until the lift reached its destination, but in them, an eternity of suppressed trauma raced through my mind. I finally knew what had happened in the mine, but I needed to remember what had happened after that.

I felt that something very important was still to be discovered, but my mind slammed shut the moment I tried to delve into the hidden truth. Too horrible. Don't think about it.

The lift doors opened. I had survived it yet again.

"What's up with you?" Eva asked when she saw me. "You're as pale as a ghost."

"I'm alive."

"You what?"

"I was a little dizzy, but it's gone."

"And we better get going, too," Steve said. "Don't want to miss the last ferry of the night."

51

My whole body ached. I wondered briefly what I was doing on the sofa in Eva's living room until I remembered that I'd stayed up for one more drink after we got back last night, thinking I wouldn't be able to sleep without knocking myself out. Obviously, I had succeeded in doing so, at least for a few brief hours.

I looked out the window without moving my stiff neck. Outside, an orange ball announced the dawn of another beautiful Sydney morning.

Eva came into the room. "Up already?"

I yawned. "Not in bed yet."

"Ouch." She walked into the kitchen and put the kettle on. "I'm making tea. You want a cup?"

I didn't feel like talking. The episode in the lift flooded back into my mind. I massaged my neck. "No, thanks. I'll try and catch some more sleep."

"Good idea, but this time, go to bed. You'll be a lot more comfortable there," Eva said. "I'm driving Steve over to Homebush. He needs to get the equipment packed and loaded. I'll be back in about two hours."

"Why doesn't he take the car? Saves you having to pick him up again in the evening."

"He'll get a ride home with the company truck. Plus, he wants us to have the car for the day. We should make the most of it. Starting tomorrow, he has a week off, and I'm sure he'll want his car back for that."

Eva noticed I was barely listening.

"Isabella?"

"Huh?"

"I said Steve will be here all week. I don't want to burden him with our problems, so I suggest we sit down with Johanna as soon as I'm back and talk some sense into her."

How long does that give me? Two hours to figure out what happened after Kurt left me in the mine and how to face Johanna. "Sure. I'll tell her when she wakes up."

Fifteen minutes later, I heard the door close behind Steve and Eva and stretched out on the sofa again, trying to sort through the images from the previous night. What was real, and what was schizoid angst? My therapist in Germany had told me my commitment problems were borderline schizoid. My desire to be independent was born out of a strong urge to avoid any type of intimacy with another person. Hogwash to justify his high fees, or so I had thought. But if the horrific re-enactment of the scene in the mine wasn't an exaggerated expression of my anger—if it was what really had happened to me—it wouldn't be surprising if I mistrusted anybody I came in close contact with.

I could feel tears running down my cheeks. Why am I crying? Is this the so-called breakthrough my therapist had hoped for? Am I finally brave enough to face the truth and admit to myself that Kurt raped me—not once, but several times—and tortured me with sadistic pleasure until somebody came, until I heard a voice? But then what?

My mind went blank every time I tried to take the next step in my long-buried memory. It must be hidden there. I must get to it to find closure.

Meanwhile, no matter how hard it would be, I had to tell Johanna. She needed to know at least this part of the truth, and we would have to take it from there.

I heard the bathroom door and then the shower running. Johanna must be up. I got up, went into the bathroom without knocking, and waited until she pulled the shower curtain back.

"Shit!" She took a step back and nearly slipped.

"Sorry. I didn't mean to scare you."

She grabbed a towel from the rack and started to dry herself.

"I need to talk to you."

She scowled. "You look a mess. Did you guys get drunk last night?"

"I slept on the sofa. Kind of."

"I didn't sleep much either."

"Why's that?"

Johanna wrapped the towel around her body and walked past me. "I suggest you take a shower, too. It'll make you human again. When we're both dressed, we'll wake up Eva, have some coffee in the living room, and I tell you all about it."

"Eva is gone," I said, "but she wants us to sit down and talk as soon as she is back. Listen, Johanna, I have to tell you something very serious."

"Me, too."

"About what?"

She raised a finger. "Later. Go take a shower."

By the time I got back into the living room, Johanna had made a large pot of coffee and was sitting on the sofa, leafing through a bundle of fax pages on the coffee table. "Look at that," she said, without lifting her head. "This came in yesterday evening. My friend Mira persuaded Bill to give her a copy of the forensic report. Do you want to know how Kurt died?"

The question hit me like whiplash. I wrapped my arms around my torso to stop myself from shaking.

"Sit down." Johanna patted the seat next to her. "I'll read the important parts to you. They are very interesting."

My knees went soft and I sank into the cushions. All the blood must have drained from my face.

"What's the matter with you?" Johanna put the report down and studied my face. "Don't you want to know?"

I took a deep breath. "Last night, I remembered part of the missing hours. Well, I guess most of them. I was in a lift at the bar we were at when the power went off. I was stuck in the pitch-black by myself and it came back to me without any warning. I remember now what Kurt did to me." I saw her wince. "I remember everything except how I got out of the mine and how Kurt died. I have to assume that I killed him, and now you announce that the report states how he was killed." I paused and took another deep breath. "And you ask me if I don't want to know? God Almighty, of course I want to know. I need to know." Tears welled up, and I wiped them with the back of my hand.

Johanna handed me a tissue.

I wiped my nose. "He lured me into the mine and then he…Johanna, he…" Oh God, I can't finish the sentence.

"He chained you up down there?"

I nodded. "And then...when I couldn't get away...he brought...he brought a..." I sobbed harder. Johanna put her arm around me, and I sank into her hug.

"And then he brought a snake," she completed my sentence.

Johanna's embrace tightened while I shook in revulsion. "You know?"

"He had a cage full of them down there. He liked doing it. You never get used to it." She stroked my back. "How did you get away?"

"I don't know. I simply don't remember. He left me lying there, and then I thought I heard a voice, but that can't be. I must have imagined it. And then the lift I was in moved again."

Johanna gently pushed me away from her and looked at me.

I slowly regaining my composure. "And that's all I remember, but it's enough to have me convinced that I am the guilty one."

"No, you are not!" Johanna's fist hit the coffee table so hard it made the fax pages fly. "It wasn't you."

"What makes you so sure?"

"Read the report. You're in the clear. Kurt was killed with a pick, not a hammer. You had no access to our mine tools. I did. It was me. When I left you in Eva's care and stormed off to confront Kurt, I was beside myself. I must have been so furious that I lost it completely, got the pick, and killed him."

By now Johanna cried, but she refused my attempts to comfort her. "All those years, I somehow blamed you. My life was ruined when Kurt raped you because, deep inside, I knew I should have warned you. I played the grieving widow after he disappeared to make sure nobody would suspect you, but now I know that I killed him. Believe me, had I known sooner, everything would have been much easier for me. At least I would have known why I was stuck there."

My mind couldn't process what Johanna had said, not immediately, anyway. It didn't match my recollection of the event, fit with my hunch that there was more, or do anything to disperse doubts about my innocence.

Johanna sniffled and wiped her hand under her nose. I wanted to hand her a tissue to dry her face but the tissue box was empty. She sniffled again, took her handbag, rummaged blindly through it, and finally emptied its contents on the low table. She pulled one tissue out and snorted noisily into it.

I noticed a key with a St. Christopher medallion on its ring. "What's that?"

"I have to give it back to Eva. It's her car key." She picked the key up, put it aside and filled her bag again.

"Where did you get it?"

"From Eva."

"I mean the medallion."

"Why?"

"Turn it around." I could not contain my excitement. "Quick. Show me. No. Don't. Don't say anything." I pressed my eyes shut. "The engraving reads, 'Dio ti protegga Bella'. Translated, that means, 'May God protect you, Bella'. " I opened my eyes again.

Johanna rubbed her fingers over the medallion's faded surface, puzzled by my certainty, until she could decipher the inscription. "How did you know?"

"It was a farewell present from my father. He always called me Bella. I never liked the medallion, found it too bulky and religious, but Dieter got a chain and wore it quite often. How did you get it?"

"I found it recently."

"Where?"

"At my mine, on the ground, close to the manhole."

Dieter. The realization bolting through me made me jerk. I hit my forehead with my flat hand. "Damn it. It was Dieter. It was his voice I heard when I was down there. He was the one calling out for Kurt."

Johanna straightened. "What are you talking about?"

"I'm telling you. He was there. I remember now. I don't know why he was there or what happened next, but I'm certain I heard his voice. Shock and shame must have blocked my memory."

"Shame?"

"I didn't want him to see me like that. Can you believe it? I was ashamed to be in that situation, but I also knew he was my only chance of survival."

"Did he come and save you?"

"I don't know."

"But you are certain he was there?"

"Absolutely."

We sat there, stunned by this new twist in the story, when we heard the door open.

Eva came into the room, smiling. "Oh good, I smell coffee," she said.

Johanna picked up the fax pages and began to put them in

sequence while I sorted my brain.

"What's eating you guys?" Eva asked. "You're both as white as those pages there."

Johanna handed them to her. "Read."

After she glanced at them, she frowned and asked what the hell it all meant. Pick versus hammer? Proof of what?

I filled her in on my new enlightenment regarding Dieter, and Johanna showed her the medallion and its engraving. Together, we pondered what that could mean.

Finally, Eva asked, "How did the medallion get there?"

"Oh please, that's irrelevant."

"Why?"

"Because Dieter could have lost it there on any of his visits. It is much more important to ask what Dieter was doing at the mine when Isabella heard him. And how he got there."

"By car, of course," Eva said.

"Jesus, Eva."

"No, seriously," Eva insisted. "He must have driven back to the mine. He probably felt bad about the fight you had and went back to apologize to you."

"Highly unlikely," I said. "It was hours later when I heard him. My timing might be a bit off, but I do know that Kurt tortured me for quite a while. Plus, I walked the whole distance to the mine, remember?"

"Uwe would have mentioned at some point, that Dieter turned back to pick up Isabella, wouldn't he, Eva?" Johanna asked.

Eva was struggling to find a logical explanation. "Maybe he didn't mention it because they couldn't find her. Still, he should have told me. Why on earth did he hide that from me?" She jumped up. "This is ridiculous. I'm tired of speculating what happened. We need to know for sure if it was Dieter at the mine. I'm sure Uwe still remembers if they turned back or not. I will call and ask him."

Isabella snorted. "Yeah, I bet he'll tell you the truth on the phone. He probably won't even take your call."

"Then we'll go see him. His company is in Harbord, only fifteen minutes from here. I will call and make an appointment. You two come along and we'll put him on the spot together."

"I doubt he'll tell you anything," I said.

"Why? All we want to know is if they turned around, and if so, what went on at the mine. Did Dieter call down to Kurt? Did Kurt come up? For heaven's sake, that's important, isn't it? I will demand an answer. I'm fed up with him giving me the silent treatment. He never talked to me then, I'll make him talk now."

I had to giggle. "Not bad, Eva. I didn't know you had so much fire in you. Quick. Do it before the fire dies down."

Eva was already dialling. After being transferred a few times, she finally got hold of Uwe. He must have asked what she wanted in an off-putting manner because she scrunched her face and lashed into him. "Listen, Mister Bigshot," she said, "I'm not interested in how important your client's call is. You'll have to put him off until later, same as you used to do with me. Tell him something—a nice little lie or some bullshit story. You're good at that, I remember." She caught a quick breath. "Maybe that was long ago, but I'm sure you haven't changed. I will be in your office at ten this morning, and you better be there. If you make me wait for even one second, I'll tell your receptionist about your dirty little habit of double bookkeeping—" She was interrupted, but she barked right back. "Of course I know about all the cash you accepted for jobs when we were still together—the money you used to form your company. And I will tell all your employees how you treated your daughter. What a miserable miser you are." She snorted. "Ten o'clock sharp." She hung up and sunk back onto the sofa. "I can't believe it. This creep hasn't spoken to me in years and he wants to give me an appointment three weeks out."

"Woo-hoo!" I said. "Who is this dragon lady?"

"What time is it?" Eva asked.

"Half past nine."

Eva stood again, rubbed her hands together to stop the shaking, and lifted her chin. "Let's go get him."

52

EVA

We arrived at Uwe's office ten minutes too early but I refused to wait in the car as Johanna suggested. I stormed into the reception area, Johanna and Isabella barely keeping up with me, announced myself as Mrs. Seybold, and was taken to Uwe's office without delay.

Uwe stood facing the window. He wore a gray suit that screamed money, and made my blood boil.

"I hear you are still using my name," he said, turning around. When he saw my two friends, he broke into a tiny smile. "Well, that's a surprise."

As always, he had himself under perfect control, which made me even more furious.

"How are you, Isabella? And you, Johanna?" He shook hands with both of them and asked us to take a seat at the elegant sitting area opposite his gigantic desk. Whatever happened to the miserly streak in him I knew so well from our time together? I couldn't stop the hurt tone in my voice. "To answer your questions, they are both well, and no, I'm not using your name anymore. My name is Taylor, but I wanted to stress to your receptionist that you and I used to be married. Just in case, you understand."

"Actually, I don't understand but I'm sure you will tell me in time." He took a seat behind his desk—his safety barrier, no doubt. "Once you cool down a little. You seem agitated. Am I making you nervous?"

Has he always been such a pompous ass? While I was groping for words, Isabella took over. "We are here for a specific reason—" she began but I had to interrupt her. No way would I let him see any weakness in me. Never again.

"It's about our last visit to Lightning Ridge," I said. "The day Kurt died." I leaned forward to better watch his reaction. A soft blush rose from his neck, spreading over his face. "The morning when you threw Isabella out of the car."

"It wasn't me who threw her out." Uwe turned to Isabella. "And to be correct, Dieter didn't throw you out either. You were angry with him, and Dieter stopped the car. You got out all by yourself."

Isabella wanted to object, but I waved her off. I had to attack before he fully composed himself again. "Let's not split hairs. You obviously remember that morning, so you will also remember what happened next."

"What's wrong with you, harping on about days long gone? Typical female. You always have to go on about the past, analyzing things that can't be changed."

"We are here to figure out a few things from the past, and we need your help."

"For what?"

I decided to put him on the spot. "We want to know why you guys drove back to the mine."

His blush deepened. "Who said we went back?"

So it was true. They did go back.

Isabella drew in a deep breath. "I did. Don't deny it, Uwe. I remember everything. I just can't understand why you went back."

His posture stiffened. "You remember?"

"Oh, goddamn it," I snapped at him. "Stop pussyfooting around and admit it."

"Since when do you swear like that?"

He must have felt my barely controlled anger. "Okay, okay. We drove back. What's the big deal? Isabella, you said you remember, so what does it matter why?"

"Aren't you surprised that I remember now, after so many years?"

He looked at me with a smirk. "No, Isabella, I'm not surprised at all. When you and Eva came back to Sydney, Eva told me that Kurt drove you from the mine back to the house, but I knew you were both lying. You see, I saw you run away from Kurt. I heard him yell after you and I saw you leave the mine in his truck. A lover's quarrel—that's what it looked like to me. I guessed you made up again soon after, and you stayed a few more days in Lightning Ridge to enjoy your affair. I wasn't born yesterday. You couldn't fool me, but I was a bit shocked that you put up with it, Johanna, and more than upset that you, Eva, would cover for her."

I was flabbergasted. "I remember you acted so strange when you picked us up from the railway station. You knew then that I lied to you? Was that the reason? Why didn't you simply ask me why I lied?"

"It wasn't important."

Not important that he thought I lied to him? Jesus, what kind of marriage did we have? I couldn't speak.

Isabella found her voice faster than me. "You thought Kurt and I had an affair?"

"Of course. Dieter told me that much."

"Dieter what?"

Uwe got up and closed his jacket. "Enough now. You may enjoy digging into the past, but I really don't have time for this nonsense."

None of us moved.

He twiddled with a button on his jacket. Nerves. "I have to ask you to leave now."

"Sit the fuck down," I said.

He paled. "I beg your pardon?"

Johanna came to my rescue. "We know how you financed your company," she said quietly, using this information as leverage on him.

I prayed he wouldn't close up on us. How long was tax evasion punishable? I had no idea but hoped he would still be worried about his inaccurate bookkeeping.

"If you don't answer our questions," Johanna pressed on, "we will make it public."

Uwe's neck was on fire now, and the dark red spread all the way up to his hairline. I had seen it before. He was ashamed, nervous and ashamed. Johanna's attack was working.

"What do you want from me?"

"We want the truth," Johanna said. "Then, we'll leave you alone. I promise we won't tell a living soul about the ill-gotten money." Her voice was calm and reasonable, and he seemed to trust her. He sat down again, shoulders slumping forward.

"It wasn't my idea," he said. "Dieter was so mad. He couldn't let it go. He wanted to go back and get our share."

I wanted to ask what share, but Isabella coughed into her

fist and stared at me.

"I had already given up on it," Uwe continued, oblivious of our stunned silence. "Don't get me wrong, I was annoyed that Kurt reneged on his word, but I didn't want to pick a fight with him. When we tried to reason with him the day we found the opal, he laughed in our faces. We didn't know then how much the opal was worth, but Dieter and I were furious that Kurt refused to give us our share, no matter how small it might be. We worked hard for that find, just as hard as him. Personally, I was more disappointed than furious. I was too proud to beg, and to be honest, I didn't have a clue about its true value, but Dieter must have had. Excuse me for being so blunt, Isabella, but Dieter picked a fight with you on purpose to get rid of you. Then, we drove on to Inglewood, had lunch and a few beers, and waited more than long enough for Isabella to reach the mine. Dieter told me that you and Kurt had an affair, and since Kurt thought we were on our way to Sydney, he wouldn't secure the mine properly in his haste to go somewhere to have a romp with you. Dieter said he knew where Kurt had hidden the opal, and that we just needed to hang out and be patient. Once we got back to the mine, a quick in and out, he figured, and we'd be on our way home."

Johanna sucked in a breath like a whistle. "Dieter went back to steal an opal from the mine?"

"Not stealing," Uwe said. "Dieter only wanted to show it to an appraiser and get an honest estimate. Then, he wanted to confront Kurt with it, and make sure we got our share. I would never have agreed if he had been planning to steal it."

Isabella was sitting on her hands but I could still see them shaking, and I could hear the angry vibration in her voice.

"But it didn't turn out as he had planned, did it, Uwe? Kurt hadn't left the mine. He was still down there."

"To make sure we wouldn't bump into him, in case he'd come back to the mine after your little adventure, we took the back road—the one coming from the cleaning pit—and parked the car behind a small hill. Dieter told me to wait there. He wanted to sneak up to the manhole and check out the situation. I didn't mind staying behind because I wasn't keen on a possible confrontation with Kurt. Dieter, on the other hand, was so pumped, he wasn't worried about it. He said on the off chance that Kurt was there, he'd force him to hand over the opal. I must say, I admired his guts. I'd never seen him that confident, that fearless. He actually went into the mine. I stepped out of the car, too. All that beer earlier took its toll. Anyway, I saw Dieter at the manhole, yelling down, and then, I guess when he heard no answer, he climbed down the ladder."

"So I heard right," Isabella whispered. "It was Dieter's voice."

"And then?" I asked Uwe.

"Then, I got back in the car and waited."

"Could you see the manhole from there?"

Uwe held up his hands. "Enough. That's enough. I told you what you wanted to know. We took the opal. I admit that I used the proceeds from the sale—my share of it—to start up this company. I was entitled to that money, so what's the problem?"

I didn't know how to reply to that. I thought we'd pressured him with my knowledge that he had accepted cash payments for many jobs in his early days as an independent carpenter but now we had a totally different perception of his guilt. Where on earth was this heading? Stealing an opal? Which opal? Money shared? Dieter back at the mine? Isabella still down there? Dieter must have seen her or heard her yelling for help. My head was spinning.

Isabella and I were at a loss for words, trying to make sense out of the onslaught of information. Only Johanna had enough presence of mind to react to Uwe's accidental, but for us, very fortuitous, confession. "I assure you again, Uwe, that we are not interested in making the theft of the opal public," she said quickly. "We only want to help Isabella sort through the events of that day. She has a few facts confused."

"If you say so," Uwe said, only half convinced.

"Okay, let's try again. You had a clear view of the manhole?"

"Only when I was outside the car. Sitting inside, I could only see the area where Kurt usually parked his truck."

Isabella finally found her voice again. "Did you see me there?"

"I told you before. I saw you running toward and getting into his truck. I could hear Kurt yelling after you. I guess he wanted to stop you. Then, I heard the car door slam and him roar like wounded boar. He was still screaming when the engine noise faded. Must have been one hell of a fight you two had."

"Kurt was screaming?" I asked.

"You bet. He sounded mad as hell. It really scared me. I thought if he found me sitting there, he'd rip me to pieces. You know how he could be when he was angry."

"He was alive after I left," Isabella said.

Uwe gave her an irritated glance. "Of course he was alive. I contemplated getting out of the car again to see where Kurt would go and where Dieter was, but it was too dangerous. I could only hope Dieter had managed to go into the mine and hide there while the loving couple was at each other's throats."

"Watch it. You are talking about Isabella here," I said. He shrugged. "Anyway, like the true hero you are, you stayed in the car and waited."

"Sure," Uwe said. "What else could I do? My heart was pumping so hard I couldn't breathe properly. I wasn't worried about Dieter so much. I knew he wouldn't do anything dangerous, but Kurt's screaming unsettled me. I didn't know what to do next. It seemed like hours before Kurt stopped but it was probably only a few minutes. Suddenly, all went quiet, and then Dieter showed up. He tore through the shrubs that covered the hill, lost his footing, slipped, rolled down to where we had parked, jumped up, and opened the door. He was breathless from running and covered in sweat and dirt, but believe you me, he had the opal."

"Were his clothes bloody?" Isabella asked.

"Bloody? No. Why? He was covered in mud and dust from the mine, of course, but I didn't really look at him too closely. He yelled at me to start the car and drive off as fast as I could, and I panicked, thinking Kurt might be right behind him. I drove like a maniac for at least ten minutes until I remembered that Isabella had taken his truck. When I calmed down and was ready to talk to Dieter, he noticed a lake next to the road and told me to stop there. He wanted to clean himself up and change his clothes."

"Did he tell you what happened then?" I asked.

"Kurt and Isabella were in the mine together, he said, doing you know what. They were so busy at it, they didn't notice him, so he hid in a side tunnel and waited until they left. Once they were up the ladder, he grabbed the opal and made his way out, terrified that Kurt might come back down."

"You believed that story?" Johanna asked.

"Why shouldn't I?"

"Because Kurt is dead. Because he was murdered."

"Murdered? What are you talking about? He died in a hunting accident."

Johanna gave a desperate sigh.

Isabella straightened. Her posture was statue-like and her face expressionless. She seemed far away. "I remember now," she said, her voice trembling while she described the scene of the past that became clearer with every word. "Dieter called down. Kurt hit me. Hard. I must have lost consciousness for a while. Next thing I knew, I was alone in the dark but I could hear voices. Kurt argued with Dieter. He called him a hen-pecked wimp and taunted him. 'Your own wife begged me to fuck her. Likes it real rough. Wants a man to show her who's riding her.' Dieter mumbled something. My heart raced. Should I scream for help? What if Dieter heard me? Found me like this? Then Kurt made the decision for me. Said, 'You want to see how she likes it? Look at what I got here.' His voice came closer. His torch shined on me. I opened my eyes, blinded by the light, and started begging Dieter to help me. I knew the shadow behind Kurt was Dieter. Kurt laughed and turned back to Dieter. 'Listen to her pretending,' he said, 'as if she didn't come crawling to me, asking for the whip and chains down here in the dirt. That's what she wanted because you can't give her what she needs. You and your limp piece of junk,' she said.

"Dieter started objecting. I begged him to believe that Kurt forced himself on me, that I was held prisoner there, that he must help me. He did nothing but listen to Kurt, who said, 'You don't believe that she screws anybody? Guess you don't know that she even fucked her boss, Hal. She told me about it. Laughed about you thinking you got the jobs for your talent while she used her cunt for making sure the whole advertising world owed her favours.' Dieter believed him. I could feel it. He'd always suspected about Hal. My God, he didn't even look at me when he walked past me, following Kurt deeper into the mine when Kurt said, 'Come, I'll show you the opal once more, so you know what else you don't deserve. It's mine. Mine alone. It belongs to me, just like your wife belongs to me.' Finally, a break. They disappeared deeper into the mine, into the labyrinth of shafts.

"I got on my knees and started crawling toward where Kurt threw the key. Please, I prayed, let the chain be long enough. Groping in the dirt, I found the key right away. Somebody up there was on my side. I fumbled, nearly dropped the key, turned it, and the lock sprung open. I crawled away from them, no strength left. Sharp rocks sliced my bare legs. I lifted myself off the muddy ground and began running toward the light. Out. Out. I needed to get out. This was my only chance. I reached the ladder, but halfway up, I heard someone below me. Kurt. He must have heard the creak of the rungs. He's coming after me. The ladder swayed from his weight. He's on it. Faster. Faster. I reached the top. Run. Run. I reached his truck and got in. Another prayer. Please, God, let the key be in the ignition. I found the key turned it. The engine started.

"A hand appeared at the open window. Kurt tried to open the door. I looked and saw a metal piece on the seat next to me. A hammer. Without thinking, I grabbed it, and I hit. Hard. He squealed in pain and let go. I dropped the hammer on the floor, put the truck in gear, and held the steering wheel with shaking hands while it jumped into action and picked up speed. Quick. Quick. Away from here. I looked in the rear view mirror and saw him running after the truck. My heart raced, thinking he might catch me but then Dieter appeared behind Kurt. I saw him lifting a pick and nearly swerved off the road. Oh my God, oh my God. Dieter smashed the tool into Kurt's backside. The truck jumped over a bump in the road. When I regained control, I looked back but both had disappeared from my view. I'd made it. I knew Dieter hit him hard. Kurt would not follow me."

Isabella caught her breath. The room was so quiet you could have heard a mouse scurry over the carpet. Then, Isabella whispered, "Dieter killed Kurt. But not for me. Not to avenge what he'd done to me. He killed him out of greed. To get the opal. I knew it even then, and couldn't face this truth until now. Dieter murdered him for a piece of glittery rock." She made a miserable sobbing sound and got hold of Johanna's hand.

I felt heartbroken and elated at the same time. What an incredible turn of events.

Johanna stroked Isabella's hand. "The medallion," she

said. "I found it not far from the mine. Now I understand why it was there. Kurt ran after the truck and Dieter followed him and attacked him from behind on the driveway leading out of the mine. Kurt was a strong guy but Dieter had a weapon. In their bitter struggle, Kurt must have ripped the medallion from Dieter's neck. Maybe Dieter didn't want to kill him but he hit him several times to make him immobile. When Kurt was out, Dieter rushed back to the mine, snatched the opal and ran back to Uwe's car. Kurt then dragged himself back to the mine and collapsed next to the manhole. When I found him, lifeless and covered in caked mud and blood, I immediately assumed Isabella had killed him."

"Are you sure he was dead when you got there?" I asked.

"As dead as he was when we both went back to bury him," Johanna said. "But we now know he was still alive when Isabella drove off, which can only mean one thing."

Uwe cleared his throat. "That Dieter killed Uwe? That is preposterous. Eva. I find it ridiculous, to say the least, that you never mentioned that you helped Johanna bury Kurt. Why on earth did you two do that? Why did you invent this story about Kurt having a hunting accident? Are you insane? How can I believe anything you crazy liars say in an effort to unsettle me? Is this an attempt to extort money from me?"

As he directed his questions at me, I felt I should give him the verbal trashing he deserved. "How dare you question our motives? You steal a valuable opal from a friend, use the proceeds to build your company, cheat me out of my share and let me believe you can't afford child support for your own daughter. You think you had nothing to do with Kurt's death? Let me tell you, you're not only a liar, you and Dieter are thieves and murderers. You creep, you—"

He raised his hands. "Good Lord, please. I had no idea how Kurt died. If Dieter murdered him, you shouldn't have covered up the crime. Why would you do that?"

I had to draw a deep breath to break through the hatred I suddenly felt for him. "You wouldn't understand, you arrogant little shit, but I'll try and explain it to you anyway. We did it to protect Isabella. Kurt raped her. He was a perverted sadist. He'd mistreated Johanna for many years, and she had a miserable life even after his death because you guys lied and cheated her out of what belonged to her. But you won't get away with it this time."

"Johanna promised to keep me out of it."

"She promised to keep quiet about your little accounting tricks, the ones I told her about. But what we are dealing with now goes way beyond cheating the tax department. We are talking theft here, which I can assure you, we knew nothing about until we got here. You brought it up, you stupid pompous ass. You conceited little louse. You murderer."

Uwe threw a desperate glance at Johanna.

She shook her head. "Sorry, Uwe. We can't keep you out of this. If nothing more, you are an important witness."

"You don't need to go to the police. Why should you? Nobody ever missed Kurt."

I enjoyed watching him squirm. "Of course we must, my darling ex-husband. Kurt's skeleton popped out of his grave, and with it, the truth will be exposed." I stood. "Ladies, we should make our way to the police station."

"I believe the station handling this case is on Parramatta Road in Glebe," Johanna said. "That's what's written on the coroner's report."

Isabella joined us. "Good idea. Let's move."

Uwe's head flew back and forth between us. "Wait. Wait. What's the hurry? No need to rush into things that might only hurt us."

"Us?" Johanna asked.

"Especially you," Uwe said quickly. "When the brutality of Isabella's rape becomes public, the media will assume that he subjected you to similar treatment, Johanna. Her defense team will have to bring it up, and you could be seen as an accomplice."

"Oh, please," I said.

"It's happened before. Couples committing sex crimes together, getting off on it. Who's to say that Johanna wasn't in on it? Kurt and Johanna, the perverted psychopath couple. They'd have a field day with that one. Furthermore, once they realize that you, Isabella, were married to the guy who killed your rapist, the tables will turn. Dieter will become the avenging hero and you will be the slut—with your best friend forever, Johanna, encouraging you to join in the sex game. Trust me, they'll make up all sorts of scenarios to drag you through the mud. You won't be able to show your face anywhere, any of you." He held his breath, and so did we. When we didn't react, he addressed me. "Eva, for God's sake, think about Nadja. How will she feel when she finds out you helped cover up a murder?"

"Keep Nadja out of this."

He ignored me. "And what about Steve? How will he like it when they whisper behind his back? Please, listen to me. We need to discuss all possible consequences of your next action. Let's not rush into something we might regret. A few more hours won't matter. Shall we go for lunch together and talk it through? Can I invite you to my club?"

Isabella waved him off. "I don't give a hoot what other people say."

"Easy for you to say." Uwe gave her a winning smile but his voice was sharp and high-pitched. "You'll go back to Germany, but what about your friends? Imagine the media circus Eva and Johanna will be exposed to."

"He has a point," Isabella said to us. "Shall we go for lunch and discuss it?"

"Sure," I said. "But without him."

Johanna grabbed her handbag. "He can't buy us with one lousy meal."

I grinned into Uwe's alarmed face. "Don't worry, honey. We'll be back at three o'clock sharp to let you know our decision. If you let us wait a single second, we're going straight to the police station."

53

We went to the Freshwater Restaurant across the street from Uwe's office and asked for a corner table on the patio so we'd be partially hidden behind a white plaster column and an enormous ficus tree. Our conversation would encompass a variety of topics for which we certainly didn't need an audience.

Uwe's warning had unsettled us but not enough to waver in our conviction that he and Dieter had to pay for their crimes.

"Dieter is going to die in jail," Isabella said. "I won't rest until he's sentenced to life in prison. I'll get the best lawyers. I don't care how much it costs."

"You must be so upset," I said.

"Strangely enough, I'm relieved knowing the truth. I always wondered why he left me in such a hurry but so many years have passed since then, it doesn't affect me emotionally any longer. But it hurts like hell that the three of us broke up our friendship, and that you, Johanna, unnecessarily suffered a life of hardship. I'll never forgive him or Uwe for that."

"Uwe won't get a long sentence," Johanna said.

"But his reputation will be damaged so he won't be able to play the successful businessman when he gets out. To lose his company will hit him harder than doing time." A picture of him begging at the roadside popped into my mind.

Isabella smashed my pleasant vision. "But would he,

Eva? He is smart. He'll put a successor in his chair to handle things while he's away, and in a few years' time, either all will be forgotten or he'll continue to pull the strings from the background."

"It may not even come to that," Johanna said. "He'll turn on Dieter, become the star witness, and only be sentenced to probation."

I wasn't convinced—didn't want to be.

"Be realistic. What do they even have on him?" Johanna said. "Sure, Uwe benefited from the proceeds of a crime, but he insists he had no knowledge of it. Any judge would believe him, even I do. Sorry, Eva, but there is no reason he should lose his fortune."

"I will make sure of it."

Johanna snorted. "And how will you achieve that?"

"I don't know."

Isabella straightened in her seat. "I do." Johanna and I moved closer. "Uwe is scared of us, especially of you, Eva, which is quite a feat, considering your gentle nature." She giggled.

"I turn into a fury when it comes to him," I threw in.

"Uwe can't afford a whiff of suspicion on his business dealings. If the tax department gets wind of his former undocumented cash deals while he has to defend himself in a brutal murder case, he's screwed on all levels. He'll lose all credibility. He knows that you've got dirt on him, Eva, so he should be open to discuss a deal."

"A deal?" Johanna said. "What kind of deal?"

"I don't want him to get impunity," I said.

"Don't worry," Isabella said. We moved closer still, until

our heads nearly touched, while she elaborated. We spent the next hour examining every aspect of her plan and considered the outcome for each player should our ruse be successful. Finally, we felt it was foolproof and realized we had only nibbled on our food.

"Better eat fast," I said, picking up my knife and fork. "It's close to the deadline we gave Uwe. To have the element of surprise, we'll have to spring this on him hard and fast."

We were shown to Uwe's office right away.

When we were all seated, Isabella got straight to the point. "How much did you get for the opal?"

Uwe had barricaded himself behind his desk again, but I could see him squirm. "I'm not so sure. As I said, it wasn't that much."

Isabella got up. "Very well. If you don't want to give us an honest answer, we're going straight to the coroner's office."

"Wait. Wait. I seem to recall it was about a hundred thousand."

I jumped up. "You seem to recall *about*—"

"Dieter sold it. I had nothing to do with it, so I can't say for sure how much he got."

"How much did he give you?" Isabella said in a dangerously low voice. "Tell the truth."

"All right, all right. He gave me one twenty five. Thousand, I mean. So he must have received a quarter million total."

"You got over a hundred thousand—" I wanted to jump at his throat but Isabella stopped me. "Now we are getting somewhere," she said to Uwe. "That's quite a bit of money, even now. In those days, it must have been a fortune."

"Kurt was stupid. If he had stuck to our agreement, Dieter and I would have trusted his word and been happy with any payout, even if he said the opal was worth only a few thousand. But once he broke his word, Dieter thought it was better to find out its true value, sell it, and split the proceeds evenly. Then, you girls came back and informed us that Kurt had disappeared and most likely died in a hunting accident. Well, then we figured we'd only have to split it between the two of us."

All blood left my brain. "It never occurred to you to hand Kurt's share over to Johanna?"

Uwe avoided my eyes and didn't say anything.

Isabella must have noticed my effort to suppress my disgust and seemed to worry that I'd lose it. She pushed me onto the sofa. "Let's all calm down and discuss our options. Johanna, how much would this opal be worth today? Half a million, maybe?"

"A million," Johanna said. "In fact, I'm pretty sure it would be more than a million."

"I find that a little exaggerated," Uwe said.

Isabella threw him a glance that could have made the Sahara freeze over. "We are not interested in your opinion."

"What do you want?" Uwe asked.

I forced myself not to think back to those difficult years when I didn't know how to get by every month while he had pocketed a fortune. Even a small portion of it would have made my struggle to raise our daughter much easier. Seeing the apprehension in his face gave me the strength to get myself under control again. I smiled. "You will pay back the money to its rightful owner. You will give Johanna the million dollars."

"Have you lost your mind?" Uwe folded his arms and his eyes narrowed to slits. "I can't get such a huge sum together."

"You can, and you will. Get a loan from your bank, secured by your company assets, and pay it off over the years, just like I had to finance Nadja's education. You stole the opal from Johanna's mine. It belonged to her. She never made an agreement with you and would not have agreed to Kurt's offer, if there was one at all. You benefited from the proceeds of this opal for years while she had to toil away in that horrible, dark mine. Consider the million a loan she gave you, a loan that is due now, with interest and compound interest."

His left eyebrow shot up. "Since when do you know anything about financial terms?"

"Unfortunately, I had to learn early on how to deal with banks when it came to borrowing money."

"I'm sorry, but under no circumstances can I get that much."

Johanna took over. "Then we are sorry, too. If you don't deposit the money into my account, we will name you as an accessory to theft and murder in our statements."

"You really want to go to the police? What good will it do? We can come to a private arrangement. We need to negotiate terms—"

"Nonnegotiable," Isabella said. "If we don't make our knowledge of Dieter's crime public, Johanna will be accused of killing Kurt, and she has suffered enough. Don't you see? It's up to us if we drag you into it."

Uwe's shoulders sloped. "What about Dieter? Shouldn't

he pay at least half?"

"We'll make sure Dieter will pay for his crime but not in monetary terms. That is your obligation—your chance to buy yourself out of this mess. We will allow you to reimburse Johanna, and by keeping quiet about your involvement, blame will fall solely on Dieter."

"Explain how you can guarantee that Dieter won't drag me into it?"

He had taken the bait. "Easy enough," I said. "As long as our stories match, Dieter is the sole perpetrator. All you have to explain is that you saw him climb into the manhole to steal the opal. He sold the opal and I'm sure he gave you cash, so there is no paper trail that could connect you to it. If Dieter ever gets caught—and that is very much an *if* since we have no idea where he is—he can argue anybody's guilt, but it won't mean a thing. He left the country and you stayed. Why would that be?"

A tiny glimmer of hope flitted over Uwe's face. "You are arguing in my favour."

"Hold your horses," Isabella said. "This only works if we support your story. If you don't pay up, we will tell the police we are convinced you were in on it—at least on the theft part, considering that you cheated the government before. My lawyers will insist on checking your books all the way back to the founding of your company to trace the funds you used as start-up capital. I bet you declared it an inheritance from overseas. Money laundering wasn't such a big deal then."

Bull's-eye. His face turned beet red again. My ex was such an easy read. "Our offer stands for twenty-four hours,"

I said and got up.

Already at the door, Johanna quickly walked back to his desk, took a pen from his elegant stationary holder, ripped a piece of paper from the notebook next to it, and scribbled her account number on it. "Tomorrow, 4:00 p.m. Not a second later."

54

JOHANNA

Steve was home by the time we got back from Uwe's office, so we filled him in on our meeting.

"A risky move," Steve said. "If he has to use his company as collateral to finance the million, and his business takes a dive, he'll lose it all."

"Who cares?" I said. "By then I have the money. And if not, at least Isabella and I can lead a life with a clear conscience again."

Steve seemed to grasp the enormity of my relief. "I agree, it was worth pressuring Uwe. You can finally leave Lightning Ridge and move back to Sydney."

"Or to Germany," Isabella said. "You can fly back with me."

I broke into uncontrolled laughter. The ideas they came up with. Honestly. So far from my own. "I will visit all of you, but I certainly won't leave my little town."

"Why? What do you want there if you have money?" Isabella asked.

"I had an epiphany while we were negotiating with Uwe,"—I gave Eva a warm smile—"which was mostly your doing, and what a terrific job you did, by the way. You should start your own business. I believe you could handle any company with great success."

"That's me." Eva grinned back. "Ice-cold business lady. But to start up a business takes plenty of money, which I don't have."

I got serious again. "Now, listen to my epiphany," I said. "Remember the day the men came back to the house, all ruffled and openly hostile toward each other? When you all went back to the motel, Kurt went back to the mine. I bet that's when he closed the side tunnel. I never reopened that tunnel since I assumed he'd closed it because it gave no yield."

Steve was quick on the mark. "Kurt closed it because quite the opposite was true?"

"A rock that size would indicate an opal street running through the wall formation. Kurt must have suspected that an even greater fortune was waiting to be mined in that shaft, and he closed it off to secure it against prying eyes—like Dieter's and Uwe's, or mine." I took a deep breath. That bastard would have cheated me, too. I was sure of that. Maybe I was lucky he was killed before he could do me in one lonely day while I was toiling underground in the deep, dark hell he had created for me. Nobody would have realized I disappeared. Nobody would have missed me.

Isabella clapped her hands. "I get it. You want to go back and dig for the fortune that might still be there. I'll keep my fingers crossed for you. That's a plan I can fully support."

"Not only me," I said.

"Who else?" Eva said.

"Mira. I'll call her later and ask if she wants to join me in this adventure. She came back from Brisbane and wanted to work with me. I could use an experienced partner in this new endeavour. We could have a lot of fun, digging away together all day long."

"And rounding off the day in the pub," Isabella pouted her lips at me. "John, John, John, my darling, I'm coming…"

"Shut up, you silly woman."

Isabella wasn't deterred. "I'm so happy for you to finally be able to enjoy the fruits of your endless labour. And for you, Eva. It must have been so satisfying to stand up to Uwe and see him squirm."

"You bet," she said. "I'm only sorry you can't experience the same. It bugs me that Dieter will get away unpunished."

Steve had left the room without us noticing and came back with a bottle of wine. "Why should he?"

"Because we only know that he went to America. God knows where. It's a big country."

"But we know his name and that he is a photographer." Steve put the bottle on the breakfast bar and reached for glasses. "I'd start the search in New York. He had money in his pocket. He'd try to establish himself somewhere flashy and fashionable."

I had to put a damper on Steve's enthusiasm. "Australian judiciary can't investigate in America. They won't even bother to look for him."

"Not even if a court finds him guilty?"

"I don't think so," I said.

"Would it help if we tell them where he is?"

We pondered Steve's question while he poured us white wine. None of us could be sure.

"It's worth a try," Steve urged. "His name is Dieter Kraus. If he opened a studio or worked as a professional photographer, he should be on social media. Let's google him."

We took our drinks to Steve's office. We were lucky on the first try. Dieter Kraus Pictures had a website.

"How creative," Isabella mumbled under her breath.

The website featured several artistic landscape pictures. Dieter specialized in the production of elegant calendars and named a list of galleries that showed his work.

"In other words," Isabella said a bit louder, "he couldn't get into the advertising world."

I nodded. "Lucky for him, he doesn't have to make money."

"At least we know where he is," Steve said. "I'll print the information, so you can hand it over to the police."

"And they'll do what with it?" Isabella asked. "File it or wipe their asses with it. What they won't do is start extradition proceedings. Way too complicated. No, no. We need to lure Dieter back to Australia. Then, they can arrest him as soon as he clears immigration."

Nice idea. Unfortunately, it wasn't feasible. "He won't come back here. He'll smell a rat from the start."

"I wouldn't be too sure about that." Steve raised his glass. "I have an idea that might work on a self-centered, greedy prick like Dieter."

55

I had filled John in last night on the latest development on our side, and he had promised to inform Bill in turn. The next morning I was already on my third coffee when John called me back. We briefly discussed Bill's reaction before John steered the conversation to a more personal level. Sounding real and honest, he said he never doubted that I was innocent. He said he missed me and made me promise I would return to Lightning Ridge as soon as possible.

I was a little flushed when I went over to the breakfast table where the others had assembled, waiting with expecting faces to hear what John had found out. "Bill went over to the pub last night as soon as John called him," I said. "Mira was there, too, and the three of them stayed up until four in the morning, talking. Bill believes what John told him, even without concrete evidence. Bill suggested the three of us go to Dubbo and make our statements there, to him. It'll be a feather in his cap if he can solve this case quickly, especially if the outcome is so spectacular that it will undoubtedly create a small media sensation. His superiors will love that so little manpower is involved to bring the perpetrator to justice, even if the guy never hits Australian soil again. Uwe can make his statement here, but if it goes to court, he'll have to testify in person, same as you, Isabella, but that could be a year away, easily."

"What about Dieter? Did you tell John our plan how we'll

try to lure Dieter back to Sydney?"

"He thinks it's marvellous. So does Bill. To pretend to be a gallery and appeal to Dieter's delusions of artistic grandeur made them both chuckle. If we are convincing enough for Dieter to drop his guard and attend our proposed exhibition of his amazing talent, Bill can arrange to have Dieter arrested as soon as he steps off the plane."

"I better get the website up, then," Steve said. "I need to register it with ozmail, otherwise Dieter can't contact us. When will you girls drive up to Dubbo?"

"I promised John to be there the day after tomorrow." I could feel the heat rising into my face again.

Isabella rolled her eyes. "Oh my. Can you wait that long?"

John's words resonated in my mind. I can't wait to see you again, he'd said, I'm so lonely without you. I shook it off. "We have an important appointment," I said quickly. "Four o'clock at Uwe's office."

The day dragged on. Steve and Isabella were busy with the website, Eva baked a cake, and I paced the flat like a tiger, torn between staying level-headed and melting into an X-rated vision of meeting John again.

At three o'clock, Uwe called and said I could pick up my check. He didn't want to do a transaction of that caliber via the usual channels, so he had a special bank account set up for it. "Sure," I said, "I bet you know all the tricks."

"As long as you get your money," he finished the conversation, cold as frozen hell.

Isabella and Eva had listened to my responses and broke into a happy dance as soon as I hung up.

Steve came rushing in. "So, it worked?"

"Yeaaaahhhh!" we squealed.

"Johanna, if you want to get that money into your bank account today, you better hurry," he said.

"And then we buy the best, most expensive, French champagne for our celebration tonight," Isabella added as the three of us raced to the door.

Uwe was still icy when we got to his office. He handed the check to me, made me sign a receipt, and shook hands with all of us as if this were an everyday business transaction. When he came to Eva, he held her hand a fraction of a second longer. "You've changed," he said, a tiny seductive vibration in his voice. "You seem so much stronger now."

"I should hope so," she hissed back while she withdrew her hand as if his touch were poison. "After all, I had to get your daughter and myself through all the hard times without any help from you."

We raced to the bank and made the deposit just before closing time. Then, I saw a liquor store at the corner and steered toward it. I picked two bottles of Roederer Cristal without looking at the price tag. This was my day, and my friends should have the best.

"Have you gone nuts?" Eva stared at the total on the cash register.

"I sincerely hope your ex's check doesn't bounce," I said.

"He wouldn't dare," Isabella said. "He's not stupid. We'd get him on fraud on top of everything else."

Isabella insisted on getting caviar and Melba toast to accompany our champagne. I tried to stop her but didn't have enough money in my account to take on that expense, too, not until Uwe's check cleared, but I already knew how I would make it up to her.

We drove back to Eva's and put the champagne on ice. "Ten minutes in the freezer should do it," Steve said. "I see you girls are eager to get the celebration underway."

"We are indeed very thirsty," I said. "I'll be back in ten." I quickly disappeared to my room, did what I had promised myself I'd do, and came back the moment Steve popped the champagne and filled our glasses.

"Hold it," I said. "I need to pay Isabella for the caviar now."

She looked at me like I wasn't quite right in my head. "But I told you I'd pay for it."

"I insist. It's my celebration."

"But you didn't have enough money in your account."

"That's why I'm giving you a check." I handed it to her.

She glanced at the check and did a double take. "Wait a minute. You made a mistake. That's way too—"

I whisked out a second check and gave it to Eva. "Not at all. Eva's is for a flat $300,000, while yours, Isabella, is for $302,000. Caviar addition to your share of our loot."

Eva stared at her check for a second and then carefully placed it on the table. She kept shaking her head, and I gave her time to understand the magnitude of my gesture. She'd wouldn't have to take on part-time jobs any longer and have enough money to enjoy a good life with Steve.

Isabella just glued her eyes on me, waiting until I got tired of just standing there.

"Say something," I pleaded.

"I can't accept this." Eva's voice was harsh.

"Neither can I," Isabella said.

Their reactions annoyed me. "Damn it, girls, of course you can. It's your share. We've been in this together, and each of us had her burden to carry because of what our exes did to us. Our lives nearly derailed, and it is only our joined perseverance that made it possible for the truth to come out. I could never have done it without you. I would have rotted in prison." I could barely control my voice. "Don't you get it? You must take it. I couldn't live with being the only one who finally profits from what was done to all of us." Tears welled up and began to wet my cheeks. My knees were shaky so I sat down. All this emotion surging through me felt like relief.

They still didn't say anything.

"Please don't misunderstand me, Eva," Steve said after clearing his throat several times. "But I think Johanna is right."

"Thank you," I said.

"But why so much?" Isabella said. "You suffered most. You shouldn't give us a third."

My burst of laughter broke the tension in the room. "I'm shocked, Isabella. I always thought you were good at math. Three hundred thousand is not a third. I'm still ahead by $100,000, but I did this split on purpose. If you agree, we will reserve that for incidentals to get Dieter back into the country, and once here, for top-notch lawyers to make sure he will never walk this earth as a free man again."

56

We knew our ruse had worked before we reached Dubbo. Eva got the call from Steve and put it on speaker so Isabella and I could listen.

"Dieter mailed back," Steve said. "Said he's available all of December to coordinate the exhibition of his work in our amazing, fabulous, newly established gallery. He could get here as early as next Tuesday."

"He took the bait," Eva said. "Hook, line, and sinker."

"Why am I not surprised?" Isabella said, loud enough for Steve to hear. "He's always been so full of himself. The chance to show off his American landscape photos clouds his judgement so badly, he wouldn't smell a rat if we dangled it in front of him." When Eva threw her a glance, she quickly added, "But in this case, credit goes to your brilliant website, Steve. You're the best."

Steve thanked her and added that we should tell Bill about Dieter's arrival. He'd mail him the details once they were confirmed. Then Bill would be able to organize the welcoming committee.

We spent the next day with Bill giving our statements. By the time we were done, we were exhausted, and John and Mira arrived soon after we got to our motel. John had closed the pub so he could meet us in Dubbo, and we all went to dinner together.

Bill brought good news. "We can get the arrest warrant

by next Monday. We'll open proceedings here in Dubbo and do the referral to Sydney at more or less the same time so a judge in Sydney can sign off on it. That'll give the police at the airport the power to arrest him as soon as he's cleared immigration. I'll drive to Sydney myself to make sure procedures are done fast enough and so I can be present at the airport when he's taken into custody. I wouldn't miss it for the world."

"Neither will I," Isabella said. "I will change my flight to Wednesday. Don't you want to come back with us to watch the happy occasion, too, Johanna?"

I shivered. "No, thanks. I've got better things to do than waste my time on that loser." Underneath the table, I let my hand glide over to John. Aware that this was the first time ever I had initiated physical contact with him, I was a little scared what his reaction would be. He leaned back, half closed his eyes, and gave my hand a gentle squeeze. I felt my skin tingle with pleasure. Please, don't let me blush like a schoolgirl. I could feel the heat, spreading from my fingertips to my scalp, but nobody seemed to notice.

Isabella and Eva were high-strung, talking nonstop about the upcoming arrest, speculating how Dieter would react and how they would feel, and congratulating themselves on their achievement.

"I guess I'm the only one not directly involved," John said. It didn't matter. By dessert time, Mira and Bill were entangled in their own flirtatious behaviour, and Eva began to yawn. It had been a long day.

I could have sat there forever, but when everybody got up, John let go of my hand and said a hasty good night, and we went to our individual motel rooms.

I kept my door ajar for quite a while, but the hallway stayed quiet. What did I expect? That he would come rushing in, throw me on the mattress and take me in a mad rush of passion just because I'd held his hand?

I fell on the bed. Staring at the ceiling, I pondered why I wasn't happy. Dieter was coming back and justice would be served at last. I had more money in the bank than I ever could have hoped for, Mira would join me in exploring my mine, and I would build myself a lovely home in Lightning Ridge and enjoy the rest of my life.

All by myself. Damn it.

I had left John out in the cold for too long. All the years I rejected his advances must have left a mark on him. He'd never believe that I, all of a sudden, turned from frigid to fiery. He'd laugh at me if he knew I simultaneously felt a terrible knot in my stomach and a longing ache in my heart every time I thought of him.

Why do I allow myself to hope for more? He didn't come to my room and may never have had any intentions beyond good-natured pub banter. I had wrongly interpreted his true level of interest. I'd blown it by holding his hand—scared him off for good.

So be it. Love and happiness ever after were not for me. My lungs constricted, and I let out a painful breath that sounded like a whimper.

Damn. Damn. Damn. Stop this nonsense.

I was angry. I got up, pulled my T-shirt and jeans off, stepped out of my underwear, and went into the bathroom to take a shower. Nothing a decent amount of cold water couldn't fix. I stayed under the spray until I shivered. Good. Freeze this stupidity. This schoolgirl crush inside a grown woman. Finally, when I was so cold my teeth were shattering, I turned the water off and got out of the shower. I rubbed myself dry, wrapped the wet towel around my hips and opened the bathroom door.

"About bloody time." John was sitting on my bed, only a few steps away from me.

My anger flared up again, except this time, instead of dark and depressing, it was refreshing and exciting like a stiff breeze. "How dare you?" I lashed into him. "What are you doing in here now? Why the hell did you make me wait—"

He jumped up, crossed the room with two quick steps, and put his hand on my mouth. "Be quiet or the others will hear us. I thought you understood. This evening belongs to us alone. If you hadn't spent so much time in the bathroom… oh my God, you are so cold. Did you take a cold shower?"

I nodded.

"Because of me?"

I nodded again.

He took his hand off my mouth and covered it with his mouth instead. His lips were soft and moist.

"You are cold and hot all at once," he whispered, slowly moving his mouth down my neck. I shivered again.

He pulled me along until he reached the bed, then lowered himself onto the mattress until his face was below my naked breasts. He looked up. "You are more beautiful than I imagined in my dreams."

I stood in front of him like a statue, closed my eyes, and prayed he wouldn't stop. His hands outlined the shape of my bosom, brushing over my nipples ever so lightly before they moved lower. I sighed. "Don't stop," I whispered, wondering why my voice sounded so hoarse.

He pulled the towel from my hips, and with it, all inhibitions I had ever felt. This was a moment between two lovers like it should be, like I had never experienced before, and I promised myself, I'd make sure the rest of my life would be full of moments like this.

EPILOGUE
Barrier Reef, one year later

The yacht was anchored in the shallow waters of the Barrier Reef, about an hour from the harbour of Cairns. I could feel the rocking motion of the boat and hear the small waves splashing against her hull. Relaxing in an oversized, canopied lounge chair, a cool drink in my hand, I let a gentle breeze stroke my skin and wondered if heaven could be any better than this sunny December summer day.

A year had passed since we had lured Dieter back to Sydney. To celebrate, John and I had chartered the yacht over the Christmas holidays and had invited our friends to join us. With their arrival, our time of quiet reflection would be over.

I stretched out, closed my eyes, and allowed myself to savour the memories that danced behind my eyelids like sparkling stars. I had so much to be thankful for.

The year had been busy like no year before. Mira was a godsend as a partner. Her enthusiasm was catching, and together, we had opened the eastern shaft within the first week of our collaboration. The reason Kurt had closed it was apparent at first glance—evidence of opalization between the boulders of the shaft. Kurt must have seen it and ushered Uwe and Dieter away. They weren't experienced enough to understand what the narrow street of glitter in the wall signified, but Mira and I knew.

We'd picked up our tools and started work immediately.

What we found over the next weeks was beyond our wildest dreams. I once said to Mira, "I wish Kurt was alive for just one day, so he could see what we see. After he'd eaten his heart out, he could drop dead again."

Mira had laughed without missing a beat in her delicate hammering around the opal street. "And I wish Dieter would know how rich we'll be when we are done here. It would make his rotting away in prison that much worse."

The court case had dragged on, just as Bill had warned us. When Dieter had arrived in Sydney last December, I wasn't there but Isabella was. She told me she'd barely recognized the overweight, balding man who'd walked through immigration's glass doors into the arms of the uniformed police officers waiting for him. They had cuffed him quickly and led him away, past where she was standing. When he'd seen her, his expression changed from confusion to disbelief to understanding in an instant. He'd then raised his cuffed hands in a defiant gesture and spit in her direction. After that, she'd vowed to come back and sit through the court case, no matter how long it took.

Thanks to a bunch of smart-ass lawyers, the case hadn't gone to trial until last month. Isabella had flown in to attend the hearings, prepared for it to drag on, but it had taken just five days. The case was documented well, the forensic evidence was indisputable, and our witness statements held no contradictions while Dieter got himself tangled up in countless inconsistencies. But ultimately, it was Uwe's testimony that pulled the noose around Dieter's neck. I had to give him that. He'd played the trustworthy, respected businessman to perfection. His short but precise account of what he had seen left no room for doubt. The jury deliberated less than four hours.

I looked out at the open ocean. Isabella was meeting Mira and Bill and Eva and Steve later and they would come to the yacht together in a few hours. I looked forward to Isabella's detailed account of Dieter's reaction to the guilty verdict and sentence of life in prison.

Would she visit him now that he was locked up for good? Did she still have a score to settle? I wouldn't put it past her. Maybe she'd drop by the penitentiary and fill him in on our good fortune. I made a mental note to give her an extra-large piece of opal jewelry to wear around her neck to showcase what he'd missed.

And one for Eva. She deserved one, too, although she still wasn't one for flashy symbols of her newfound wealth. She had put all her money into a company for part-time secretaries, providing well-paid work for many young moms who needed an additional income but couldn't commit to full-time employment. She'd worked hard and succeeded in getting her company on major companies' radars within the past ten months. So good of her. So very Eva. She deserved this holiday as much as all of us.

I stretched my tanned legs and let out a long breath. Life was good, just a bit too hot.

"We should go downstairs and turn on the air-conditioning for a while," I said to John as he came up the few steps from the galley carrying a jug with ice cubes clunking in mint-flavoured water.

"Already done." He topped off my melted drink with the refreshing fluid. "It'll be cool enough in a few minutes."

I fished an ice cube out of my drink and rubbed my wrists with it. Then, I rubbed my forehead until the water dripped down my temples. I closed my eyes.

Suddenly, I felt another ice cube on my skin. John let it glide up my right arm, along my shoulder, moving down the straps of my bathing suit, exposing my breasts. I kept my eyes closed and concentrated on the sensation of getting hot while being cooled down by hands that used a rapidly melting ice cube to totally undress me.

"If you don't stop, we won't make it downstairs, and I'll have a heatstroke up here," I mumbled. "At least, you'll be a very rich widower." I smiled inwardly at the word widower. Perfectly correct, as John and I had secretly married a week ago—something else to celebrate with our friends.

He stopped what he was doing. I opened my eyes and couldn't hold back my excitement. I slung my arms around his neck and breathed into his ear. "So, how about it? You want to become a rich widower or not?"

He pulled me away until he could look into my eyes. "I don't want to be a widower. Not a rich one or a poor one. I can't imagine a life without you anymore." With that, he got up, pulling me with him.

When we reached the last step, I hesitated. The cool darkness of the galley should have been welcoming but a sudden memory made me shiver. Down, dark, on a chain, a life of dependence and degradation. Have I truly left all of that behind or will it enter my mind at odd moments, poisoning my ability to find true happiness?

John's hands rested on my shoulders. Heavy. Protective. He could feel my doubts and knew my fear of dark places.

"Shall I turn on the lights?" he asked.

I concentrated on his presence, vowing not to allow the memory of a pathetic past infiltrate my newfound desire for love. "No," I said loud enough to exorcise the ghosts waiting in the darkness. "I don't mind the darkness." Not anymore and never again.

For the first time, John and I made love in pitch-black surroundings, and when I felt his body on top of mine, I forgot all that had happened before and knew I was whole again.

CPSIA information can be obtained
at www.ICGtesting.com
Printed in the USA
LVHW042039020419
612749LV00002B/104/P